Date, Love, Marry

Today is ours; let's live it
And love is strong; let's give it
A song can help; let's sing it
And peace is dear; let's bring it
The past is gone; don't rue it
Our work is here; let's do it
Our world is wrong; let's right it
The battle is hard; let's fight it
The road is rough; let's clear it
The future is vast, don't fear it
Is faith asleep? Let's wake it
Today is ours; let's take it

Originally written by Beah Richards, recited by Ruby Dee

I extended my hand to receive my grocery receipt from the checkout lady. She couldn't help asking: "If you don't mind me asking, you look familiar. Are you an actress or model that I've seen in several movies or covers of major magazine covers?"

Taken by surprise, I laughed and immediately turned to see if she was referring to someone behind me. Still, she repeated her question and pointed at me.

So, I responded: "Oh, no. Not at all. A few people have asked me that, but I've never pictured myself in such a chic way. I'm just a regular next-door girl," I replied.

I felt embarrassed and uneasy when people were so quick to place a judgement value on someone based on looks. So, I immediately started thinking of an excuse to tell her I was in a hurry. Best to save face and to avoid public stare or undue attention.

Of course, I consider myself attractive but not remarkable fabulous in terms of looks. People have always complimented my tall height and slim figure. Perhaps, also due to the fact that my forehead and mouth harmonize with sensual full lips. I've got an angular chin that equally balances against my nicely shaped nose. And I also do have well-arched eyebrows and large animated dreamy eyes. Physical appearance is often a resemblance to one's parental lineage, which is a unique beauty in all human species.

If I had a choice, I'd prefer for people to be drawn to me based on my general appearance and charm, exemplified through the vivacity and grace of movement; to my face and eyes that often express plenty of feelings, kindness, calm, candor, and care. And maybe, my elegant, tasteful dresses and a bearing which unites and makes appealing the dignity of a woman that is often portrayed by actors of notable repute.

She was looking at me suspiciously as if I was lying to her. It's obvious she didn't believe my answer. So, she decided to be insistent in seeking the 'truth' or whatever she considered an appropriate response. I know I was in no obligation to give her an answer or engage in a conversation with her, except for the courtesy of public politeness. Since she not only asked me the same question thrice after my response, I decided to respond because she was murmuring to herself that some famous people play god whenever they're around average folks like herself.

So, I said to her in as calm and gentle a voice as I could: "Actually, I just completed my master's degree program and am pretty happy that I can channel my energy to engaging in what I'd always dreamt of doing with my life. Pursuing an entrepreneurial venture in my childhood dream of art and craft café that provided international snacks and gourmet coffee for local college students and young professionals to hang out and socialize with their friends." I concluded quickly so as not to hold the checkout line.

I glanced behind me and saw that another customer was directly behind me and didn't appear to be in a hurry. The elderly woman was reading one of the tabloid magazines, '*The National Enquirer*,' with a sizeable full-page caption, "The first man in the world ever to get pregnant." Could it be true or another sensational article to make money?

I wonder about the unbelievable story headline on the tabloid cover these days. Especially during our era of social media boogeyman that's permeated by fake photoshop, news hype, audio, and video fakery. I'm also thinking about what the checkout lady is asking me. She reminds me of one of those individuals who are always dissatisfied and at variance with themselves and with the world around them.

She perseveres: "So, what program did you major in, and at which of the local universities?"

The speed and pitch of her voice sound hurried and obstinate. When she asked this time, she drew her upper lip up to show her dazzling white teeth, which looked like veneer. I could see curiosity written all over her face. I couldn't tell if she was bored from not being very busy or simply trying to be friendly. Either way, I decided to answer her inquiry.

"In marketing and business communication and at Case Western U," I replied, feeling calm that a stranger like her appeared to be interested in my academic success, even under no obligation.

However, I was more disposed to believe that she was bored because she was without customers to keep her busy. But again, the cashier could conceivably be one of those sociable creatures or friendly people that genuinely care about others, especially her customers and their personal stories, regardless of who they were or what they did in life.

And in answer to her last question on what I'd be doing since I graduated, I told her that I intend to work for myself as an entrepreneur.

-

Being self-employed has been in my mind for some time, considering the boring experiences I've had as a part-time worker or an intern. I knew going into sales and marketing as my dad did or opening a coffee place like my mom back home, were not what I wanted to do. However, a combination of their career interest and background might be appealing, from a self-employment point of view, especially with the types of customers around here.

A coffee place with mini relaxing couches, Wi-Fi, a reading area, and laptop hookups would be attractive since I'm surrounded by several neighborhood colleges, universities, and eateries.

Maybe an art gallery and a cafe would be a good combination to attract a younger, educated crowd since the population around here is mostly college students and suburbanites.

My gut feeling tells me the area and business idea would be perfect for a neighborhood made up of several colleges and universities within the city and suburban area. So, a good location should be East 4th Street, in downtown Cleveland, which, from my judgment and head research, is an ideal hangout, seven days a week, plus being within walking distance between several campuses and residential houses.

I remembered a call to my mom back in France last night yielded excitement too, but with a hint of sadness or worry on her part. When I asked about her concerns, she worried about how I'll cope in a foreign country alone as a twenty-something-year-old female, and more so, trying to start and run a business. I told her not to worry, and she asked if my boyfriend would be helping me, and I broke into laughter before responding.

I told her we broke up a few months ago and hastened to lie to her that I had a new boyfriend now and that he was more mature and stable, and yes, he promised he would help me if I needed any help.

I couldn't answer her question about why I kept going from boyfriend to boyfriend. Plus, why my relationship experiences within my US city are different from what she went through as a young female back in rural France, or the outcomes from such relationships are not one hundred percent under the woman's control? I ignored her question. I drowned her voice quickly by raising mine, stating: "mom, I'll be just fine because several of my American friends and the new guy I'm dating have promised to help me."

"Marie," she said softly, knowing that I was eager to shorten or end our conversation. "If you plan to remain in the States, I hope you know we are here to help. Whether you decide to remain there or decide to return to France."

Before I could thank her or say anything further, she cleared her throat and continued: "And who is this new guy, and didn't you say your boyfriend, Aaron, and you were inseparable the last time we chatted? I wonder why you can't have one good guy and stop changing boyfriends like underwear."

Realizing that she won't let this subject die a natural death and trying not to get upset with her relentless line of questioning, I responded as calm as I could: "I have to run, mom. Why not we talk some more when I'm less busy?" and hung up. She makes me feel frustrated and upset because I'm not a kid anymore and would prefer to live and learn independently.

To set the record straight, I'm neither a serial monogamist nor a girl with a preference for friends with benefits. When I like someone, I give the relationship my one hundred percent.

It may sound unusual. Moving from Europe to the States, straight out of high school to attend university for most young girls, it would be thrilling to meet a handsome young guy in a college environment. And fall head over hills in love, or rather, engage in several romantic flings while navigating college life.

It didn't take me a long time to realize that most college dating revolves around casual relationships that seem promising at first, only to find out before long that sometimes, these relationships fall apart after a couple of weeks or before the semester ends. I call it "the three-month hitch." It involves a series of texting or phone calls. And late-night or weekend hookups. Eat-outs or drinking parties, picnics, or multiple heartbreaking encounters, as well as picnics and short trips, among other mutually agreeable interests.

From my first year until graduation, my relationship with Aaron was similar to most of my college or university dates, from my first year until graduation. We started talking while taking an elective course together. He said hi to me and asked if I could share my notes for the previous week that he missed, and I said yes. After making copies, he thanked me, saying he liked my accent and wanted to share a cup of coffee or drinks whenever we had time. He wanted us to exchange numbers. I was reluctant because he wanted more from me than just friendship.

"Maybe next time we meet because I'm in a hurry right now. Going for a bite before my next class," I said.

"Can I join you now? Briefly?" he responded instantly.

"As in a date?" I replied, trying to smile at my choice of words.

"Yes, kind of like that," he said cautiously. "Any interest?"

I hesitated before answering: "I don't have much free time," I said honestly, but it didn't stop him from asking, even though he was also between classes. I knew he wanted to go out with me from his persistence, however irregular or fragmented our separate schedules might be.

"You have to eat," he pointed out to me, "and from what I can see, you'd be cheap to feed. You don't eat much."" He is associating being slim with starvation, I thought. However, I don't mind talking and getting to know him.

I laughed at what he said and relaxed my demeanor. "Sure. Maybe. I guess. Why not?"

"I wouldn't call that a vastly enthusiastic response, but it'll do." He smiled at me.

"I just hesitate to go out with anyone right now. You know, I have a hectic schedule, that's why. Every time I plan, I must cancel. I juggle classes and a co-op that is sometimes virtual, as part of my program. I'm on standby sometimes, and they yank me in, and I must leave before the food comes. It pisses normal people off. And it gets old fast. How sexy is that?" I lamented, with the hope he understands and doesn't take it personally.

He thinks I'm a beautiful, intelligent woman and seems determined to go out with me from how he sounds and looks at me. I believe he likes everything about me and has a crazy feeling that we're meant for each other. I think he has never met a woman he likes as much. All these thoughts were going through my head as our eyes kept feasting on each other, trying to figure out our head or heart intentions.

"I get it. I'm busy too, but I can't help wanting to meet you so badly. Maybe our lives were meant to cross each other. If true, you won't regret it," Aaron said hopefully.

"Maybe not," I said frankly, "if I give us a chance."

"So, you're going to take a vow of chastity?" I grinned at what he said.

"No. But I hate disappointing people, and I always do. And dating is so much work."

"Dinner is easy. We can meet for as long or as short a time as your heart desires." He looked as though he meant it, and I smiled.

He was making it easy for me and hard to refuse. And I liked him too. I couldn't see into the future, but I liked the idea of having dinner with him a lot more than some of my recent dinners with a guy that thought he was God's gift to women because he's a part-time model and stage actor. At least we're taking a course in common, and we both have crazy schedules.

"Okay," I agreed. "Dinner sounds good. It's a deal."

"How about Friday or Saturday? Someone screwed up the schedule and gave me the weekend off." He stated, laughing.

"Lucky you. I'm working Friday and free Saturday. We could give it a shot." I replied.

"Perfect."

We exchanged cell phone numbers just as I was receiving a text message. I glanced at him regretfully and told him I must go now and asked him to give me a call anytime. Glad we were able to establish a reasonable basis for a friendship or anything else that happened.

It had been a pleasant exchange, and I felt surprisingly more comfortable with him than with most men I meet on campus. I don't like the games you have to play and that most men seem to expect on a "date." I'm not flirtatious and often say what I mean, which frightens many men.

He didn't seem to mind it—on the contrary, he liked it. And I wonder how he would get along with my girlfriend, Elisa. He wasn't her 'type', and I suspect she would find him boring, which I didn't find in him.

Our conversation was lively and thoughtful, and I liked that there was no pretense about him, and he didn't seem to have a big ego, which I don't like in males. Many of them think they walk on water and are full of themselves. And I like that he seems able to laugh at himself and is relatively modest and respectful of me.

We left where we were standing, and he walked me back a couple of steps, thanked me for the time, and headed back to his next chore.
"See you Saturday," he said more casually on his way off. "Don't forget to wear your beauty," he teased me, maybe literally. "That way, I can wear mine and don't have to feel shy." I laughed at his joke.

"I'll try my best," I promised, and as he walked down the hall, there was a spring in his step and a smile.

"What are you so happy about?" I could hear a female voice asking him. "Are you on drugs?" She smiled at him. He's probably a friendly and likable guy, and the females like him, plus he was a good-looking guy.

"I have a date," he confided, looking like a kid in a candy store. It was hard to believe that was a big deal to him.

"Lucky girl," she said to him. She looked years older than him, so she wasn't interested but thought he was a catch. One of them said he was a "hunk," unbeknown to him. He was unaware of what they said about him, which was just as well.

"Lucky me," he corrected her. He could hardly wait for Saturday night. And a couple of females walking by were smiling too.

—

 We finally arranged to meet at a local restaurant and bar the following Saturday, at approximately seven-thirty, at a local eatery near campus. We met at Bodega restaurant and lounge by Coventry at the suggested time, and when I arrived, I noticed he was already there and waiting in the reception area. Dressed in business casual, he walked up to me with a big happy smile, and he gave me a bear hug.

With one hand on the nape of my neck, he gave me a hot, quick kiss on the lips as if we'd had a dating relationship previously. His confidence excited me, so I returned the kiss and felt increased physical chemistry.

After our warm kiss that seemed forever, we followed a waiter to be seated at a table near the bar area. Because we were both hungry, we wasted no time placing our order of seafood stuffed salmon, mixed veggie salads, and two glasses of white wine from an extensively long list of choices.

Aaron and I enjoyed our seafood meal and had an animated conversation of an easy volley. He was very relaxed, had a quirky sense of humor, and seemed intelligent and passionate about his classes.

He talked about his favorite sports, especially tennis since he was on a tennis scholarship at the university. Among other things he said, he added, "last but not the least; I'm honored to be with an exceptional girl – you." I blushed and thanked him for the compliment. We finished our meals, refilled our wine glasses, and moved to the romantic lighted lounge area to listen to live music.

We enjoyed each other's company for a few more hours until close to midnight.

He told me more about his childhood years. He is the youngest of three children, with two older sisters, Jane and MaryAnn. Jane is married and living in Columbus, Ohio, with her husband, while MaryAnn, the oldest, is finishing graduate school at Cleveland State.

Their mother, Laura, an accounts manager with a local bank in Columbus, raised all three children. His memory of his dad is based on his mother's account since he passed away less than a year after his birth due to prostate cancer. Half an hour later, he wanted to know if it was alright for us to call it a night. I told him I didn't mind and thanked him for sharing his family background with me.

Aaron and I headed out of the restaurant and walked to his parked car. As he opened his car door for me to get in, he kissed my hand and asked if I wanted to see where he lived, about five minutes away from the university.

"By Shaker Heights," he added, looking at me mischievously.

I accepted his request and followed him to the car. A photograph by Ed Sheeran was playing on his car stereo as we arrived at his place. He took long and quick steps over to the side of my car door as I was trying to open it. He held it wide open, touched my left hand, kissed my fingers as he helped me out of it, and walked me to his apartment unit.

As he opened his apartment door, he held me close and whispered into my ear, "I can't restrain the fire of love which is consuming me inside. I feel like I'm about to commit a carnal sin," which made me laugh because of the sound of his deep voice, and choice of words. Yes, he sounded trite, but I liked him and enjoyed his company.

As we entered his living room, I could see a massive sofa across the large room through the dim light on the wall behind it. He pulled me closer to himself and forced a kiss on me, which I resisted. I tried to pull away from his strong hands, but I couldn't because my efforts were useless.

I was thrown backward on the sofa instantly while his hands took possession of my longing body. My resistance weakened as the furor of lust was upon him, yielding to his physical strength and hunger.

I closed my eyes as if afraid to see how he exposed himself. He roughly forced my thighs apart, throwing his weight upon me, as I could feel the hot soft head of his cock, forcing its way between the lips of my vagina.

I struggled and contracted myself as much as possible, and since I was not very wet, he experienced significant tightness as he entered my pussy. I cried as I was experiencing real pain because his enormous penis was hurting me.

happiness and excitement. It is okay to spend a lifetime with one person until old age or death. We only have one life, and it's okay to promise whoever is your significant other to be faithful for the rest of your lives. Still, as a pragmatic person, we know feelings could change in a few years or 10 or 20 plus years.

"So, as someone who came to this world alone, you must be honest with yourself and the one you decide to live with because we all know love, romance, or sex will change over time. I believe in what I call the French way, which is having sex with someone else besides your significant other, should not have any consequences.

"That should not be considered a crime because we all came to this world alone and will die alone, regardless of how we lead our lives. As far as I know, ordinary people, regardless of what they believe in, desire and consummate sexual or romantic acts with someone outside of their profound relationship regularly.

"Maybe in some part of the world, very old people close to a hundred years, and those of legal age of sex or marriage, believe that crushes or straying from your significant other does enhance commitment with the one you love. Unless a couple has other unrealistic expectations or other personal problems that only a shrink can fix," she said.

"Hold that thought for a minute, Elisa, let me get us some snacks and more drinks, please," I requested and hurried to the kitchen area. She was definitely getting my curiosity in high gear.

I returned with two plates of sliced salmon, grilled meats, fresh veggies, avocados, and dried fruits. Plus, a refill of wine and small water bottles, and I asked her a follow-up question on her thoughts about sex in a serious relationship.

"I believe people begin to have problems when they put too much pressure on sex," she continued.

"For me, kissing and spreading one's legs is a physical act or new experience, with zero emotional involvement."

I don't know about you, but if I have sex today. And the next day, I'd feel like a virgin each time. Because the first time is when you are both trying to be your best romantic and passionate self. As if you are expected and eager to please yourself and your partner.

The first night with someone new is when we try to act safe and pleasant. Authentic and doing everyday things like kissing, hugging, touching, taking off clothes, engaging in oral sex, and penetration and the end of the sex act.

If all goes well, and one continues with the relationship, you become more confident and experimental. Sharing secrets and fantasies, and whatever intimate desires one has, and discovering each other more and more."

I expressed gratitude to my friend, Elisa. And, of course, I'm glad her dating style has worked for her, but it might not exactly work for me. Although I heard and understood her persuasive reasoning, it is possible that some people also have different or some other points of view.

I think my feelings and expectations in my relationship with Aaron are identical to some of my other friends, either on campus or city.

And just as people have a different outlook on life and relationships, they are also bound to have different experiences, which are true within siblings or relatives and swats of any segment of a population. It is also true that guys can be spoilsports, especially when they see themselves as indispensable or have unlimited choices, but so are girls.

After a week of silence, I decided to accept Aaron's "friends with benefit" arrangement, which started great. He was much better than the fewer crazy guys I dated previously. Not as extreme in character or behavior, plus we were able to talk through our issues.

The pressure was off since we openly discussed and defined our relationship, bringing us closer. It could be only my feelings, but I thought about Aaron more and wondered what he was doing when we were not together. Sometimes if I were at a party, I'd wonder why he wasn't there. If something funny happened that reminded me of him, I hated feeling like I wasn't "allowed" to text him because I didn't want him to view me as insecure or anxious.

I kept pushing this feeling aside but felt I was not true to myself. When a guy at the party starts talking to me about dating, I discover that they're talking to many of my other friends. And when I ask them what kind of relationship they're looking for, they straight away tell me "open relationship," which in my head means friends with benefits. It made me feel that the best thing is to continue with Aaron instead of starting with someone who could worsen.

I concluded that the right thing to do was be patient and wait for him because, again, connections like ours didn't come around often.

As the night party was long past midnight, and everybody was drinking more, getting louder, and some of my girlfriends were hooking up with different guys, I decided to text Aaron and tell him I'm coming over. He didn't reply, but I went to his place anyway.

Upon arrival and ringing his doorbell, he opened his door but didn't seem excited. I hugged him anyway and pushed my way into his living room. I kissed his neck and then his lips and allowed my left hand to wander around the front of his pajama pants, which immediately made his penis increase in size and hardness.

Evidently, in an excellent state of excitement, Aaron picked me up and took me to his living room sofa, mumbling, "you little slut, I can't help myself." I did not respond but noticed a substantial long fleshy-looking thing sticking out of his buttonless pajama pants, hard and stiff, with a ruby-colored head, bobbing like a lizard searching for food.

I took hold of it with one hand and moved closer to the shaft, rubbing it up and down.

"Oh! Ah! I can't help myself. I must have you," sighing.

His face flushed, and his eyes seemed ready to start from his head, and immediately, some hot liquid spurted from between his legs. The drops fell on both of our hands and legs. Some even fell a yard or two over the floor. This action of his seemed to complete his state of ecstasy.

He held on to me tightly, but sank back quite listless for a few minutes, then rousing himself; he started undressing me and kissing me hungrily. I moved my lips from him, kneeling on the floor in front of him; I took ahold of his limp penis and gave it the most sensual sucking, to the great delight of Aaron, whose face glowing again with pleasure. I noticed his instrument was similarly rigid and ready for enjoyment.

He pushed me aside and quickly went down on his knees and glued his lips to my pussy, sucking and kissing furiously to my delight as I was sighing and squirming with pleasure. And when he could no longer restrain himself, he got up on his knees between my legs, bringing his shaft to the charge, and to my astonishment, he ran it straight into my open dripping crack until it was all lost in my belly.

We laid still for a few moments, enjoying the conjunction until I heaved up my bottom, and he responded with a shove, followed by the most exciting calisthenics. With the reflection from his living room wall mirror, I could see the massive shaft as it worked in and out of my sheath, glistening with lubricity, while the lips of my cunt clung to it each time of withdrawal, as if afraid of losing his delicious sugar stick.

This action did not last long as our movements got more intense. We both met a spasmodic embrace as we almost fainted in each other's arms. I could see a profusion of creamy moisture oozing from the crack of my pussy as we both lay in a kind of lethargy of enjoyment after our battle of love. Aaron was the first to break the silence. "Marie, will you be free to spend time with me?"

I suggested that he should take me back home to pick up some change of clothes and for him to bring me back to his place afterward, and he accepted with a mischievous grin on his face.

Upon returning from my place, we went back to bed and slept like babies, and when I woke up in the morning, he was nowhere to be found. I called his name, and he answered from the kitchen area and told me he'd be right with me. A few minutes later, he was in the bedroom with a breakfast tray for us.

"Seat up, Marie," smiling, "I've got your favorite breakfast – look, some French toast, French scrambles eggs, and freshly squeezed French grape juice."

We fed each other, ate as starving pigs, and rewarded each other with lovemaking, and body parts exploration with our tongues and hands, which lasted about two hours, followed by a nap and a bathtub scrub. Now I see what my girlfriend Elisa meant by the feeling of having sex the first time, each time one makes out. Aaron and I drove to Little Italy for seafood pasta, salad and beer, then dropped me off at my place with a goodbye kiss.

A few weeks later, Aaron had not called to say hi or see how I was doing. I texted "what's up" twice but got no reply, knowing he read the texts. I couldn't help remembering that I've been the one that has initiated our last two dates, and his behavior never improved, even after our last time together.

One of my friends told me that Aaron was seeing another girl. that lived near or around the Coventry area. She thought it was me but noticed the female companion was shorter than me. Anyway, this lack of communication and effort told me all I needed to know. That he's not into me, he likely never would if he's not making any effort to ask how I'm doing or say hello.

Plus, I didn't have all the time to pursue him or worry about us, so I must channel my energy into final exams and prepare for graduation. Even though my feelings for him have been consistently strong, I've decided his idea of friends with benefits arrangement is not for me. Ghosting him is not an option either, so I must move on.

On Thursday after class, for several weeks, a female friend that lived across from me when I was roommates with Elisa asked me to meet her for a drink, and I accepted, which was a couple of blocks away from campus. An hour when we were walking back to our apartment, someone touched my shoulder, and I turned to see Aaron and one of his friends I've seen around but don't remember his name. They both hobbled and blurred in speech like they were drunk. I ignored him, but he followed me to my apartment, and I reluctantly allowed him to follow me in.

He said he wanted to talk, but e fell asleep no sooner than sitting on the sofa watching the television show. The second day, which was still a weekend, he came over drunk again, and he again fell asleep on the couch watching a movie. I watched him sleep for half an hour. I went to my bedroom, locked my door, and left him a note telling him to let himself out and call me after he got some sleep.

On the third day, when he came the third time, I excused him by the door, went inside, wrote a third note, and told him to go home and never come to my place again. I never saw him again. He never showed up at my door any longer, and I figured three strikes, he was out.

As I kept thinking about my love connection here in the state of Ohio and my desire to remain in the States and find a guy with that we can build a healthy relationship together, my mind kept wondering about my parent's relationship during my early childhood, growing up with them as a child and young adult. Case in point, I remember asking my mom how she met my dad, and she was reluctant to share any details with me, except turning the questions back at me, like a lawyer or police officer in an interrogation, or simply providing me with answers that weren't meaningful or sensible.

Over time, she volunteered more information during the tail end of my high school years, days before she and I were to accompany dad on our first trip to America for his sales marketing conference. Although his trip was work-related, he decided to take us with him because he was going to be gone for a little over a week. Plus, it was an all-expense paid trip by his company.

He has been working in marketing for the Bordeaux wine grower's organization, which represents the wine produced in the Bordeaux region of southern France. Bordeaux is centered in the city of Bordeaux, on the Garonne River. To the north of the city, the Dordogne River joins the Garonne, forming the broad estuary called the Gironde and covering the whole area of the Gironde department, with a total vineyard area of over 120 000 hectares of land, making it the largest wine-growing area in France. Anyway, my dad was working for this group and later met my mom, whose family was one of these small family-run winegrowers that were blended and sold by wine merchants under commercial brand names.

Anyway, regarding how my parents met and fell in love the first time, mom said she saw this young, good-looking fellow looking her way and smiling. She looked back, and he responded with a wink. He didn't say any word to her but blew her a kiss on his way out after his meeting with senior management. Within weeks, they were sneaking around and making out in a car during short secretive dates because they didn't want anyone to know what they were doing. As they took a stroll along this shady footpath and field pasture, where one is likely not to meet anyone at this late evening or night, he commented on her appearance by saying, and I quote: "I can tell that you are in love the way your eyes are smiling at me, and the way you are heaving your bosom."

She blushed and was shocked by his choice of words. She couldn't believe he said those words, and before she could think further, he pulled her closer by her waist and kissed her lips. She reluctantly responded and, in a few minutes, they found themselves on one of the wooden benches, ripping each other's clothes off and making out. She believes that is how or when I was conceived.

So, it was not long before my mom became pregnant, and as their secret affair was becoming obvious, with my mom's pregnancy becoming noticeable, my parents had to get married because of it. It was strange because they hardly knew each other at this time, except through physical intimacy. Since I was considered an accident, my mom told my dad that he was free to do whatever he wanted and not obligated to marry her, but he went ahead and married her. Spin forward to my adolescence period, I began to think about the nature of their relationship as they were together. I increasingly wondered if they would be divorcing because they were literally quarrelling on a regular basis.

Often, my father would do as he pleased, like leave the house without telling anyone where he was going and engage in whatever activity or indulgence, he wanted. My mom, on the other hand, would not dare step outside the house without getting in trouble with his tongue lashing and screaming voice. Even when she went to choir practice the day before Sunday service, it was trouble. Or going to job-related travel or meetings that, in his mind, took too long or because his head or heart was consumed with negative thoughts. The outcome was trouble or reason for an argument. Once during one of their argument, I became so hysterical that my mother had a hard time calming me down. Family relationships at home were essentially toxic or noxious.

When it came to my and my dad's relationship, I don't remember my father ever praising me for doing anything good, touching me to show affection, or taking me on his lap, when I was much younger. Maybe I have a distorted memory, but I can't recall a single emotionally positive incident involving my father. Our relationship consisted solely of control and punishment. My school grades were always good, but if any grade was less than an A-minus, I was punished as if I failed the course. His reaction or behavior towards me made sure that I had to be extremely careful when I was writing because every ink blot or correction was the potential to have to re-write the entire notebook.

Thank goodness I graduated from my elementary school with distinction, as shown on my certificate, but even on seeing it, my father did not praise me. Instead, he stated: "someone needs a beating," which, for him, was his idea of a joke. Once, he had to physically smack my backside for going out of the house to play with neighborhood kids at a park across from our home. Even after explaining that I was not there alone, that there were other kids with me, he would not listen. "You are not 'other kids,' he said."

Even as a young child of a little over seven-plus years old, I was just as terrified of my dad when my pencil didn't have an eraser, or it fell off. A type of situation that is generally common to just about any child. His propensity for anger or fury would scare any kid, wondering when an unpredictably and irritated parent would physically or verbally hurt them. Although he never lets you know when you could potentially be hurt or beaten, the fear itself could be equally distressing and keep a child trembling like an animal that's about to be slaughtered.

At age seventeen, just before high school graduation, I started to go to house parties to celebrate pre-graduation and passing precollege or university entrance admissions with my friends. Before I was able to get out of the house, there was always a huge commotion because my father didn't want children "roaming about alone." My father only saw his own positive qualities and good intentions because he was always correct.

To this day, he has not changed in this respect. It is impossible to change someone who has such a virtuous belief in himself. As a child, I was very close to my mother, and she loved me as well. Perhaps the bond between us was way too strong. Early in my childhood, she started to treat me more as a friend. Like, she told me about her work, her worries, and so on, but I was not able or expected to ask her any questions.

To be quite honest, I don't recall telling my mother any of my own problems since puberty, unlike my friends' mothers. I had learned early in life that all I could expect in return would be a few soothing words like: "it will pass," or "nothing to worry about," "be strong," or "don't worry, be happy."

There was never enough time to explain the problem fully so that it would become clear to both of us or to me since I was still confused or immature in many ways. Yet she was a great comfort to me during my period of severe despair. Our relationship is of a paradoxical nature - on the one hand, a close attachment to each other, but on the other, mutual suspicion. Very often, I would go to her and put my head on her lap, sick with worry or fear, but when she asked me what was wrong, I refused to tell her or express my feelings to her openly. The current problem we have is that she keeps saying she understands my having become an adult, but on the other hand, she denies this to herself and refers to me as childish when my thoughts or ideas are unacceptable to her or contradict hers.

Besides the bits and pieces of stories about me and my parents, my other family members that were aware of childhood traumas were my grandparents – that's my mom's parents, who weren't living far from us. I was practically growing up alone during the first six years of my life because I was kept in a nursery school. For only about two months because my grandmother refused to let me continue to be traumatized, as I cried so excessively every morning before departure from home.

After that, I was left at home with my great-grandfather, that's my grandma's father. Later my parents moved to a newly built apartment building, much larger and spacious than the one we lived in. I joined a larger group of children, but during school hours, I was still alone because students were grouped based on ability. In this elementary or primary school classroom, I was considered the best student, which didn't help matters, considering I wore glasses and became an object of ridicule. The only time anyone spoke to me was when we had a difficult assignment. My self-esteem was practically nil.

Middle school was another story. There, I found friends with whom I have kept in touch since. As I reflected on this entire earlier account of my early childhood and eventual departure to the United States for college or university education, I wonder how much of these early life experiences and situational background have made me who I've become, for better or worse, or perhaps, it's a combination of all of these, plus my personality traits. One way that has helped me in finding myself is to seek and search for information on any unknown phenomena, whether of things, self, people, our environment, or planet earth.

Just as I was done with childhood and family contemplations, my phone rang, and it was Elisa, wanting to invite me to a house party later at nine-thirty pm. "Okay," I said. She wishes for me to be ready in three hours and to 'dress to impress' because she wants me to meet someone named Greg – Mike's boss. Sounds like a 'blind date?' Anyway, she'll pick me up in the company of Mike, her husband-to-be.

An hour and a half before picking me up, I spent some time getting ready. From the inside, I wore a seductive, glamorous lush, soft dusky-pink mesh and red lace harness bra. The fresh pink set features an enticing detachable harness, and to look the modern and millennial that I am, I decided to wear a light blueish Gucci gown and nude-colored high hill shoes.

At exactly the appointed time, my doorbell rang, and it was Elisa. I met her at the door, and we walked to her boyfriend's black G-550 Sports Utility Vehicle and drove to downtown Cleveland's Ritz-Carlton.

After handing the keys to valet parking, we were directed inside by the concierge, walking across the hallway to the large room that was set up for the party.

According to Mike, Elisa's boyfriend, the party is meant to celebrate the investment management company's third-quarter success and socialize with key accounts' customers. It is slated to be informal, including lavish door prizes, a full course meal, dancing, and of course, an open bar. Uniformed servers were available to seat people, provide food items, or anything requested by the guest, as needed.

As we were walking further into the massive open space, Mike waved at a set of couples, two older gentlemen and their wives. He whispered to Elisa and me that over ninety percent of their clients were multimillionaires. His sight directed us to a shorter guy to the left and his wife. He owned a chain of restaurants and cafes across the state of Ohio and neighboring states. And the other couple owns a dry goods chain, headquartered in Cleveland but with branches on both coasts of the US and overseas.

Seated at the table to the left of us, we could see several more couples chatting among themselves, laughing, and sipping their drinks. Further in the middle area are seated dozens of relatively younger guests, made up of some famous athletes with both the Cleveland Browns and the Cavaliers, as well as media and medical tech moguls.

Next to them but standing are three charming animated people, a stout man that looks about sixty plus, according to Mike. His name was Mr Holcomb, a billionaire farm equipment manufacturer that was sold in over a hundred countries. He also has hardware chain stores scattered across America. The younger attractive female, Deborah, is his daughter, a final year medical school university student at Case Western.

"And the tall, slim, dark, distinguished youthful guy is my boss, Greg Davies," says Mike, as he smiled and winked at me.

Greg and Mike attended Case together and were roommates, and both majored in economics. Mike went on to work in investment banking, while Greg went on to pursue a Harvard MBA and took up employment, working for Goldman Saks briefly. He later returned to Cleveland to run his father's yoghurt and ice cream manufacturing business. He took it globally and sold it two years ago for almost two billion dollars. He retired his parents and decided to pursue his first passion, which was wealth and asset management. "Anyway, that's the guy Elisa, and I would want to introduce to you tonight," Mike concluded.

Meanwhile, we were seated next to another couple, exchanging greetings and tête-à-têtes while being served several courses of meals, ranging from choices of Korean style grilled skirt, steak with red wine-shallot sauce, steak with olive salsa, London broil steak with onion marmalade, Spanish steak salad, pan-seared T-bone steak, plus bite-size dishes of salmon, scallops, shrimps, and servings of any drink or juice of choice.

At precisely an hour and a half later, dinner was ended, and the guests were ushered through the right-side double doors exit of the dining hall, crossing the pillared and balconied corner, into the concert hall where a live band was playing a mixture of irresistible melody of waltz, and slow listening and sing-a-long songs.

Next to it, was a high wall opaque glass door that led to the DJ hall section, lit by the blaze of the electric chandeliers, with a large dance floor space for those that preferred urban and top-forty hits. As we walked toward these sections, we could see that the slippery, glittering floors were crowded with dancing guests. Men were in suits or formal semi-casual wear, while women were variously attired. My friend, Elisa, was wearing a white dress, high at the neck, with a large hat of black velvet to match her shoes. Her pearl earrings, dress pendant, and wristwatch were also matching.

Minutes later, we were joined by Greg, Mike's boss, who quickly tapped his shoulder and said, "Hello, Mikey." Mike returned his greetings and proceeded to introduce me because he'd met Elisa once previously.

Looking my way directly, with a smile and deep voice, he reached out and shook my hand, saying hello and nice to meet you. He looked at Elisa with a smile and thanked her for coming.

He looked my way again and couldn't help but complement my fair hair fluttering in the breeze from the A/C, adding that my elegance, dress, and looks resemble some

Hollywood movie star. I blushed, muttered some thanks, and looking sideways, I noticed Elisa's frown of jealousy at hearing the words of admiration. Greg looked a handsome sight himself in some exquisite blue trousers with a silk shirt, a pale blue blazer belt, and a cap.

Greg looked to his left, and a bellboy immediately came over and he requested that we should be taken to a private compartment through an entrance directly across from the DJ section. As I came to understand later, this compartment was set up for Greg and his team to meet with clients and dignitaries that wanted to privately discuss the further business. Or to share a drink informally or simply to introduce themselves and say hello to the head of the investment management firm. This gesture was not unusual because they all knew of him, but most have hardly spoken to him, except through the company portfolio management team. Mike explained that the company was well run, with an effective and efficient delegated role for each well-trained, self-managed team member.

As we were getting settled in, with drinks on hand, the door flew open, and we could hear sounds of laughter and music from the music hall, and several people were walking in. As it was beginning to look packed, an older good-natured couple came in, with drinks in one hand, holding each other's free hands, singing a lively popular song, and causing much merriment.

Greg paced forward at the sight of two newcomers. He greeted them with a handshake, stating, "it's a pleasure to welcome you guys," turning around, he introduced us to the females since the guests already knew Mike. Greg stepped by my side, walked me a few steps away from the group, and asked if I'd like to accompany him to meet some more guests, and I gladly accepted without hesitation. I told him he did a good job organizing the party and thanked him for allowing Mike and Elisa to invite me. He smiled and immediately stated that it was an honor to have me, and he hoped to get to know me more in time.

He asked, "do you live in Cleveland, or are you visiting from another country since I sense an accent?" His deep voice sounded slightly raised since the loud music from the dance hall was making it harder to speak in a low tone.

 "Well, yes, I live in the city now and just completed my academic program a few weeks ago, but originally from France."

"Oh, I see," said Greg, "I'll formally introduce myself to you much later, but first, shall I introduce you to some of my friends that are also at the party?"

"Of course," as he touched the tip of my nose, smiling.

He disappeared into the crowd and immediately came back with a distinguished well-dressed gentleman, whom I remember Mike saying, owned equipment manufacturing company. "This is Mr Holcomb," he said, "my friend, Marie," he added warmly.

"Nice to meet you Mr Holcomb," I pretended to look surprised, acting as if I'd never heard that name previously. I pointed out that I overheard his name earlier and proceeded to explain to Mr Holcomb that one of the investment management team members, namely Mike, pointed him out as one of their major clients when he and his daughter arrived for the party. The old man and I went on to make chat.

Greg was slightly confused, wondering if Mr Holcomb and I had ever met, but played along. In any case, he excused himself and left us to continue chatting, saying he would arrange some drinks for us, as well as for Mike and Elisa. He turned to me and promised he'll be introducing me to more guests later. Smiling, he walked towards the large glass exit doors and signaled one of the bellboys to where I was standing.

A bellboy showed up, and I could not believe my eyes. Behold, it was Aaron, my previous boyfriend. He didn't recognize me until I called his name. I had lost some weight and toned up from regular exercise, and now wearing beautifully designed and elegant dresses styled in ways he had never imagined nor seen in me before.

"Aaron," I called out, "what are you doing here?" Aaron was flabbergasted and stuttered and responded, "M-a-r-i-e, is it you?", more a statement than a question, his face turning a dull yellow.

"I work here," he said, "and how did you end up here at the party?", he asked, sounding malicious and irritated. Looking contrite, he quickly muffled sorry for sounding stupid, for not responding to my calls or phone texts and diverting his love interests with other dates, and so on.

"If you're trying to be honest with me, why not tell me the real reason for changing our relationship to friends with benefits?" I asked him, looking directly into his eyes.

"To be honest," he said, "I truly don't have a good reason, except that I started dating one of your single friends, and because she didn't want to be the reason for ending a good friendship with you, we both kept it a secret, to spend more time together. That was why I suggested an alternative relationship with you instead of breaking up."

I retorted, "no worries, I've moved on, just like you moved on," feeling uncomfortable and annoyed by the direction of the conversation.

"Well, I am glad you are enjoying yourself," said Aaron, startled at my sudden transformation and confidence.

Abruptly realizing that he was at work and on duty, he looked sideways and noticed that another bellboy was attending to Mr Holcomb, Elisa, and Mike. He proceeded to continue his conversation with me, lowering his voice, almost in a whisper so as not to be heard: "I don't know why you should turn against me, Marie."

I caressed the left side of my hair and ear lope and looked very mockingly at Aaron, stating, "I see you had forgotten when you told me we should either become friends with benefits only or call it off. And that you are young and not ready for anything serious or waste time and youth with only one female."

"Not at all, Marie; you must know I was wishing to marry you someday," he said, blushing, with his face turning a deep red.

"This is news to me," I cried out, feeling upset.

Aaron's voice was reduced to a murmur and trembling in his chest, "I may add that I have always loved you, and now I seem to do so madly," he added passionately.

"But I don't love you," I responded.

"But if you marry me, you might get to," said Aaron.

"I think not," I replied, "but it is very kind of you to ask me," as I smiled more nicely at him, even though I wanted to run far away from him for what he did to me.

"This is agony," he cried out loud, clutching to the tray and cloth towel he was carrying as one of his accessories while providing drinks or supplies to guests, "my life will be sour grapes and ashes without you."

"Be a man," I said in a calm whisper, and not making a scene in a crowded hall, "anyway, I shall always think of you in an endearing, warm manner, I promise."

"Well, ok. Half a loaf of bread is better than none," he replied, his voice sounding miserable and thanking me, and cleaning some perspiration from his glistering forehead, as he walked away to continue his work chores.

Just then, Greg reappeared with a very impatient woman in a tight silk dress, who was referred to as Justice Richburg, a member of the judiciary whose husband was a prominent property developer but had been dead a few years. He has been managing her family's assets for the past year and a half.

"So, this is Miss Marie," she began in a rather high-pitched condescending voice.

"Oh, yes," I responded, pondering what Greg must have told her.

Greg chimed into the conversation now and again as Justice Richburg told rather witty legal stories and jokes to enliven the party and maybe to impress me and others. She shook our hands goodbye after a couple of minutes, and I was further introduced to a few more people, such as local entrepreneurs, sports reporters, and professional athletes. And after engaging in some interesting conversations that ranged from the business of money, sports, and some community-minded issues, Greg again thanked them for coming as we each wished them goodbye.

Finally, our team, which was made up of myself, Greg, Elisa, and Mike, walked towards the dance floor to dance a little; have some refreshments; greet some more people, and then call it a night. Greg exchanged numbers with me and hugged Mike and Elisa good night. Holding my left hand and gently pulling me closer, he kissed my hand, whispering into my ear and saying, "I'll call you tomorrow at noon, and thanks for coming to my company party."

6

My phone rang a few minutes after the noon hour, and I picked it up to say hello, and immediately, I heard a deep male voice ask if he could speak to Marie, and I responded, "this is she."

I recognized the voice from the night before. It was a pleasure to hear from him because he looked too good and very important to be bordered by someone average like me, in a sea of many fishes.

"Hi Marie, it's Greg, and how are you doing today?" sounding very business-like.

"I'm fine, thanks for asking, and you?" I replied, smiling to myself.

"Great. Hope you had a nice sleep?" he stated, as guided and professional as possible.

"Yes, of course, it was a pleasure to meet you. And, sorry we didn't have enough time to get to visit one on one." I replied, making sure I didn't say the wrong thing or turn him off.

"Glad you mentioned it because I'd love to come and take you out on a formal date today if you don't mind?" he asked.

Smiling to myself, I said, "that sounds like a sweet deal." I will be lying if I say I wasn't nervous when he said, 'formal date,' just in case he forgets and starts treating me as one of his clients.

"Great. Would it be alright if we go through some shops along the way first?"

A little surprised and puzzled but responded, "oh! Yeah!! Sure!!! what time?"

We settled for four pm, and I hung up. I went to the kitchen to fix an omelet and a glass of orange juice, relax awhile, and then prepare for his arrival, as scheduled.

Maybe I'm nervous because this is my first time dating a professional man instead of my fellow students. And strangely, our age difference is very close. He sounded like a nerd, but I guess it does not matter, except he could turn out to be so boring and uninteresting. Maybe I was worrying too much because he was very sociable and in complete control of his guests at the party. And only a well-developed, highly intelligent, confident, and global-minded person would exhibit such attributes.

A few hours later, I hear footsteps outside of my door, and I can see Greg through my white clear window blinds. Walking to open the door for him, I feel an intoxicating pleasure, an invisible force that rushes through my soul and plants a smile of joy on my lips. On opening the door, I see a broad smile on his lips and his big soft brown eyes. I rush with open arms to reciprocate his and collect the bundle of rose flowers from his right hand.

As he entered the apartment, our lips met, and we automatically started kissing like starved poppies. His kisses tasted like flowers, and I couldn't help teasing him by implying that he kissed them before bringing them to me or whether his warm lips tasted naturally like flowers. He laughed and explained that his garden has several types of perfume flowers. So, yes, he smelled some white, yellow, and red perfumed flowers and violets plucked from his garden prior to coming to my place; but no, he didn't eat or taste them.

He decided to tease too, by stating: "why are your lips with emotion," and I smiled, saying, "because opposites attract."

And since we were still standing by the door, I told him I was ready. We then stepped out, locked the door, and headed to his car. He opened the passenger door of his Ferrari F-1 spider 2-door convertible to let me in; looking into my eyes, he reached for my hand and kissed it, closed the door gently, and walked to the driver's side.

"What's on the agenda?" I asked with excited curiosity.

"Since it's a weekend, are you available for a two, or one-day outing?"

"Two is fine if we'll return to my place to pick up some items," I said.

He responded, "what if we're able to pick the items while out and about?"

Sensing he was thinking about shopping, I replied, "if you prefer, I'm fine too."

"Deal," he stated. "We are driving to Beachwood Place now. Do some shopping first. You can pick up a couple of clothes, footwear, and related female items. If we have extra time today, we could visit a spa and salon, which could take a while because it will involve a foot soak in oatmeal or some other natural ingredients, and indulge in deep tissue massage or rubdown with a variety of ointments to loosen those stubborn knots that keep your muscles tied up and tense, followed by a milk bath."

"Wow, you planned or arranged all that already?" I asked, amazed by his many suggestions.

"Not yet, but an appointment can be done a little in advance anytime," he stated.

Continuing, "It should probably take an hour plus. Else we can reschedule another day and time."

"Yeah, sure. Considering we have to factor in dinner time too," I added.

"True. Dinner, drinks, and duration would depend on location and kind of meal. These definitely should take the rest of tonight through the wee hours of the morning," he laughs.

"I see why we need at least two days to sandwich your huge agenda," I replied.

"Absolutely. And if my guess is correct, the next day could start about high noon, with a drive to the riverfront district for lunch, followed by a walk by the pier, or we could cross the river to see one of the outdoor concerts at the Nautica Pavilion, or just hang on the East Bank and listen to the music drift over. Then followed by dinner and call it a day as we approach late or early hours. Does all that sound like too much?"

"Wow! Omg! That's a heck of a lot to jam-pack for a two-day weekend. Sounds like something we could do over one to two weeks' break," I shouted, laughing so hard with anticipation.

"That's a lot of pleasurable adventure, the likes of which I've never dreamt of in my entire lifetime." I lean over to kiss the corner of his lips, as well as his chiselled jawbone, just as his soft, strong, warm, and beautiful free hand on my knee was caressing and generating heat and quivers across all sensitive parts of my body.

I couldn't help leaning and hugging tightly to his right side and wishing his strong, firm body could melt into mine right this moment, as I felt some tingling spasm from head to toe. I'll have to find a way to let him know that he should not be in a hurry to make me happy because I am happy to just be with him, around him, to touch him, feel him, or just know that he's in love with me and his heart is with me. This is the ultimate priceless gift I'd desire from him.

Meanwhile, we arrived and parked outside the major Mall at Beachwood Place. We held hands as we headed inside. Smiling, and at the information booth area, he pointed to the directory, saying I should not forget to celebrate my day, and headed to our first stops at Sephora, MAC, and LUSH, which were on the first floor. I picked up all the beauty supplies needed to make myself look and feel gorgeous, inside and outside, from lipstick to bronzer.

We walked inside each store together, going through many options as I picked my selections; choices, as he was patiently smiling and teased me with some outlandish or colourful items. The store attendants are also nice and very helpful in helping me decide between a few items. I thanked Greg as he used his credit card to pay for the things, as we headed to another floor for other things. We then headed out to Saks and Nordstrom, Victoria's secret and a few boutique outlets for women's wear, from bikinis, undies, and bras, as well as several women's essentials for the hair, body, and feet, from formal to casual or comfort and relaxation. A shopping extravaganza indeed.

Since the shopping outing consumed most of our time, we were somewhat tired, and our hands were full of shopping bags. I stole a glance at Greg, and he immediately whispered in my ear, "Marie, can we take the shopping bags to the car?"

"I think you're reading my mind," I responded. And we walked towards one of the major exit doors and onto the parking lot.

"I can eat an elephant," he said, laughing, after hauling bags of my items.

"I'm hungry too, and my legs are tired from our long shopping hours," I echoed.

"Plus, since the day is winding down, and it's getting dark outside, can we move the spa to tomorrow and go find a place to feed our hungry palates after we put your stuff in the car?" he suggested, with his eyes probing for affirmation from me.

"Sounds like a sweet deal," I said to him as he opened the car door, helping to place the bags both of us were carrying.

He then helped me into the passenger door.

"You're a perfect gentleman, Greg," I said to him, and he quietly responded by kissing my forehead lightly. He walked over to his side of the door, got in, and we drove off.

As he was driving, he touched my thigh gently and asked, "what are you hungry for?"

"Something international and authentic. Like Sushi or Mexican?" I suggested, smiling and massaging his warm arm.

He laughed, saying, "that was what crossed my mind when you uttered the word internationally."

We headed towards Cleveland Heights, then drove to a Mexican restaurant and Bar. We parked, went in, and were seated near the bar section, where a live band was playing some mariachi music.

The Fajitas, guacamole deep, enchiladas and margaritas were good. As the dinner progressed, I felt more and more relaxed and comfortable with Greg and prompted him to share with me about how he grew up, his family, and the close, loving, caring, nurturing relationship between himself and his parents and twin brother.

I opened up too and shared with him about how I grew up, my early childhood experiences with my parents and grandparents, and how it has impacted me, as well as my past limited relationships, hopes, and fears about the future. He assured me that, although he experienced what is described as stable family life, he said he valued my honesty, candor, and positive outlook and expectations.

He added that he usually trusts his first impressions. He liked me the very first time he set his eyes on me and has enjoyed every moment we've spent together so far. He sees me as levelheaded, funny, and beautiful. He then asked if I was willing to explore our relationship further, and I accepted, and he thanked me for sharing my family tree.

As it was getting close to midnight, he suggested that we could call it a night, and I agreed since we'd been out and about for over half a dozen hours already. Upon getting into the car, he whispered, "Your place or mine?" and I told him mine since he bought lots of stuff for me, and I needed to offload them back into my apartment.

He wanted to know if I could still come to his place to start our day early or should he pick me up in the morning instead? Noticing that he was very interested in being with me more, I agreed to return to his place, which would afford us more time to get to explore our relationship further.

And more importantly, he has a genuinely happy smile and deep beauty about him, which I see in his big brown eyes, warm and strong hands, gentle touch, and athletic body. Besides, he's only a few years older than me, but extremely very mature, kind, caring, thoughtful, funny, loving, and has a spectacularly successful professional career. So yes, I'm grateful for his time and generosity.

We arrived at my place, and he helped me carry my shopping bags. As I went into the bedroom to pick up some overnight items, he remained standing and curiously looking at my living room wall pictures and artwork. He complimented me on the art décor and pondered if the paintings were commissioned and were of family members, and I said yes.

And as I wondered about his statements, I asked him, "how did you know all that?"

He said his family has similar works that they got made while travelling through Europe. Of himself, brother and parents. I told him that all the pieces were from my grandparents because they were instrumental in making me the woman I am today.

Smiling, he turned around, his soft brown eyes hypnotizing and putting me in a trance, he slowly walked towards me, holding my free hand, and I slowly let go of the overnight bag from my other hand, as I was eager to melt into him with excitement, by gently dropping it on the floor.

As he pulled me closer to his chest, I could feel his heartbeat and the hardness of his upper body against my breast. As my nipples were getting hard from a touch of pleasure, the magnetism and melting of our lips were instantaneous. We hungrily sucked, tongued, caressed every part of our embrace. My blood was in a boil and I could no longer resist the impulse to enjoy the beauty of Greg's wholesomeness.

As if he could read my mind, he immediately lifted me up, and I instinctively wrapped my legs around his middle. With his lips still glued to mine, he moved a few steps back and placed me on my couch.

Somehow, my left knee touched his pants, just outside the most intimate part of his anatomy, and I could feel his penis quickly harden and throb as my knee rubbed against it, while his face was glowing all over as our lips were still scurrying through every part of each other's necks, lips, eyes, ears, and faces.

Just as all the exciting movements were going on, I felt a perceptible tremor passing through his frame as he struggled to take my clothes off while I was doing the same with his clothes.

He was, however, quicker in getting my clothes off when I had just slipped off his jacket and began to unbutton his pants. Pulling them down, my eager hands wandered under his shirt, feeling the firmness of the ivory-like flesh of his deliciously rounded buttocks; my hands and eyes noticed that his underwear was saturated with sperm.

My roving hands took possession of his very beautiful long, and large penis that was still throbbing, and holding with my two hands, I licked it with my lips, tasting his delicious warm sperm. I sucked it for a moment or two and stopped just before he was about to spend again. He quickly took control, kneeling, reclined the sofa, and opened my legs to expose my slit, my dripping, wet swollen pink cunt. In a second, his mouth was glued to it while letting his tongue run wild inside of me.

As my body was having spasmodic convulsions, voluptuous fluids were flowing out of my cunt, like an overflowing river embankment. My mouth kept emitting involuntary Ah! Oh! Yes! With tears of joy streaming out of my eyes.

In a second, my ecstasy doubled as I felt the slow insertion of his penis. It swelled inside the juicy cunt which received it lovingly. We continued to kiss and cuddle slowly while our bodies lay almost motionless. Then I began to move my buttocks in a slow motion and instantly screamed from excess emotion as I spent and felt his hot cream of life shoot into my hungry womb.

7

A little after half an hour of a quick clean-up, we were approaching Greg's house. Turning into a large manicured tree-lined lane, I glanced at the large mansions on both sides of the private lane. In less than a minute, we turned right, facing a lake in the foreground; we were driving directly towards an imposing gate of his mansion.

At the entrance, he pressed a button in his car, and a voice from the intercom at the gate instructed him to proceed to the end of the drive, which was surprisingly a long minute as it swung open.

There were enormous old trees on either side of the drive along the way, and with the bright light posts, I could see a glistening pond. A park and manicured gardens in the mansion foreground. As we got out of the car, an older stocky grey-haired gentleman appeared from a side pair of bungalows attached to the three-story mansion. As he was hastening towards us, Greg whispered that it was his house manager, explaining that the manager and his wife doubled as butler and housekeeper.

"Welcome home, sir," the man exclaimed happily as Greg stepped out of the car.

"Hi Cooper," he responded, "please collect her bag and my briefcase and take it to the house."

He quickly carried out his task and walked ahead of us towards a huge front door with tall and large pillars on each side. Approaching nearer, the doors flung open as if by magic, causing my heart to skip a bit.

Cooper, the house manager, led the way, followed by Greg, who was holding my hand. The long entrance hall was filled with impressive paintings that covered entire walls, at which I was staring in awe.

As Cooper flipped a second switch at the hall wall, I could see the paintings better as he led the way into an enormous living room, which had even more paintings on the walls, beautiful antiques, and two huge fireplaces.

Beyond it, I could see a porch overlooking the pond. The mansion sat on a hill, facing the bond, and I could see a boat as Greg was squeezing my fingers. I squeezed him back, looking at his smiling eyes. "It's beautiful here," as I admired the mansion and the scene beyond, and he was pleased by my reaction and rewarded me with a broad smile.

"That's why I sometimes tend to work at home because it's so peaceful here."

Reappearing after dropping off the bags, Cooper asked me, with an expressive smile, what I'd like to drink. I asked for water as Greg, and I walked to sit down in the living room.

Two small bottles of water and two cups of tea, and homemade chocolate cakes were brought in a tray for us. Since it was already past midnight, Greg said he would show me the bedroom after a brief relaxation. We chatted about our itinerary for the next day, with a probable starting hour of noon, with an outdoor lunch by the riverfront district, followed by a walk along the pier or the river. Or, depending on our mood, to simply hang out by the East Bank and listen to music, followed by dinner much later, before returning home.

"I suppose you would now like to unpack and unwind for the night and start our day bright and early," said Greg, as he was stealing his eyes between the wall clock and myself. Maybe his thoughts were based on observing that I was looking a little tired.

"That's rather a good idea," I replied in agreement.

"The rooms are on the 3rd floor and have high ceilings and large windows that open out to the view of the pond and flower garden," he said, as he led the way up many winding stairways till we came to an oak door with some lovely swan and bull emblazons painted on it.

"Here we are," he whispered calmly as I noticed my carry-on luggage by the large walk-in closet. The room is magnificent, with purple silk curtains and a 4-poster bed, draped with the same shade, with a large walk-in closet on one side of it.

The toilet set is white and mauve, and there are some violets in an expensive vase; across from it is a marble paneled shower and a large bathtub that doubles as a jacuzzi at one end.

Next to the room is a pair of double doors that lead to an identical room, but slightly smaller, which includes a tip-up basin with a hose, all in pale yellow and wild primroses.

At the opposite end of the floor that covers the space for the two rooms is located a huge master bedroom suite with a fireplace, a spa tub, dual closets, and a terrace with several extra luxurious fixtures of comfort. And overlooks the pond from a second-story balcony and rooftop deck floor. On this same floor, he mentions, is a large living room that features custom shelves and a built-in projector screen, and a mini-library.

"Well, Marie, since we've taken our water and you've patiently listened to me describe this floor, I suppose we should have some rest to enable us to start our day fresh; what do you think?"

"I think we should sleep too," agreeing with him, "and thanks for introducing me to this floor. I hope you'd be kind enough to give me a mini-tour of your beautiful property when next you have the time. You are a beautiful and kind man, and I'm glad to have met you."

Smiling, he held my hands in his while I responded by squeezing his fingers against my palms. He lifted me up effortlessly, kissing me with his sweet, warm lips, carried me to the room with my luggage, placed me by the edge of the bed, and sat by my side with his hands wrapped around me.

We kissed passionately for what seemed like an eternity, and upon opening our eyes, smiling, he asked if he could be excused to process and upload some work project to meet a deadline, and we will see each other again in the morning.

After several moon hours of deep baby sleep, I was awoken by the room intercom, and a female voice said good morning and asked if I wanted a cup of tea or coffee brought to my room, and I responded, "coffee."

I then got up and used the bathroom. Freshened up. And upon hearing a tap at the door, I said, come in, and to my surprise, it was Greg, carrying two cups of coffee for both of us.

"Top of the morning to you, Marie. Did you have a nice sleep?"

"Yes, I did," I replied, smiling and looking into his big brown eyes.

He appeared thoughtful and reflective, and I asked him if he was okay. His reply was quick and affirmative as if he was caught off guard, which made me wonder if he sometimes feels lonely, but I couldn't bring myself to ask.

As if he knew my thoughts, he sat by my side and summarized what he was thinking and feeling after we went to our separate bedrooms last night: he said his brother and himself had been involved in adult duties growing up. Such as in helping in his parents' businesses and in everyday life chores, which essentially have been all work and limited play

Although they'd taken numerous trips overseas together, his joys and happiness were subsumed by that of his parents. And although he engaged in several sports recreationally, he tended to lead a solitary, reflective life, preferring books, creative arts, and economic endeavors. He said he literally only dated once, which he described as more a friendship than an actual boy-girl relationship. Such as, going out to the theatre, walks, eating, and engaging in family-oriented events or group activities were the norm. He thought it was romantic but not intimate enough to build a deeper connection.

For a moment, he was silent and looked at me. I told him I understood and that he was not alone. He nodded and thanked me. We held each other close, kissing very slowly and hearing each other's heartbeat.

He whispered in one of my ears, "I love you."

And I did the same in his other ear, "I love you more."

He called the butler to bring the breakfast to us by the terrace. While seated on the terrace, we couldn't help enjoying the fresh breeze and sunshine, as well as the spectacular view of the sky and beautiful pond below.

While glancing and enjoying the view, I noticed he was watching me with pleasure, as he was also scanning the outdoors too.

And when I smiled back, he stated with an affirmative curiosity, "hope you truly like the States, so far." I sense his statement is coated in a deep desire to build a long-term relationship with me, but I'm not confident enough to as him what's in his mind.

He proceeded with his monologue while I listened with interest, punctuated with a word here and there and gestures of acknowledgement.

In short, he explained that when Mike, his employee and Elisa's boyfriend, asked if they should invite me to meet him, he wasn't as enthusiastic about the idea but glad he accepted. He said when he first looked into my eyes and my appearance and our eyes met, he felt instant chemistry. I told him I thought he looked like those kinds of guys one only sees in the movies or GQ magazines but only dreams about.

He agreed with my assessment but explained it as one of those social constructs that define and divides people, but deep down, we all have the same fits of hunger, emotions, feelings, and desire to give and receive love. He was quiet as if to gather his thoughts and then continued.

That when he spent more time with me and got to know me more, I turned out to be surprisingly poised, attractive, personable, intelligent, and mature. He said he meets females often but professionally and is never relaxed enough to stray outside his goal of finding passion in business success, just like his parents before him. In me, he confessed, he could talk about everything else, which he found very relaxing, enjoyable, and refreshing. He thanked my friend Elisa and Mike for making it possible.

At the terrace, breakfast of eggs, bacon, toast, tea, orange juice, and a bowl of fruits were served. He moved his chair closer, like placed next to mine, so that we could have the same view. He cracked a joke about Siamese twins, and I laughed and pulled him closer, kissing his lips and ear lobe. After murmuring I love you to him, we continued our chatty hour and looked at the outdoors' lush landscaping and a beautiful pond.

And to answer his question about my experiences, I told him it has been a mixture of fun, heartbreaks, and the resolve to grow up and make something good out of my life. I explained to him that although my situation was not unusual, it had to do with me coming from a different culture, being raised by parents that cared but were not as involved in parenting, as well as my personality or character traits. He laughed and agreed with my analysis, chiming in with the idea of him growing up surrounded by luxury and opportunity but not necessarily, being consumed by it. His brother, on the other hand, decided to pursue medicine and combine practice and teaching at the UCLA medical school in California.

He concluded by saying, "you seem to have had an interesting adventure in academia and social life here in the States so far, and what are your next dream goals?"

I responded by telling him about my desire to open a small art gallery and bistro by East Fourth Street here in the city of Cleveland to take advantage of the young college crowds and play with the competitive niche as the market dictates. And that I've signed up on a lease and looking to get started before the summer is over. He kept nodding his head throughout, and when I stopped talking for a moment, he said he was very impressed and said I shouldn't hesitate to ask him for guidance, or rather, if I'd be open to a partnership with any form of modification, or a 'silent investor.'

"Absolutely," I shouted out my excited agreement. I could see a winning combination with him on all fronts. Considering his business acumen and management expertise, his kindhearted and supportive personality, and our love for each other, what woman would say anything other than a capital 'yes!'

When he asked if he could show me his second floor. We stood up together, held hands and headed down the hallway, and took the stairs down. It was a huge floor, much bigger than the third. Not only did it have two guest rooms on one end, but a walk across the hallway were many conveniences, including a gym, game room, media room, and conference center. And through large double doors leading into a minibar and wine cellar, an open private terrace overlooking the outdoors, colorful flower beds and miniature palm trees, and a man-made waterfall that runs into a heart-shaped swimming pool. I asked him when he gets to enjoy all these, and he said his company usually hosts holidays and end-of-year parties or similar special occasions, like family visitations. He teased me that I would be welcomed as a special guest anytime. Since we had planned to visit the spa in town the day before, he suggested we should try and get ready. We walked the stairs back to the third floor and parted ways to our respective rooms to use either the shower or bathtub and meet again in less than an hour.

 An hour and a half later, he called for us to meet downstairs in the living room for take-off. We drank glasses of freshly squeezed fruit juices that were prepared by the butler prior to heading out to the spa. I suggested that we could skip the spa for another day or use the one in his home since it has everything. He thought my idea was, in his own words, "brilliant."

We both laughed and agreed to just go for lunch, take a walk by the pier and enjoy the fresh air outdoors, and then hang out by the East Bank or Nautica Pavilion. We dressed in casual wear and walked out to the car. In less than ten minutes, we arrived at a local famous French restaurant downtown. Greeted with smiles, the waiter took us to a comfortable terrace seating area facing the river.

Greg asked for me to suggest our meals since I was French, and I picked up the menu, smiled, and ordered a French-style leg of lamb with lots of garlic, mashed potatoes, and string beans. And for dessert, I picked tiramisu. Greg suggested a red wine, which tasted exceptionally good. We were so relaxed, enjoyed the animated conversation, and I explained to him about various types of French wines and the traditions surrounding each. I explained that I enjoyed cooking or experimenting with different foods, to which I could see the excitement in his eyes, like a price fighter, in anticipation. He then asked if he could be honored to enjoy my cooking one day in the future, and I promised to invite him to satisfy his palate.

We finished our meal, headed to the door, holding hands and smiling, and walked towards the East bank to enjoy fresh outdoor air along the boardwalk. There was some solo singer playing multiple instruments, using his feet for drums, hands for guitar, and mouth for both the harmonica and singing. His various song choices ranged from pop, rock, reggae, country, and urban mix. One fascinating final act before our departure was his dancing on sharp-edged, pointed, broken bottles without being hurt or injured.

We bought some small bottles of fruit juice and walked away from the crowd, and in less than two minutes, we found a bench and sat down. Greg was quiet for a minute and appeared thoughtful, so I asked, "how are you doing, my man?"

He looked at me and smiled. Squeezing my fingers in his big warm palm, he said: "You're wondering what's in my mind, right?" he said.

I agreed with his guess, and he continued, "you are very good at reading emotions. I just thought about my parents and remembered I've not spoken to them for a while. Especially mom. I wonder how they're doing."

"Please go ahead and call them. Turn your thought to action, my dear. I should think there's a reason for thinking about them, and naturally, it should be followed with a call, even if just to say hello or just to hear their voices," I suggested.

"You're right. I'd call in a few," he concluded. "And by the way, how about you?"

"Well, to tell you the truth, I don't call my folks much. As you know, the way I grew up and the nature of our relationship never lend themselves to normal closeness. Only my grandpa and ma cross my mind now and then because of the special bond I had with them as a kid. Other than that," I started laughing nervously, "promise you won't laugh at what I'm about to say, ok?"

"I promise," he replied, smiling.

I continued: "Since we started dating, I feel as if we are a family, literally and metaphorically speaking."

"Gee, thanks, I never thought about it that way. Yes, you're correct. We're in love and have a deep connection and understanding. That's what is referred to as chemistry, right?" he asked.

Before he could finish, I jumped in: "Of course. I've never had a guy or anyone care for me as much as you have. Very genuinely and unselfishly. I notice you speak about your family pretty much, regularly, and very fondly. I hear it in your voice, and even Stevie Wonder can see it in your eyes too." I said good-humoredly.

"But seriously, being close to one's family, laughing and sharing or doing things together, comes naturally to you. It's obvious when you talk to them or about them."

He reached over and pulled me closer with his strong hands, kissing my forehead and then my lips. His fruity, warm lips tasted delicious, and I wanted more, but he adjusted my body sideways, slightly.

Wrapping his hand around my waist, he whispered in my ear: "Wow! A girl like you comes around once every hundred years. Who is this girl? When you're in your element, your accent sound so sexy; plus, you feel and look so hot. You are a goddess. Believe me, I'm smitten.

"When we first met, It didn't take me a minute to know that you were a hot girl. And being realistic about your having roots outside of the States and not knowing your future goals after graduation, I couldn't imagine anything between us other than to take it a day at a time. I acknowledge the fact that our modus operandi is honesty: I'm thankful for your great qualities of beauty, intelligence, plus other- centered thoughtfulness and nurturing personality. So, dating and being in love with you suits me very much. What do you think?" He concluded, searching my eyes for a response.

"Honestly, from what my upbringing has taught me so far, love and trust are more important than marriage. So, wearing a white dress and throwing a big party is not necessary because we're 'husband and wife' in my heart, and a certificate or state or church cannot erase that from me. Meeting you is like winning a lottery." Like the Americans would say, 'you are the best thing since sliced bread that has ever happened in my life." I giggled and couldn't believe I actually spoke those words.

Laughing hilariously, he touched my arm momentarily and asked to be excused a few minutes while he returned a missed call. Standing up and removing his cellphone from tho loft oido pookot of hio windbroakor, ho dialod a numbor. I oould hoar everything he was saying because it was on speaker.

"Hi dad, it's your son Greg; how are you and mom doing?"

"We're doing pretty good, son, and how about you?"

"Great, dad. May I speak to mom to see if I can arrange to visit you guys morrow?"

"Hold on a second." Silence. "Honey, Greg is on the line." Silence a second more.

A female voice on the phone: "Hello son, I've not heard from you for a while."

"Hi, mom," he responded, "how're you and pop doing? Hope well."

"Yes, son, we are in good health and doing pretty good," she replied, sounding very pleased.

"Nice to hear, mom. I wanted to see if I could drop by tomorrow for lunch or dinner. Your choice." He looked at me as if to confirm or be reassured.

"Oh, sure. You can drop in anytime. Lunch would be fine since we have a bridge game at the Hamilton's, our old friends, you remember them, don't' you?"

"Yes, of course, I do. Would twelve-fifteen be okay? And mom, I'll be coming with a female friend of mine, if it's alright with you?" he asked her.

The Hamilton's, as he explained later, was his parents' neighbors he's known way back during his preteen years. He said he got hooked on chocolate cookies and apple cider juice growing up because Mrs Hamilton had a habit of bringing over the two items for him and his brother once every weekend when both families were off and wanted to visit and exchange neighborhood gossip or just conversated about anything that caught their fancy.

"Great idea, son. You work so hard, and it's good to take time out and enjoy some company some time. Anyway, we'll see you and your friend any time after the noon hour, okay?"

"Yes, mama. Please give my love to dad and see both of you tomorrow," he said.

"Okay, son. Oh, before I forget, your brother Bill, and wife Sara, arrived an hour ago from California for a three-day conference. He said he was going to call you after he got out of the shower when they got in. Or maybe he has already. They're in one of the guest rooms, so I won't know for sure. In any case, we will all see you tomorrow," she concluded.

"Sure, mama. Bye for now," as he hung up.

Before placing his phone in his jacket, he said there was a missed call from his brother that came through as he was talking to his mom. He smiled as he was putting the phone away, saying he'll call his brother back later or see him tomorrow anyway.

I opened my arms for a bear hug, and he reached out and pulled me in, almost melting me into himself. He hugged and kissed me hungrily and whispered in my ear that it would be a good idea if we went home and continued since it was getting dark outdoors.

We walked to the car quietly, and he opened my car door first, let me in, and then his side. Squeezing my knee briefly, he took off for home. When we entered the gates with a remote sensor, I didn't see his house helpers and sensing my curiosity as our eyes met, Greg informed me that he'd text them to go ahead and sleep and he'll see them in the morning.

As we entered the house, we headed upstairs and into his master bedroom. I told Greg I'll jump into the shower, and he said he'd be next. Just before I was completely undressed, he handed me a glass of orange juice while guzzling his, making some throaty noise. I laughed, and he simply said, "Yeah, sure, that was a taste quencher. See you shortly, or I'll come to scrub you myself."

I told him the second option sounded ideal and headed to the shower. As I was quietly washing some soapy foam off my neck with my eyes closed, I felt a light touch on my shower cap, and upon opening my eyes, I noticed Greg standing naked next to me and asking if I needed some help. I said yes but added that it was conditioned upon him letting me do the same for him. We scrubbed each other simultaneously, and as his hands reached between my thighs, I felt a tingling sensation and started hugging him as the washcloth fell off my hand. He responded and started kissing me passionately, moving between my lips, neck, and ear lobe. He turned me around, bent me forward, and with one hand, he curbed my breast, and with the other, he squeezed my backside, opening my pussy, and glided into my oozing orifice. Our sensation was unbearable and, in a few seconds, we both spent and were dripping juices between our thighs.

Holding each other very tightly, we turned around, facing each other; we kissed quietly, slowly, and longingly, and returned to our continuation of soaping and scrubbing each other until we were done. We then grabbed a couple of towels from across the shower stand for each, helping to clean each other, and walked back to the bedroom. After putting lotion on each other, we decided to get under the sheets naked, melted into each other's arms, and fell asleep shortly afterwards.

8

We woke up a little early and walked to the downstairs terrace for coffee and a quick breakfast, as well as enjoy the outdoors-fresh air from the flower garden and pool, before going to Greg's parents for lunch. For breakfast, Cooper prepared for us some French toast and eggs, cups of orange juice, as well as honey-flavored coffee.

After the meal, Greg excused himself to call his brother Bill. A few minutes afterwards, he hung up and said that his brother and his wife would accompany us to an outdoor concert by Avon Lake, not far from his parents' neighborhood home. I thought it was cool, because it would offer me an opportunity to have fun, socialize and get to know his family more.

We took a walk around the garden, smelling the roses, and chatted for a few more hours. Then went back upstairs to get ready. Looking inside my allotted bedroom closet, I decided to wear casual clothes since we were going to be outdoors after lunch. I wore a white lacey waist-length top, paired with wide-leg cargo pants, and added some eye-catching color with some bright purple converse sneakers. When Greg walked into the room shortly for us to see if I was ready, I noticed he was dressed nicely too, wearing a white polo designer shirt, a brown belt over a blue jeans, and dark blue tennis shoes to match his looks. When our eyes met, we both smiled as he further admired my top to bottom outfit, with an obvious pleasure and animal magnetism that pulled him over to my side, with him holding and pressing his hand against my arm. He gushed, "you look beautiful, girl" as he gave me a quick kiss.

Hand in hand, we headed to the stairways. Taking baby steps, we kissed several times until we got to the ground floor. He helped me into my side of the car, and we drove through the gate to our scheduled get-together lunch with his family. Going through the traffic, we eventually arrived at Avon Lake and navigated through a gated community until we rang the doorbell. Greg's brother opened the door to let us in. Bill was a very tall and handsome guy, as he reached out to kiss my extended hand and gave his brother a bear hug with acknowledgements of chitchats, signifying they've not spoken for a while. On entering the house, a beautiful young female, probably around my age, reached out with her arms open for a hug for both Greg and me.

"I'm Sara, Bill's wife, and you?"

"Marie. Greg's girlfriend," I replied, with my eyes glued to a slim, tall, strikingly beautiful twenty-something-year-old female.

"Nice to meet you, Marie," as she smiled and walked me further into the large panoramic living room.

"Look who's here," Bill announced with his booming voice as we were in the living room area. His voice sounded like and could be mistaken for his brother Greg.

Looking straight ahead were two people sitting on a large couch, facing the big screen TV, and they both looked up simultaneously. Greg walked up to them, and I followed closely behind. I could see a strong resemblance between the two siblings and their dad, with beautiful brown eyes and naturally lush well-lined eyelashes like their mom.

"Hey, dad. Hey mom," echoed Greg to both parents.

Both stood up, taking turns to exchange hugs and kisses.

"Dad and mom, meet Marie," said Greg.

"Hi Marie," uttered his dad, extending a handshake.

"Hello, Marie. Welcome to our home," his mom reached out, extending open arms, and we both responded with a kiss on either chick.

Both parents did the same with Greg with exchanges of humor and laughter. His mom proceeded to request for everybody to move to the kitchen for lunch. The dining room looked beautiful. The table was decorated with flowers and ornamental decorations. The females sat on one side, with Sara and me on either of our hosts. And Greg and his brother Bill are on either side of their dad, across from us females.

Sets of plates, spoons, and glasses were placed in front of each dining chair. We started out with cocktails and alcohol-free fruit-based drinks. Sara and I had a tequila that was flavored with cider. It was a lip-licking sippy drink that prepared my appetite for the meal. Greg and his dad had a watered-down Black Lapel, which they characterized as smooth. His mom stock a glass of freshly squeezed fruit juice. While Bill settled for some California glass of white wine.

Next was a combination of salads, but primarily lettuce salad, which came with several flavored dressings from cheese to a combination of nuts and earthy ingredients. This was followed by the main course, with various options or combinations, ranging from grilled octopus with garbanzo beans and olive tapenade. The seafood risotto was also provided with abundant creamy flavored fresh chunks of clams and lobsters.

Greg's family was nontraditional, very conversational throughout the delicious meal, and very openly discussed their professional and social relationships. As physicians, Bill and Sara shared a lot about their medical orthopedic and pediatric services or programs, respectively. And Greg, about how he and his team are adapting to sustainable investment market-driven models for the maximization of his company's bottom line.

After a full course meal, Greg suggested we should go relax more comfortably in the living room. Bill and Sara excused themselves to their room to get ready for the Avon Lake outdoors party. Our hosts remained in the kitchen awhile, with Greg's mom putting the left-over foods away, with help from her husband, and appearing to be in a very good mood, laughing and chatty.

"Would you guys want anything to drink or snack while you're relaxing?" said Greg's mom.

"No, ma'am. We're fine, thank you." Echoed Greg.

"I hear you guys are heading to the Lake for a live music show?" she continued

"Yes, mom, it should be fun, I'm sure. Are you guys coming too?" replied Greg.

"No-o-o. We think it would be more fun for young people like you. Plus, you might meet some people you knew way back when you were younger. Besides, you'd be enjoying your brother and wife's company while they're in town."

"True, mom," he responded, then turning to me on the couch we're sharing, "Marie, I know you've heard me say this before, and know you don't mind hearing it again. I want to let you know I love you very deeply, and I'm going back to the kitchen to tell my parents I'm in love with you, okay?"

"Oh! Oh! With tears streaming from my eyes, "I love you so very much too my sweetheart. You're my everything. You're the best gift I've ever had in my life. To cherish forever."

He stood up quietly and, holding my hands, he pulled me up and wrapped both his hands around me, and kissed me passionately. Excusing himself, he walked back to the kitchen to talk with his mom and dad.

Then he returned to the living room with a glass of water for me. I drank it till the last drop and thanked him for knowing I needed it. His mother and dad walked by moments later, one behind the other. They sat on the large sofa, facing the wall TV and fireplace. His father asked if I'd been to Avon Lake before, and I said no but was looking forward to the experience.

He mentioned that it's been a long time since he last visited the place himself but remembered it fondly when his two sons were little, and they used to hang out there on weekends, chatting with other young parents, while the neighborhood kids played together. He added that over the years, the local city government expanded and modernized the outdoors landscaping and surroundings, such as flower beds, seating areas, a playground for younger kids, all-season open space gym, and exercise fixtures. Plus, a hardwood all-season stage for occasional performances or for people to hang around and watch fireworks and other related annual holiday events.

Greg chimed in that one of his favorite childhood activities was to use the sand to build castles. And during his teen years, to playing beach volleyball with his friends.

They then excused themselves as Bill and Sara joined us in the living room. Greg said to no one in particular but suggested that we could go ahead and relax for a while and drive out to the lake whenever we were ready.

I overheard Greg's brother Bill and his wife, Sara, talking about medical events pertaining to nurses' c-sections, patients, recovery, and so on. I know they're both physicians, so I decided to ask them about their specialities.

"Sorry to cut into your conversation; what area of medicine did both of you specialize in?" I enquired, looking first at Sara, then Bill.

"We are both in obstetrics and gynecology, often abbreviated as OB-GYN," said Sara, with a smile, looking at me and then turning to Bill, probably to see if he had anything else to say.

"Yeah, sure," added Bill. "These two subspecialties, namely obstetrics, cover pregnancy, childbirth, and the postpartum period. While the gynecology aspect covers the health of the female reproductive system - vagina, uterus, ovaries, and breasts." He concluded and quickly apologized for being too academic. And I reassured him that I'm very grateful to learn about it from an expert like him, for free.

 "It must be a very busy and stressful job, I suppose?" I chimed in with a smile.

"Yes, but we enjoy it. Never a dull moment," he added

"Absolutely," echoed Sara, with an enthusiastic voice. "We sometimes have big emergencies during labor or delivery, but we're glad it's not all the time."

It is obvious to see that she's very passionate about her profession. Very easy to see what binds them as a loving couple, in addition to their other common personality traits. As she spoke, she noticed her husband was looking at her with a grin, and both busted out laughing together. They are a beautiful couple and exude ease and comfort that is common among compatible family members, like its resemblance to what I've found in the man I've fallen in love with.

"Where were you born," I asked Sara, out of curiosity and wanting to get to know her more.

"Manhattan Beach, California," she responded. She's stunning in physical beauty and would've easily become a model or actress. But choosing an option of medicine with her smarts instead of playing doctor on television or in the movies. And as if she knew what I was thinking, she added, "I had a degree in biology and film studies but ended up in medical school to follow the footsteps of my mother, who is a cardiologist, while my father is a movie producer. An excellent decision that led me to my handsome husband." She concluded and laughed heartily.

"I'm lucky too," stated Bill, smiling, "else, I won't have met her either. And for me, my parents say I've always played doctor as a kid. Not necessarily wanting to play one on television," busting out with laughter, which made us laugh along too, "but to become a real doctor, although I didn't know in what specialty. As I thought about it while in the program and talking with my mom, I naturally gravitated towards OB since my mom mentioned that she had two miscarriages before my brother and I were conceived, and it has been a very rewarding career for me ever since," he said, with a glowing sweet smile on his face.

"That's beautiful, Bill. And do both of you like or enjoy living and working in California?" I asked out of curiosity.

"Oh yeah," they answered in unison. Looking at Sara, Greg nodded, "we love it."

"And your living area is further away from work?" I asked further, not being able to hide the excitement and fascination I had with my boyfriend's beautiful family.

"Not exactly, because we live pretty close to the university teaching hospital, which is a block away, and a short walk or bike ride to work in our beautiful year-round weather." Said Sara.

With a glimmer in his eyes, Bill added, "we have plenty of room for you guys as guests any time. Our four-bedroom space is available whenever you and my brother come to visit. We would make time to show you around and introduce you to our friends who are made up of people from across every continent in the world," looking at both myself and Greg with a radiant smile.

"Yeah, sure," added Sara, with joyful excitement. "We are pretty close to my younger brother's condo, a former Olympic medalist, now turned Silicon Valley venture capitalist." She went on further to state that her brother has an actor girlfriend that shuttles between out of town or country shoots and staying with her brother.

Hearing them talk about close and happy family relationships makes me envious and wish for the same too. With resources and close distance, loving families are a skip away from each other, whether spending weekends or holidays together.

"Families, like from both your sides, are very rare these days," I said after listening to them. "Most people I know, including myself, live all over the country or far away countries, from their siblings and parents." Although very busy, their lives seem very normal and balanced. Their family backgrounds are stable, and they can make time for each other as necessary.

"So, what do both of you do for fun when not working?" I asked, noticing that they were a little thoughtful and tentative prior to responding.

They laughed, realizing that typical physicians hardly have to time off. "Work, work. We enjoy what we do," Said Sara. With a sense of honesty and compassion in her voice.

"Well, we enjoy events or short trips outdoors whenever we can. Such as concerts, movies, wine tasting, skiing, sailing, fishing, hiking, playing tennis, or watching professional sports." Bill added, quietly and candidly. From my observations, they both make an excellent, caring, and loving couple. Both are beautiful, smart, and levelheaded. And I thanked them for sharing a slice of their family history, as well as their professional and personal life.

Greg came back into the living room after briefly using the washroom. He asked if we were ready to drive to the lake, and we all stood up. His parents walked in from their inner rooms to hug us goodbye. The six of us stood up, hugged, and kissed while we waived their parent's bye for now as they saw us off to the door. We thanked them for the nice lunch and warm hospitality. They acknowledged our visit and asked for us to stop by some more, anytime. Greg and I drove in our car. Bill and Sara rode theirs right behind us.

Arriving at the car park at the lake, the four of us got out and headed to the raised stage, which was beginning to be filled with many local and out of town young and not so young people. One of the strikingly stunning girls recognized Greg and walked up to us to say hello. Greg introduced her to Sara and me, and we shook hands with her while she hugged and kissed the two brothers as long-lost friends. When she walked back to the stage to join the other musicians, Greg told us that he and she were high school classmates; she left for New York City to study music and later formed a pop band with her fiancé's boyfriend; and was home to visit her family and share her first successful album, by opening with her popular single, and providing a free concert for her home crowd.

All eyes were on her because she was famous, successful, and very attractive, combined with her stunning and glamorous looks. She wore a black and blue sheer, vintage celebrity-styled dress. The dress was ankle-length with long blue sleeves and blue paneling with eye-catching lines on the dress. I realized why she drew so much close attention from looking at her chiseled abs and glowing, toned long legs. Her upper body sported nothing but a lacey blue bra and thong underneath the sexy sheer ensemble, paired with black strappy sandals, bronze jewelry, and blue eye shadow to accent the dress. Her hair looked cute and sexy in a high ponytail with bangs that framed the sides of her beautiful face.

The audience was dancing along as they heard the high tempo and beautiful voice of the singer that complemented that of the guy. Greg ordered us some drinks to stay hydrated. And Sara enjoyed the music, chatting, laughing, and singing along. Her black and white striped sweater paired with a black mini skirt and ankle-length boots looked beautiful on her. The crowd was excited and loud, and you could hear various voices saying how hot the female singer was and some guys in the rows behind, in front, and around us, echoing similar sentiments of excitement and jubilation while pumping their hands in the air, to fit the rhythmic sound of the music. The large crowd made up of the young and old, men and women, were everywhere like an invasion of locusts, to see and be seen. We were told a choreographed dance parade had ended just before our arrival.

Dozens of empty beer cans and plastic bottles of water, beer, and soft drinks were scattered all over the grassy and sandy lake area. It was also obvious that the crowd was from Cleveland and the surrounding suburbs and cities, especially when the singer thanked everybody from neighboring major cities and counties for coming out and for supporting her music. This gesture increased the feverish tempo of the crowds.

While this was going on, I was busy taking pictures of the scenery and events as they were happening on my cell phone. I was most especially happy to hang out together with Greg and his family. I felt grateful, especially, for the opportunity to thoroughly enjoy easy, natural clean fun and make beautiful memories that are likely to last a lifetime.

When the concert ended two hours later, we decided to walk up to the stage and greet the musical duo and acknowledge their spectacular showmanship and fantastic performance. We then headed back to our cars to bid goodbye to Bill and Sara with hugs and kisses on their chicks and thanked them for a beautiful time together.

In the car back, I reflected on when I first asked Greg once about his family, and he said he'll introduce me to them and would want me to be the judge whenever I met them. And after meeting them, I now know what he meant. His modesty doesn't allow him to say glowing things about his parents. But based on the little he said, plus anecdotal statements I heard from Elisa and Mike, who have met them formally during previous get-togethers, I agree with their assessment that they are a close, loving family with deep love and care for each other as well as for others.

I could also see what Mike, who has known them for several years during his college days, described them as a "very close family whose daily tasks revolve around work and business," and I see why they've provided their children with those necessary professional skills through education, in order to assist the family business, if necessary. This is naturally reflected in Greg's passion for enhancing and sustaining the family business. It's also true that they're a very tight and well-adjusted family that is caring, nurturing, funny, and involved in social and civic projects outside of their busy schedule.

It made me realize how and why I'm so attracted to him as a person, his personality and his different background when compared to mine. It's obvious that his parents' nurturing family values and guidance, just like my grandparents were, have had a strong impact and influence on who and what he has become. I could also see why his active athletics and extracurricular involvement and hands-on academic studies with tutoring sessions would leave little time for socialization and interpersonal relationships. A situation that is often viewed by some parents as a distracting influence on the future growth or focus of their offspring, although such thinking could just as well result in a negative outcome for some children.

As we were getting closer to Greg's neighborhood, I placed my left hand on Greg's thigh, squeezing it, bending over to kiss the side of his face, and slowly rubbing my palm and fingers on him more tightly and feeling the touch getting warmer and warmer. He stole a quick glance at me, smiling, and used his free hand to place on top of mine, slowly lifting my hand off him and kissing my palm before letting go. He then reduced the car speed as he was about to turn into the large gate. Pressing the car auto- gate button, then accelerated straight ahead.

Parking closer to the door entrance, we entered the large front doors that were just opened by Cooper. When his eyes met his boss, as is often the case, and without him saying anything, he was told, "go ahead." And holding my hand and pulling me closer, Greg and I took the stairways to the 2nd floor and entered the master bedroom, hand in glove.

Inside the room, and as an afterthought, he said, "oh, I was telling the caretaker to get dinner ready, so we can eat in the next few hours." And without saying another word, we began to undress each other very rapidly. Just before my bra and undies were off me, I was lifted off the ground and placed delicately on the large comfy bed. I could feel his large penis, proudly erect as a flagpole, with its lizard head bouncing up and down, looking for an entrance to enter and take care of business. I must say that I was already wet from so many hours of starvation, especially as I could not take my eyes off a well-endowed, solidly built, glowing prick.

"Please feed me," I begged him. "I'm starving!"

He was silent as a lamb, except his face that was wearing a beautiful smile that I could only interpret as a "yes." With his soft brown eyes reading the naked hunger in me, his strong hands wrapped around my midsection and laid my back in the middle of the super king soft bed. Getting between my legs, he penetrated the wet opening between my thighs. The moment I felt the head within the further recess of my cunt, I spent profusely. He worked on me for a long time, holding back coming inside me, as much as possible. Perhaps, to give me as much pleasure as he could. This made me spend three times. The bed covers were getting wet with my flowing juices just as I was dissolving my very vitals into sperm. His ever throbbing and exploring organ met my demanding orifice and injected the seed into my womb. Tears of joy and sobs of satisfaction were streaming off my face as I continued to thank him for a job well done.

9

Waking up early from a sound sleep, which was marked by an enjoyable dinner together last night, Greg rolled over and kissed the back of my neck, and when I turned towards him, he whispered in my ear that he'll be busy in corporate meetings and conferences with his team, on second-quarter reports, as well as on sales and marketing projections for the rest of the year.

Just as he was talking to me, his phone rang, and he excused himself and whispered, "a minute, please, I've got to transmit some files and delegate some tasks to Mike asap."

He got up, wore his bottom pajamas and walked over to his mini office across from the bedroom. I decided to use the free time and go to the adjoining bedroom that has my personal effects to shower and freshen up before planning his birthday for tomorrow.

As I was thinking and jotting down some to-do items at the dresser, someone tapped my shoulder, and it was him. He informed me that I should go ahead and eat breakfast and lunch without him, and he'll have a hectic day until late afternoon. I got up and gave him a hug and a quick kiss and told him to have a nice day.

"Oh! Before you take off, would you be free to celebrate your birthday tomorrow?" I asked him before he vanished.

"Yeah, sure, just for the two of us." He replied. He thinks birthdays are like any calendar day, except for a desire to celebrate and make happy memories.

If you're a hundred percent free, I'd love to have the pleasure of hosting your entire twenty-four-hour b-day as my king."

"What do you have in mind?" he grinned as his curiosity was aroused.

"Good. First, I'll love to take you out to the Cleveland Museum of Art for an exhibit of some romantic paintings during the AM hours.

"Second, I'd like for us to take your yacht for a special champagne lunch and cake to celebrate your birthday by the river in the afternoon.

"And third, if you don't mind, I'd love to decorate twenty percent in the sections of your mansion that we spend the most amount of time, to celebrate the end of your birthday as well as my thanks for your love for me, over dinner and drinks, during our late-night hours," I concluded.

"Wow! That's spectacular," he responded, opening his arms to hug me.

Rushing into his embrace, we hugged, kissed, and mumbled inordinate love words for what seemed like forever.

"You're beyond my girlfriend, honey," he said, as his big brown eyes searched my face as if to seek reassurance.

"I love you very dearly," he muffled between our mouth full of roving tongues and conjoined lips. Feeling his phone's vibration, he peeled himself from me slowly and hurried away to get ready for a long day ahead, saying, "I'll text or call you later."

When he was gone, I reflected upon my life experiences since my arrival in the States, a place I now call home. Until I met Greg, I was focused on my studies, enjoying college life, just like any other young college-age person. My relationship experiences were nothing to write home about, and I'm glad they didn't plant any negative seeds in my head or heart about men.

As time passed and I was nearing graduation, I began to feel a disconnect with where I grew up, as well as to try to erase the bad aspects of how I grew up and replace them with how I want to grow up going forward.

Although I cannot predict the future, my body and heart feel like I'm in the right place. I'm thankful to my friend, Elisa, for helping to explain and inject hopeful ideas into my head. Her explanation of looking at being in the 'friend zone' when in a dating relationship is not necessarily a bad idea, considering life is about living and learning. More importantly, I clearly understand when she explained the fact that, what one person considers perfect, can be considered horrible by another.

So, moving forward, I still cannot believe my friend and former roommate was able to introduce me to someone I couldn't have met on my own, and I'm thankful for that too. As it's now obvious, meeting Greg has been great. He's unlike no other man I've ever known, except I read about or watch in some romantic movies.

He's an embodiment of beauty, brains, and a character that, in my judgment, is flawless. His confidence excites me. His kisses excite me. His touches excite me. His voice excites me. His smell excites me. His chiseled body and every part of it are not only well created and put together but maximized when he puts it to use.

Believe me, if I say that he's an excellent lover, consider it an understatement. As a lover, he transports me to another planet, every time and always. I feel he and I have the type of combustible chemistry that was meant for each other.

When we talk, we talk for hours. Our conversations are an easy volley. I believe we complement each other because I'm deeply in love with his high intelligence, extreme passion, and peculiar sense of humor, which is very similar to mine.

I'm smart but don't consider myself as highly intelligent as he. I agree when he says I'm funny, laugh easy, have kind and caring manners, and being inspirational.

Probably, without him knowing it, he had helped me overcome personal challenges and insecurities, which were common when I dated guys that felt smothered or overwhelmed while juggling multiple relationships and trying to find their inner self-identity.

I consider myself attractive and would easily be a model if that was my chosen career path. However, what's important to me now is that Greg and I are very happy together and glad he regularly refers to me as his beautiful exotic angel. We are not only fascinated by each other's differences but also love, respect, and enjoy our common bond.

To prepare for his b-day ahead and get some planning out of the way, I intend to take Cooper, the caretaker, to the Mall and the outdoors market to buy what I'll need for home decoration.

"Hi Cooper, this is Marie. Can you come to the 2nd floor for a moment, please?"

 "Yes, Marie, I'll be right there," he responded.

A few minutes later, I could hear some steps outside the door, and I proceeded to open the door and let him in. His forehead had some perspiration, which leads me to think he was busy in the outdoors heat. I handed him a pad and pencil to jot down a few things that we might need to get the ball rolling.

"Welcome, Cooper," I cleared my throat and started on what I'd like for us to do. "I am making plans for your boss' b-day tomorrow and would need your help. To create a fun and memorable occasion for him. First, I'm thinking of some decorations, such as a variety of fresh flowers, maybe some fairy lights and candles. And I'm also thinking about some ornaments that could bear his picture or something special about him. Even paint or do some handcrafted gift for him. What do you think?"

Straightening himself up in the chair, and with a grin on his face, he responded: "Oh my god, Marie, it sounds like you'd probably need some professional assistance because he has always celebrated this kind of special event with the help of those that specialized in entertainment consulting. Anyway, why not we discuss where you'd like to place some of these decorations. So, we can envision where and what the place would look like afterwards. Finally, whether the celebration would be intimate only or open to guests." He concluded.

I thought about all the issues he raised and asked him further: "If it's just for two and limited to the living room area and bedroom floor only, what would you suggest?"

"Now I understand," he smiled and nodded his head. "I suggest you should limit the decorations to the bedroom area with a variety of aromatic flowers, which I can assist you with, from our garden here at home. Since the living room already has all sorts of accessories and open spaces that open out to the garden, waterfall, pool, and variety of fixtures, I can help you adjust a few things to provide the ambience you desire.

"And I'm not sure if you intend to celebrate the entire day at home or also go out too. Should you plan to go out, I would also suggest you eliminate most of what we've discussed. Focus on the bedroom area, as I mentioned, and get him a special handcrafted gift or painting that he will treasure forever. As an old man and someone that has been around my boss and his family for many years, I'd say that he would be more pleased and prefer spending quality time and making lasting memories with you than an indulgence in material items unless such indulgence is directly linked to enhancing the pleasure of your time together."

"Thank you so much, Mr Cooper, for your words of wisdom," sensing the wisdom of his suggestions.

"I'm very good at drawing and painting from my art classes of over a decade before coming to America," I continued. "I would put that experience to good use. So, two to four things I'll be doing for the b-day with your help.

"And you're welcome to add any further suggestions after I share them with you:

"One, you go ahead and take care of the flowers in the morning.

Two, arrange to have his yacht available and ready for the pm hour

"And while you are at it, plan to make two French sandwiches and bake a miniature French birthday cake with a single candle to accompany it; fetch a vintage bottle of French champagne, plus French décor napkins, and place everything inside a French themed lunch basket.

"Finally, and probably after our conversation, please pick up some drawing accessories or kit, which usually include a variety of oil paints, pencils, mini brushes, papers, etc., for me from an art and craft store," I concluded.

Smiling pleasantly and showing a glow of his agreement with what I was saying, he held his hands together in the form of a clap and exclaimed: "Consider everything is done, Marie. I think you are doing what my wife would have done half a century ago if she were in your shoes.

"But one question before I visit the art and craft store. What exactly do you intend to draw? Before you answer, please do not consider my question rude, but rather as a curiosity to enable me to select the appropriate drawing and painting tools for your intended use," he said with a smile in his sparkly eyes.

Recognizing the wit of his questioning, I immediately told him I'd be sketching and painting two mating butterflies to capture an expression of the beauty and passion of love I have for Greg. As I'm telling him and explaining why I notice a look of the puzzle in his eyes. I hastened to clarify to him that it does signify the universal appeal of romantic love, albeit its eroticism and tenderness. When he realized I was reading his expression, he quickly thanked me once again. Then, he slowly walked away to take care of his day's chores and uttered the word "brilliant love birds, brilliant love birds" twice.

10

It's obvious that Greg arrived late because I slept before he got home, which was not long after I completed his b-day painting. I think he must be tired from a long day of work, considering he's usually awake at about seven a.m., and it's pushing past a quarter after the hour. Anyway, today is his special day to relax and enjoy himself, and I'm glad he's given me permission to be his designated driver to usher in the next twelve months of his life. I consider it an honor and must make it a cherishing and memorable experience for him.

Looked at him lying next to me with his eyes closed, sound asleep and breathing softly. I'm tempted to kiss his charming lips or forehead but would rather continue to enjoy his handsome looks. Especially his beautifully formed eyelashes. Well-lined lashes that would be an envy of every woman that has had the experience of acquiring such delicately shaped female facial attribute that is acquired with the help of paid beauticians, or from spending endless hours in front of a mirror to create something only half as good.

As a woman in love and someone with art training during my early childhood education, I can't help but continue to watch in admiration at his handsome head that is comfortably pillowed on one well-defined, muscled, round arm, partially covered by the bedsheet. His beautiful chiseled face is facing my direction, his brown skin glowing with abundant health and vitality.

As my ravenous eyes continue to roam through my charming sleeping king, the happy smile on my face has gotten stronger. Not even a ferocious tidal wave or a strong tsunami can wipe out the blissful feelings I'm going through at this moment. One can say that I cannot help it because I'm consumed with strong admiration, pleasure, and joy, which can only be attributed to my proudly acknowledging and professing the deep affection I have for him. Not only now, but I have realized that it has increased since we both set eyes on each other. As my eyes continue to stray at his relaxed, healthy body, arms, and legs, I see a guy that is not selfish or consumed by the strength of his physical beauty and good looks, but in the use of the gift of his intellect and passion, by mastering the art of converting working hard, to working smart.

Turning my head to glance at the wall clock, I observed the time was showing close to nine a.m. I then decided to make a quick call to Mr Cooper to get some hot water for tea or coffee and fix some omelets for us within the next hour and a half.

And to get my birthday king ready for the day, I have decided on a naughty idea that is sure to wake him up. As he is laying sideways, facing me, I've decided to do similarly, but with my head facing his legs. More like between his thighs since he is taller than me. Placing my hands on his thighs, I began to play with his private part, which I often refer to as my favorite gift from the one I love. Anyway, with my head resting on his thigh, I placed his member in my mouth and tickled it with my tongue. I used my other hand to slowly massage and play with the two balls between his legs. I squeezed his butt, hugged and kissed everything between his thighs, pressing his privates to my breast, squeezing between them, and gently rubbing and putting the tip of his member between my lips, softly tickling and biting it with my tongue. As I was busy enjoying him, his penis grew so huge that the small lips of my mouth could hardly clasp it.

The result of my naughty behavior awakened him with a glistening, hard, erect penis. He raised himself up. Without saying a word, he picked me up, placed a pillow under my butt, and laid me down facing up. I could feel the flow of sticky wet drip all over my thighs and into my butt hole. He didn't waste any time injecting his hard-throbbing warm penis inside me, resulting in an instant and profuse outpouring of my fluids. And, as he continued to rapidly shove it in and out of me multiple times, we both came simultaneously. I licked his face in search of his lips, and he responded enthusiastically.

His excitement in my body was extensive as I could feel the thrill of his mouth stirring from my lips to the neck, and from neck to ear lopes. He whispered, 'good morning honey' into my ear, and I responded, 'same to you too, my birthday boy.' He smacked my butt, and we both laughed. I asked him to get ready for the day, and he raised himself up quietly and headed to the bathroom. I decided to do the same but in the other large bedroom.

Thirty minutes later, my beaming, smiling 'birthday boy' walked in and wrapped his strong arms around my waist and a planting kiss on my neck. He was all dressed up, in a white long sleeve shirt, over dark blue slacks and a pair of beautiful, matching, comfortable men's fashion sneakers. Knowing that we'll be outdoors for a while, starting with the Cleveland Museum of Art trip, I also decided to dress and feel comfortable by wearing relaxed hangout gear too, from a white designer t-shirt tucked into a high-rise corduroy pants over a pair of towering baby soft leather trekker sandals.

"We're both ready about the same time, I see," he stated pleasantly.

"Oh certainly, my dear," I chuckled, turning around to hug him.

"You are smelling yummy," he stated, holding one of my hands out, and looking at my manicured fingernails with a pleased smile on his face.

Grinning appreciatively, I gave him a longing kiss on his lips and whispered: "thank you, my love," into his left ear. "Are you ready for a quick breakfast before we hit the road," I inquired?

"Of course, I'm ready when you are. Let's go downstairs right away." He said

We took the stairs together, with me leading the way. Thinking about two lovers holding hands and their bodies touching, and taking slow steps downstairs, created an exquisite sweetness in my heart. Gives me a melting feeling of two fragile and delicate intertwined hearts about to become one, creating a strong inseparable bond.

As we continued our slow walk downwards, I perceived the smell of lilies and daffodils from afar and noticed that the windows were open, oozing in the fresh air that increased the circulation of the sweet smells. Realizing that the entire hallway was full of perfumed air, it occurred to me that Mr Cooper must have taken care of it, as we'd discussed the day before. God bless his heart.

Downstairs in the living room, it became obvious that there was a combination of beautiful flowers everywhere. The perfume from these flowers not only penetrated and enchanted me but impressed in me the idea that my boyfriend and I were entering a world where love reigns supreme.

Just as my heart was filled with these thoughts of love and beauty, Greg drew me closer, pulled my head towards his, and we exchanged one long slow, and closed kiss, mingling our souls, uniting our hands, penetrating our melted bodies into one. Upon opening our eyes, we realized the dining table and breakfast next to us, and we went ahead and sat down to our omelet, fruit bowls, and freshly squeezed juice.

I took multiple bites of my omelet and noticed he had finished his and was eating off his bowl of the fruit bowl, a spoon at a time, in quick succession. Brushing my index finger over my eyes, I stared at him through the corner of my eyes, and he caught me looking excitedly. His smiling eyes and soft facial expression were charming and beautiful. We both chuckled at the same time, without saying a word.

"I'm enjoying my food, are you?" he said between his mouthful as he slowly chewed his fruits.

"Me too," I responded, noticing he was eating twice faster than me. Either because he was hungrier or needed to boost his energy, considering he worked out more, he was much bigger and taller than me.

"So, you've got our day planned from morning through nightfall?" he said, his eyes teasing me and curious about my creative plans.

"Yes, I have and will disclose each detail as the day progresses. So, in summary, we'll be going to the museum shortly. Then a yacht ride by the river, thereafter, followed by a dinner party for two. I'll reserve the details to myself if you don't mind." I concluded, looking thoughtful and serious, which immediately prompted a combination of a chuckle with an uncontrollable heaving of his shoulders.

As he was finally able to stop the laughter, he said that my last words sounded both funny and serious at the same time. I couldn't help but laugh at his thought afterwards.

Meanwhile, we drove into East Boulevard and turned into the main parking structure with car spaces provided for museum visitors. We walked a few steps to join the mini-guided tour that was already in session. This tour session was initiated at about the same time on each floor.

Along the walkway, we picked up a few gift items from one of the floors outdoor shopping stands. He turned to me and patted my hair, and when I turned to look at him, he drew a long breath, as if oppressed with happiness, then murmured my name and kissed my forehead.

We both looked at each other and smiled. He sensed I was feeling such an exquisite pleasure from his kiss, and he immediately looked into my eyes and silently thanked me with a very expressive glance, then let me know that we had arrived at our desired exhibition spot. I whispered happy birthday to him, and he responded by stating his love for me. I feel he will enjoy and connect this exhibit to our strong love for each other, and the beautiful paintings will stir feelings of love between us as we continue to love and cherish each other.

The first masterpiece that captivates our attention, especially for me, is "The Kiss" by Gustav Klimt, an Austrian who was inspired by the style of Japanese mosaics and the universal appeal of romantic love. A curator, Franz Smola, described it as an embodiment of sentimental feelings of tenderness and love that speak to all generations of love. Spending time and looking at it as if hypnotized, I couldn't help squeezing my boyfriend's hand and arm and kissing him repeatedly like a hungry bird pecking at food. As a girl with lots of emotions, I'm happy to know that my boyfriend Greg has just as much and is willing to express it with me whenever we're together. Most importantly, I feel fortunate to be with a man whose gifts are not only limited to his professional career but also overflowing with sensuous qualities of passion, love, romance, and willingness to satisfy my deep hunger and equal zeal to satisfy and inspire him, both equally, and beyond.

The next painting we're looking at is "The birth of Venus" by Sandro Botticelli, who was commissioned to produce it by the renowned Medici family. The painting portrays the goddess of love as an idealized standard of perfection and purity. When my boyfriend noticed I couldn't take my eyes off the painting, he squeezed my fingers twice, and when I looked at him, he pulled me closer and whispered to me, 'love is never fully realized, except by divinity. Meaning, we only experience it unexpectedly, when we least expect it.' he continued: 'For example, when a person courts another for a long time, thinking they're loved in return. Only to find out they're snubbed when they least expect it. Then, out of the blue, they're invited, as a replacement for someone that has every attribute and qualities to die for, someone you consider to be way superior to you.' When he was done and noticed I was in deep thought, he continued, 'that's life.' I smiled, and without another word, our lips melted together, and we kissed for a little over a minute. We opened our eyes just as another couple was looking at the same picture to the left of us. So, we decided to move on to the next picture.

The next image was a more modest painting by Edouard Manet, titled "Che Pere Lathuille." It depicts a couple's passion, in which they're engaged in indulging themselves with deep gazes, at a close range as if they can feel each other's breathe, as well as heartbeat. Although the portraiture is of young models, showing the same guy but with two different females, it reflects the intensity of a young lover, especially. But with respect to love in general, between two people whose body and soul are likely to be melted in love, whether for a minute or eternity.

"In Bed: The Kiss" by Henri de Toulouse-Lautrec captures a moment of unadulterated passion between two women. This artist captured mostly same-sex intimacy since his documentation was primarily from the lives of Parisian brothel workers. It's interesting to note that the artist shows a departure from his usual paintings of commercial Moulin Rouge posters, thus ensures elevating advertising into art. As this painter has naturally recognized, certain environments provide opportunities for different shades of love and passion, ultimately leading to intimacy and sensuality.

The picture "Flaming June" by Sir Frederic Leighton is acknowledged to be his ultimate masterpiece, considering it showcases his classical training with top-heavy Greek erotic imagery. It can't get better than that. As a woman that has slept alone and dreamt often, a very soft and comfortable colorful bedding would certainly provide an alternative setting to experience an intimacy that would qualify as an unadulterated and clean romantic escapism or a precursor for an anticipated love note. Very similar to an athlete, like Lebron James, Simone Biles, Serena Williams, or Tiger Woods, preparing twenty-four seven for a certain future event.

Thinking about the Flaming June painting further, I decided to seek my boyfriend's opinion on his observation: "Greg, my king," I sputtered his way to get his attention, and he quickly turned from looking at the picture to facing me:

"I have two perspectives, based on this painting, based on men and the other on women. I believe the picture reflects the behavior of women more so than the behavior of men. For example, a man pursues a profession, such as a hedge fund manager or lawyer, or engineer. A woman does too, but stick with my logic, all things being equal, okay?"

"Yeah, sure. I'm with you, all the way," he reassured, looking very attentive.

"Good," I smiled and continued. "Based on the example of a man's profession above, he is more likely to think of something, like work, other than love. But a woman is more likely to only think about herself, her beauty, and her body. The supreme art is to give himself as much pleasure as possible. This is the primary purpose of his life. She, on the order hand, is to provide herself, the capacity or ability of the man, so that he can desire her. Am I making sense?"

"Yes, of course," he replied, smiling with his eyes. "Your ideas are very refreshing, and I agree with you in terms of the fact that women are more likely to be more curious and daring, less shameful, and more focused when it comes to love. So, when it comes to the 'Flaming June' painting translation, a woman is more likely to use the comfortable, colorful beddings as a training set for her love adventure ahead, while a man in a similar situation would see it; as an end in itself."

"I agree with you, one hundred percent, because you're in harmony with your feminine side," I notched him on while we moved on to look at the next painting.

Our next painting exhibit is "The Grand Canal of Venice (often referred to as Blue Venice)" by Edouard Manet. Of course, the city of Venice has been billed as the world's most romantic city. That makes it perfect for capturing and painting a dreamy feeling of floating down a canal in one of the city's famed gondolas. The painting builds an adventurous desire in my heart. To take a gondola anniversary ride, create sets of audio and video clips for the purpose of making sweet memories to last a lifetime. Not only a ride alone but to celebrate with an expensive drink of champagne, and enjoy some Spanish love banjo song, and mini entertainment live band, as one slowly cruise through the canal, to share and enjoy the video clip, plus snapshots with friends and family, to enjoy and share among themselves.

Several hours after we finished the Museum exhibit of romantic paintings, we headed home to prepare for our second event to mark the b-day expedition. At home, I changed into a designer mini dress with a light floral print, plus a throw of windbreakers in a matching darker shade. Since we were essentially going to be outdoors by the lake and in a yacht primarily, I decided to pull back my hair in a voluminous curled ponytail and added shades to protect against the sunshine. To be comfortable around the grassy area by the lake, I wore some light blue color pumps to match my outfit. Greg wore a pair of blue jeans, a light brown polo shirt, and matching cowhide boots. He had a matching male version of shades too.

When the sport utility vehicle was loaded with Mr Cooper's lunch basket that included other necessary items we would likely need for the outdoors trip, we were ready to hit the road.

After nearly an hour of driving, Greg finally turned off the main highly onto an asphalt road that ran into what seemed like a valley. I noticed a sign on the left that stated: 'Private Road. No trespassing.' As if Greg knew I was curious about the signage, he quickly uttered, "Oh, the sign you just saw is there because this particular section of the lake is owned and managed by a country club organization, of which I'm a member, and the yacht belonging to me is anchored in front of my cabin. Members have an option to rent and use the facilities as needed instead." An option that Greg thought was better is one he seldom used.

Just as he finished explaining, the vehicle came to a high metal fence that blocked the road, which also had huge letters, smacked right in the middle: 'Private Property. No trespassing.'

Greg got out of the vehicle, walked to the gate, and pressed a button on one of the metal gate posts. After a split second, there was a metallic click, and the gate swung open. He got back in the vehicle, and we drove on; when I turned my head around, I saw the gate swing shut behind us.

In a little over a minute, we arrived in front of his cabin, the engine was turned off, and we hopped out. He handed me the cabin keys and went back to carry the lunch basket while I picked up the rest of the other items. The inside of the cabin was neatly arranged with high-grade wooden couches, coffee tables, kitchenettes and related accessories, a single furnished one bedroom, shower area that was combined with a toilet. The atmosphere of the cabin was charming, and the backyard area provided a jacuzzi, fireplace, outdoor umbrella, and chairs, plus a magnificent view of the river. This lakefront part of town is perfect for camping out during short holidays and overnight or weekend getaways.

Halfway into drinking our two mini cups of ice-cold water, we walked out by the backdoor with our lunch basket. He untied the yacht from its base, and we entered and rode away into the sunset. As the yacht propelled forward and afar, we began to enjoy the ride as much as the beautiful surrounding scenic views by the lake. The richly cushioned seat covers were so comfortable that, combined with the sunny outdoors and breeze, I increasingly began to feel lazy for a half and an hour in the waters. Greg suggested lunch, and I quickly accepted the idea, and we came off the river by the moss-grown embankment.

Fine weather was in the air, so we placed a large lightweight blanket that was packed inside the basket on the grass, directly under one of the shaded trees. A white sheet was also placed on the moss to act as a tray for food items, such as sandwiches, spiced beef, mini salad bowls, small birthday cake, mini water bottles, a bottle of champagne, and paper towels.

I placed some plates down and made two sandwiches, fruits cups, juices, napkins, and other food items in the basket. After we had consumed most of the food, I opened the champagne bottle and poured it into our cups, followed by me singing the birthday song. He laughed because of how I twisted the song and added some benefits I've gained as a result of his rush to add a year to his age. I concluded that I wished for him to have a birthday every day so that I could cherish more of his unconditional deliciousness that comes with experience and maturity. He said I'm witty and very funny, and asked if he could open it, and didn't hesitate in telling him to go right ahead.

Upon opening the gift box, he gently removed the painting and the instruction at the edge it has four parts and should be placed on a flat surface, facing up, one piece at a time, side by side, from part one to four. He did as was directed, and in an intense voice, he exclaimed, "wow, this is amazing. Where did you order this delightful beauty?"

"Sweetheart read the letter that came with it. See attached on the back of part four." I directed him, laughing.

He tore the envelope and began to read: "My dear Greg: This modest painting from yours truly, is birthed on the eve of your special day in memory of your earthly welcome. It expresses an intense mating dance between two affectionate butterflies that desire their intimacy and passion for translating into a naturally loving renaissance. Notice the colorful claws of the female butterfly with nectar, ready to transfer between the hibiscus to ensure perpetual pleasure and life.

"So sweetheart, whether us, as couples locked in a tender embrace, or as the butterflies, engaging in sensuous copulation, or the classic painting we enjoyed at the museum of art earlier today, love has an enduring appeal to all living creatures on earth, whether animals or plants.

"And throughout human history, artists have used such works to capture the beauty of passion and love. I hope that you and I can use these rich expressions to inspire our feelings of romance and intimacy, anytime, any day, any place, anywhere.

"The more we love, the more we want to love. We can perpetually renew the desire in us, just the same way the sea is renewed on the beach with the tide.

"I conclude by wishing you unlimited wishes of health, happiness, and a prosperous loving relationship between us, family, and all your loved ones.

"Forever yours,

Marie."

 We hugged and had pecking kisses like birds. I noticed he was eager to say something, but I told him to wait a minute. I refilled our champagne cups and gulped down our throats in two takes. I then ushered him to continue.

"I'm feeling really good right now, Marie. Let us bask under the green tree and grass. As well as watch and enjoy the fresh river water flowing downstream. More importantly, let us enjoy each other's company to the max. You are the best girl that comes around only once in a lifetime. You are a very beautiful, thoughtful, caring, and sweet girl - always.

"So, thanks for making my birthday special. To create a memorable bond between us. For setting up a standard that we can replicate every year into the future that we have ahead of us." He concluded with a passionate voice that combined every ounce of emotion inside of him, ending in a very satisfying exhilaration.

Hearing Greg talk, I am reminded of who he is. A charming, fun, down-to-earth handsome, compassionate guy. The most likeable person I've ever met. I pulled him closer to me and kissed him passionately and thanked him for being the best guy I ever dreamt of. Looking a little shy, he pulled me down to the soft blanket and asked that I should relax while he poured a glass of champagne for me. I took two gulps, and the glass was empty. He then handed me some French pastry, saying, "this is for you, my sweet Frenchie." I took a couple of bites, and chuckling, he said, "here's some chocolate from Mr Chocolate himself." He made me take small bites at a time, licking my tongue in the process due to the sweetness of it, in combination with the fingers that were feeding me. When he noticed I was done swallowing the last bite, he handed me his champagne glass, and I took a sip and handed it back to him. I then rested my head on the blanket and closed my eyes, but far from falling asleep.

Feeling his warm body next to mine, I turned over, facing him, and gave him a kiss. He responded passionately, none stop, almost like someone starving for kisses. Simultaneously, we undressed each other as if we were in a hurry. He turned me over on all fours, doggy style, and kneeling behind me, I guided his hand around, and instantly, two of his soft, strong fingers were gently stroking my clitoris while his hard-throbbing penis was penetrating my wet dripping vagina at the same time. As hungry for each other as we started out, he took his sweet time, moving in and out slowly, gingerly, and gently, building momentum until we both exploded in orgasmic spending.

After resting on the blanket for a minute, he sat back up, picked up his champagne glass, and gulped the last drops. My eyes were half-closed, while my body and soul were in ecstatic bliss. He looked across to the river and then up to the sky, which was beginning to get dark. Turning over, facing me, with his smile of contentment and eyes of joy, he placed his mouth to my ear. He whispered my name, "Marie."

"Oh! Am I dreaming, or did I hear my name?" I said, startled and sitting up.

"I'm trying to find the right words to say. My passion for you is very strong," he slowly uttered. And continuing, "we have grown day and night since we first met, and never conceded a single second."

"True", I repeatedly nodded, temporary surprised. "I don't know how to react, Greg."

He sat up and placed one arm tightly around my waist. "When will you marry me, Marie?" he uttered, "you must be my wife. That moment is now. I love you so intensely. If you say no, I would just hit my head against a hard rock by the river and be eaten by some sea mammals." He concluded, sounding very serious with a trembling voice.

"Oh! Please, my dear, don't you ever say or think about that." I pleaded.

 "Then look me in the eye, and say you love me and are ready to marry me." He crooned.

"Of course, Greg." I breathed eagerly, "I certainly love you with my whole heart. You are my earthly god. I consider you my second half and would give my life to be with you forever." And looking at his masculine, handsome face, I added, "I will definitely marry you."

"How soon?" he shot back before I could finish my last word, deeply gazing at my expressive longing eyes.

"As soon as possible," I replied, gently closing my eyes.

"My sweetheart," he whispered, as he seized my arms, "we will be married in the next few weeks."

"Oh Greg, this is so sudden," I responded inaudibly.

"No! No!" he bellowed back, and proverbially taking the bull by the horns, he kissed me aggressively all over my face. "You are my bride-to-be," he repeated three times. "My sweetheart, I will give you all the love a human heart can render you, the dearest of love and a new life."

He regarded me passionately, anxiously, and entreatingly.

I trembled with joy as I heard the magic words. He is full of passion and energy.

"Oh Greg, little did I ever dream our relationship coming to this," and I suddenly fainted into his strong, stretched arms.

"Oh my gosh!" he gasped, and laying me gently on the blanket, he rushed to the river yards away and filled two empty cups with water to pour on my face to revive me.

Seated next to me, holding my raised head and fanning my face, I came back to my senses, and with a weak smile, I whispered for him to take me back home.

"With pleasure, sweetheart," he responded, "I will pack up our stuff and place it into the yacht right away."

I emptied the last drops of champagne in the bottle and tidied my hair while Greg finished packing. Then holding my arm, he walked me gently to the yacht.

Helping me into the yacht, he thought out loud, "I hope you're not getting sick."

"Oh no. I'm as strong as a tiger," I replied, laughing. "I fainted from joy and excitement of the unexpected good news."

He smiled fondly; he reached over and clasped my trembling fingers in his strong hands; turning my face towards him, he planted a warm kiss on my gaping lips. He turned skyward as if he was glancing into heaven and said in a low voice, "you'd never regret the step you are taking with me."

"You're wonderful," he giggled, handing me a couple of yacht pillows to cushion my sides as he powered down the stream. The water was flowing silently under the golden moon, in combination with the electric pole lighting from the river crest. I could hear and feel the quiet silence as we glided along. I couldn't help smiling inwardly, knowing that our hearts were engulfed in love and passion and our faces filled with radiance and joy. The added sound of the mysterious water slurped against the vessel to break the monotony of the night until our onboarding homeward drive.

11

For the next couple of weeks, Greg has gotten up early, showered, and dressed in his usual designer working gear – white or blue long sleeves shirts, hand-crafted dark hue shoes and suits, or business casuals, topped with beautiful silk jackets as the weather demands. Being an extremely busy businessman, he'll continue to split his time and hours, adjusted to his tremendous responsibilities. According to the nature of his business, he had several meetings and facetime scheduled with a couple of high-tech billionaire clients at this time of year. Clients that are willing and ready to have their money placed with his investment firm. He says he courts these clients all year round due to their busy schedules. He gets great referrals from many of them whenever he makes profitable investments and expands and enhances their portfolios under management.

He is very good at doing his homework prior to meeting them. He's organized, reviews his computer notes and dots, and crosses his T's prior to every formal client meeting. He says his team, which includes Mike, is very good at what they do, each providing excellent contributions. One of them, a female, is a genius, he says, because of excellent communication and organizational skills. He admires her quantitative and numerical skills. That she can generate spreadsheets faster than his accounting staff and can spot an error easily, if any. He also has similar glowing remarks when he talks about his stock analyst, whom he describes as a genius in spotting winning IPOs. So obvious why he's proud of his team is because of their meticulous and versatile expertise that he combines into fine art in his investment practices.

I'm so happy to have him, especially when I think about his combined qualities of good looks, professional success, interpersonal skills, and humility. I see why he has kept to himself most of the time because every gold-digger and beautiful woman with a great deal of money, too, in Cleveland and across the country, would want to have a piece of him. The rich ones would feel safe with him since he has deep pockets himself. Since being with him and getting to know and observe him, he's very brilliant at everything he does. He is as smooth as silk when interacting with clients, even those he is meeting for the first time. An excellent lover I've ever had. The most generous and terrific guy I've ever been with and does not mind taking me everywhere, spending time with me, dotting and loving me every day since our first contact. He's a dream come true.

His love for me, and generous passionate personality has afforded me an opportunity to get my business venture off the ground and running smoothly. Everything has been possible due to the able management of an excellent, experienced workforce; put together, courtesy of my smart, handsome hunk. I can't help thinking about him all the time and exude a feeling of excitement whenever he takes time out to send me a heart emoji or some love notes or whenever he randomly delivers some flowers to me. He's the gift that keeps on giving.

Which girl would not want a wholesome, total package guy like Greg? A very smart, handsome, kindhearted, vulnerable, funny, serious-minded, and desirous of a family, like how he grew up. As the saying goes, an apple does not fall far from its tree. Every day and every minute I've spent with him has been perfect, whether lounging around the house, taking walks, biking, penchant for travelling the world, making love, and going out for lunches or dinners. More importantly, he is extremely, very close with his family. Thanks to them, his standard and expectations for a stable, successful, happy marriage look like the sky is the limit. I'm ready to grow old with him because he has treated me like his queen, and I consider him my angel and king. He's a keeper in my book.

And yes, he has given me a blank notebook to plan and execute details. Plus, he literally linked me with several fashion designers for our entire wedding outfits from head to toe, from suits to my wedding dress, shoes, and accessories; plus, as wedding planners and catering firms. Our ultimate decision would be geared to fit our expectations, the number of quests, and the choice of location, which we're yet to confirm. I'm so excited and would go ahead and share the good news with my girlfriend, Elisa, that introduced us, as well as let my parents know since they're the ones that brought me to this world and to the States.

"Hello, mom," I called my mom after what seemed like ages.

"Hi Marie, long time indeed. How have you been? I bet you've been pretty busy and adjusting to your new environment." She voiced, sounding ecstatic.

"I'm good and happy to hear your voice again, mom. And how have you and dad been doing?" I smiled and was glad she sounded happy. "I got a couple of news to share with you. First, I started my business, and it's going well. And I know you'd asked me about the financing, logistics, and so on previously. My boyfriend has been a tremendous help, a thousand percent." I concluded; in case she had any follow questions.

"That's amazing, dear. I'm so proud of you from the bottom of my heart. You're doing what I could only dream of. Believe me, your father would be happy too. And by the way, he's travelled across the country on some marketing assignments. So, I'll share the good news with him when he returns later tonight." She said.

"Guess what, mom, my second good news: Greg, my boyfriend, plans to marry me," I exclaimed, blushing with excitement.

"Really? You are kidding me. Did he propose to you?" Sounding surprised

"Yes, mom. We recently moved in together. We eat our daily meals together. We go out and do things together. He's very much in love with me. I'm madly in love with him. He is a very passionate and caring gentleman. And sees equally complementary qualities in me. He openly gushed out his desire to marry me when I took him out on his birthday. Now, we are arranging our wedding." I enthusiastically and eagerly share my good news.

"I see and feel what you're saying, my daughter. That's wonderful," she stated as a wave of emotion surged through her.

"Thank you, mom," as I reflect on how she's thrilled for me.

"Out of curiosity, my dear, is your boyfriend rich?"

"I haven't the least idea, mom. What on earth has that to do with it?" I replied, feeling disappointed.

"Sorry, my daughter, don't be upset. I'm just wondering how he'd afford to take care of you and himself."

"I see why you're asking. Your future son-in-law and I are not lazy. So, you won't have to ever worry about that," I assured her with a giggle.

We both bid each other goodbye, and I decided to contact my girlfriend Elisa to share the good news too. After a couple of rings, the call went into voice messaging, and I requested for her to call me whenever she was available.

Elisa called back several hours later, apologizing that she was on the phone with her father back home. When asked if he was okay, she replied unenthusiastically.

"Are you sure he's alright?" I pressed further, showing concern.

"He said he was, but that my mom is upset at him for cheating on her. Maybe, he's going through a middle-age crisis or doing what is typical in an unstable relationship. I asked him what he found in the woman, and he said, 'she's a very kind and delightful woman you'd ever meet.' And when I asked him, 'in what way?' he added, 'she does not ask anything of me, but only wanting to make me happy,' he stated.' He seemed very convinced by his action because he claimed, if he was happy, it would increase the happiness between himself and my mom." She added, sounding doubtful and philosophical.

"Did you get a chance to talk to your mom directly?" I inquired further.

"Yes. I then asked to talk to my mom, and he handed the phone to her. She said he started out saying he was going to the Country Club to hang out with his friends. While there, he took an interest in this lady who was working at the clubhouse, serving drinks and snacks. Suddenly, he increased the frequency of his supposed club visits. When my mom became suspicious because he was beginning to skip his lunches and dinners at home, she confronted him to tell her the truth.

"Marie, you won't believe it. My mom found out that he would visit this woman every day, in the name of his club. Apparently, she *was* his club," and she paused for a moment.

I busted out laughing hysterically because of the way she described it. I suppose she felt a little disappointed in my reaction, but she understood it was simply a natural reaction on my part. I'm sure she felt that this woman acted like a vulture; but also understood that her father's vulnerability did not excuse his culpability.

"Father said he wants to continue the relationship, as well as stay married to my mom." She continued, her voice listless, dismayed, and helpless.

"Did he say so?" I asked, surprised and anxious to hear more.

"Yes. He has fallen in love with her. And he claims she is too." She stated.

"Oh! No! Is he serious?" I exclaimed, disbelieving.

"Yes. Seriously. Very selfish of him! He ought to think of mom's feelings!" she wailed, decreasing to irregular sobs, in an expression of her helpless anguish.

"Yeah, sure!" was all I could say in consolation.

"They were very happy as a couple, and now he's throwing it away. His behavior is like an insult to her, as if she's not worthy of his love, instead of finding and fixing the source of his unhappiness. He has always said his mom held a sacred place in his heart and life. And I know she's had an exquisite influence in his life, fortune, and career. As well as the entire history of our family and the welfare of our home," she continued, reflecting on earlier family experiences.

I cleared my throat to assure her I was listening, not knowing what else to say. Maybe I shouldn't tell her why I called and wait for another day and time.

"Well, Elisa, don't make yourself miserable till things calm down and check on them from time to time," I encouraged her, after finding my words, "and please let's talk again soon or meet for a drink or coffee; sometime, okay?"

"Thank you so much, Marie. I really appreciate your listening and kind words.

"Oh! Before we hang up, Marie, I forgot to ask you: what's new with you. And how's your boyfriend?" she inquired.

"Thanks for asking. He proposed to me a couple of weeks ago." I shared with a big smile on my face.

"Congratulations, my homegirl," snickering, "I'm definitely happy for you," she expressed with exuberance. "By the way," laughing, "have you heard the expression, 'she came, she saw, she conquered?'"

"Never," I responded.

"Anyway, I just made it up. It means we both came from somewhere, met our sweethearts, and got married to them." Ha! Ha!

"Cool idea Elisa, but we're not married yet, technically speaking. Only engaged." I clarified.

"I hear you, Marie. I am. We had a civil marriage but will have a ceremony sometime soon. And I'm sure you'll get married officially soon, knowing the kind of man that has proposed to you. A serious-minded guy like him won't engage for too long, I'm sure." She concluded confidently.

"You are correct. We are making plans already. That's why I called to tell you in the first place." I replied, chuckling.

"Great, Marie. Don't hesitate to let me know if I can help with anything. We can meet and share ideas whenever you are ready, okay?" she stated.

"Thank you so much for connecting us and for being there for me. Greg is an angel, and I consider myself lucky. A very selfless and passionate man I've ever met," I professed my true confession from deep in my heart.

"You are lucky indeed, Marie. I am too. The expression 'you are the company you keep' rings true in the case of our partners. Greg and Mike go way back in high school, and I've never met such a pair of cool dudes previously.

"When Mike introduced me to Greg, and we later met his parents and heard about the kind of guys you were attracting, I told Mike to help me introduce you to Greg if he was single. And after he asked me a couple of questions about you, he decided to give it a go.

"I'm not an expert in relationships, but two things I saw in him that I thought he'll be perfect for you: first, nature by way of his parents, have given him a kind of gift, tall in stature, handsome in face and endowed with an enterprising spirit with the confidence in himself which these qualities give. Men like him don't need to read anything or seek advice from outside of themselves, to set themselves up for success. Beauty, and qualities of intelligence and heart, triumph over ugly, as day triumphs overnight.

"The second attribute is rare in men that are imbued with the first example, and I'm going to express it like an allegory: when we're up a staircase, we pass closed doors, not thinking that the keys are under the doormats. We never think for a moment that the place we rub or clean dirt from our feet hides the tiny tool that opens the door or gives us access to a mansion that houses rare and delicate paintings, furniture, and expensive household accessories.

"So, how do these two examples combine in your Greg? I may be wrong, but based on what I see in him, he has not only the first gift but also the second 'doormat' gift, of intense, undivided passion and energy that all women dream of in an ideal man. Based on your personality and temperament, you are perfect for each other." She concluded her sermon and excused me to prepare a meal for her; Mike called to let her know he'll be home for lunch. We bid each other goodbye and make time to meet in person sometime soon.

As I hung up, my phone rang, and it was Greg, calling to be ready for him, so we could go grab a bite before he returned to meet some clients afterwards. While thinking of what to wear, I couldn't help but remember how supportive Elisa has been to me. I consider her my best friend and sister more like an older sister. Always providing me with words of wisdom and trying to support me with necessary and helpful suggestions whenever I'm going through an unhealthy relationship conundrum. I can't forget when she told me to control my enthusiasm when it came to relationships, whether I was in it for fun or serious. It's been dozens of months ago, but it seems like yesterday when one thinks about it. Whatever the situation, I consider her a good judge of character in the relationship department. She's right; we sometimes must pass through several exits to find our way to a destination. She's like a sister, no doubt. I have in her a friend for life.

While still in my reflective mindset, my phone rang.

"Hi, sweetheart," Greg's voice was on the other line.

"Hey, babe," I responded, smiling as I heard his voice again after so many hours.

"I'm in the car, downstairs. See you shortly," he concluded.

"Fine. I'll be right there. Almost done wearing my clothes." I replied, and we both laughed when he volunteered to come to help me.

"Do you like sushi?" he asked when I was about to enter the car.

"I love it."

"There's a nice place a couple of blocks from here. The food is great, and the service is fast. That would allow us enough time to bond and have some laughter before I return to work." He said and let me know that I looked lovely in what I was wearing. His corduroy pants, starched blue shirt and khaki jacket and loafers looked good on him too. He reminded me of those action movie actors.

We walked a few feet from our parked car. Talking about our day and enjoying the warm sunshine weather. Just being with him, sharing little things about us, was very pleasing. And he was correct, the food at the restaurant was delicious, and yes, it was served quickly. Over a cup of tea afterwards, we talked about how far I was going with preparations and arrangements. He suggested we could take time off to nail down some specific options once he takes care of a couple of investment portfolios. He thought we could engage in any of our pet fun activities, such as outdoor sailing or favorite books since we liked several of the same authors.

"So, are you enjoying your date so far?" he asked me, out of the blue, while smiling.

"Of course," I responded. We still have it. good food, good conversation, fresh outdoors breeze, and excellent company – whether we're indoors or outdoors."

 "I'm a little disappointed," he said, looking slightly sad. "You never mentioned sex. That's not in your fun date plan?" he concluded, and I couldn't help but laugh out loud.

"I'm sorry, I forgot," I replied, looking at him with bashful and honest eyes. "Make it number one on my bucket list."

He made me remember my college days when a guy would expect to take you to bed after buying you a drive-through hamburger or sandwich or a real expensive dinner, and act like you're a gold digger if the guy is refused a hug or kiss.

"Actually," looking serious, he responded, "I'll admit, old fashion guys like me might not anticipate it but continue dating a girl many times until both people develop strong feelings and fondness for each other."

"Yeah, but many people would move on because they'd think there's no physical attraction," I replied, smiling. "Plus, some might actually jump into it, and maybe even take each other seriously, and get married, and lose interest after they've been together and had a couple of kids. Then either divorce or begin to sleep on a separate bed."

"I don't know if I agree with that completely," he stated seriously. "My parents still behave like they're in love and make out every chance they get. I remember my brother and I caught them making out and driving them crazy whenever they were spending too much time together, especially with their door closed. I think if two people get along well and build on their relationship regularly, they would enjoy each other and their marriage."

I nodded my head in agreement in response to his statement. I suspect my parents do not have such a relationship because my dad saw me as an accident that forced his hand in marriage. However, they're still together. Being compatible in many ways makes a difference. And since I met Greg, I strongly feel we both love and care about each other and are open to pleasing each other without reservations or excuses. His story about his parents and his brother sounds like the kind of family I dream about, instead of a moody, temperamental or crazy relationship that is plagued by negative energy, neglect, abuse, and/or absenteeism. In any case, I know he's busy, but I'll ask for a quickie before he returns to work this afternoon.

"So, do we have any plan for today?" I enquired.

"Plan?" looking puzzled for a moment, then followed by a mischievous smile. "Oh sure, I'm always ready for your snacks and full course meals." We both laughed as we headed out to the car and drove home. Upon arrival minutes later, he immediately got out of the car and hurriedly opened the passenger door for me. Helping my step out, he pulled me to his bosom and wrapped his two strong arms around me; and our lips immediately glued together like magnets. We enjoyed each other's soft, warm lips for a better part of over a minute with our eyes closed. Slowly disengaging his lips and opening his eyes with a coy smile, he whispered an apology in my left ear for wanting to rush back to his meeting and promised to make it up to me when he got home later. He then watched me walk to the mansion's double doors while getting into the driver's seat and closing the door. Entering the house and turning to look at him one more time prior to his driving off, our eyes met with a knowing, longing promise of a sweet end-of-day reward. The smile from me was followed by a goodbye wave to him. He responded with a quick wave. Then, blowing me a kiss and driving off.

12

Back in the second-floor bedroom, I changed into some comfortable house robe and hushpuppy flips. With my iTunes music machine and a tall glass of fruit juice, I went to the terrace to relax on one of the outdoor couches and listen to some contemporary jazz and soft rock music. As I was mentally reviewing our wedding plans, I couldn't help thinking about the joy and growth I've experienced since I met Greg and how impactful my life has been transformed for the better ever since. Smiling, I realized how, for the first time in my life, I've come to feel completely happy and thankful for a healthy relationship that my heart wasn't even dreaming about prior to this time. The expression 'what does not kill you makes you stronger' is very true in my case, especially when I think of relationship growth and knowing what's good for you and what's bad for you.

Several years earlier, as a young first-year student leaving home for the first time, it has been quite refreshing for me to look for and connect with people that provide or appear to provide the various needs I've desired as a female, ranging from a parental role model to friendships with same-sex and opposites. And prior to my present love relationship, I started out dating guys that are considered good people in many ways but not good for me. As well as those that only exploit or take from you but give nothing in return. Those that are good but for someone else. Some play the role of a father figure or abuse your trust along the way. Some are only good to fulfil an immediate thrill or void for the moment; others, to satisfy a combination of economic, emotional, psychological, or physical needs.

As I grew up and learned about myself and life, I'm thankful things got better, from dating men that people would consider bad for me to those that could be regarded as just okay. Regardless of why, I'm grateful my best friend and former roommate, Elisa, was able to counsel and, through action, was able to rescue me from an illusionary relationship, and literally, handing me over to a real man that was willing and ready for a relationship. The type that comes around once in a blue moon or that I could only read or watch in a romantic television show. Through her pragmatic and persuasive power or skill, her guidance catapulted me into my current lovefest with Greg, of whom I consider to be a gift that keeps on giving.

To put everything in context, let me open a window into events that directly and indirectly combined to bring me into my current state of mind and 'lucky' love life. From the beginning of my arrival in the States, both my parents have helped with my education cost, but the bulk of expenses have been shouldered by my mother and grandparents. They've shouldered the total costs for my tuition, room, and board. Not being alone in experiencing financial hardship, Elisa, my roommate, suggested we should move out and rent a place and share costs. Due to our tight budget, we also decided to take on some part-time jobs or internships for the job-related experience.

Since we didn't have transportation, we decided to rent a condo unit by Shaker Heights, not too far from campus, which is also a ride or walks away from most eateries, watering holes, museums, parks and recreations, ballparks, casinos, orchestra, clubs, variety theatres, and art centers, botanical gardens, shops and Malls, sports arenas, and countless fun venues. So, there's plenty to do or see, twenty-four-seven, within Cleveland and surrounding suburbs.

Our remodeled brick building was not extremely old but has been around longer than our two ages combined four times. The space was large with a huge living room, concrete floors, two large bedrooms with walls painted in off white color, a large storage room that was almost the size of a bedroom, a clean redone bathroom, a good redone kitchen with gas stove, refrigerator and basic essentials, such as utensils, plates, glasses and dining set. Other items included bedroom and living room sets, but we had to provide pillows, beddings, and everything else to make life livable. The beauty of it was that utilities such as water and heat were included. The bottom line was that it was reasonably priced and very safe. Good enough for us to share the unit until after graduation, become more independent financially, and cut costs and other expenses.

And since Elisa was a few years older and graduated before me, she moved in with Mike, her boyfriend, to the suburb, who works as a hedge fund manager. When she moved out, I also did but to a single unit, and shortly afterward, she introduced me to my current boyfriend, Greg. And while she has gotten married in civil court, I'm engaged to be married in several weeks too.

Before we both moved out, Elisa was working as an intern with the investment company, while Mike was in management with the same organization. I, on the other hand, took up a waitressing job at a restaurant and juggled my classes. For the years we lived together, we helped each other out, and we're like sisters, and our friendship has gotten even stronger. For years, we lived together and enjoyed our time together. We regularly talked about our desires, aspirations, dreams, fears and secrets, and future career.

In terms of personality, Elisa seems to be driven and knows what she wants. She says she's more like her father, unlike her mother, that spends more of her time and energy taking care of her father. Because of her focus and determination, she was hired full time after graduation, and although she's now married, she told me, she's not in a hurry to have children. She says marriage gives and take between two people and equal in every respect. While I on the other hand, do not mind taking care of and supporting a man that loves, cares, and respects me, and the essence of a happy relationship.

I suppose I'm more like my mother and derive my happiness from supporting and seeing the man happy. I do not think marriage should be about deprivation or diminished status for a woman if the couple is compatible and complement each other on many levels. I believe Mike is a good guy for Elisa, attentive to her needs, and does almost anything she asks for to make her happy. Greg does long-term planning and consulting with clients, handles major accounts, flies to major meetings as necessary, assigns major investment portfolios and tasks to Mike and his team, and provides management oversight and long-term support for the success of the firm. His employees admire him deeply and are happy to have him as their boss. Despite his hectic schedule, he makes time for us and tunes in to me, and easily understands my feelings and needs. I love him unconditionally.

When Elisa and I moved in together, and I was working in waitressing, I dated a guy that came into the restaurant one day for lunch. He left a tip after paying for the meal and wrote his number on the ten-dollar bill and asked me to call him. I told Elisa about him, and she thought he was creepy when she asked me to invite him over, but he claimed he was too busy. He repeated the same line each time, but he convinced me to come work for him as his secretary in a small advertising agency. Two weeks later, when I started working for this forty-seven-year-old man named Jonathan, I noticed he hardly had any clients.

Jonathan convinced me to start writing his ad columns, stating that I wrote better than him because I was tuned into his market niche than himself. I believed him because he claimed Engineering was his college degree, just like my major is in business studies. He even promised he would make me a partner in his business, but since the business was not generating any profit or revenues, he increasingly became very grumpy and crabby.

I asked him why he was not working in Engineering, and he said he lost interest when it became boring. I don't know why I believed him, but I did. Maybe because he kept saying things would get better, and when I told Elisa, she said he was a fraud and manipulator. When fewer and fewer businesses were advertising with him, he switched my role from typing and paperwork to sweeping, vacuuming, and cleaning his office, which was in an old business district with several empty office spaces.

When I asked him about his family or friends, he said he has been married three times and had three children, one from each of the women. When I asked him when he saw his kids last, he said their mothers were terrible women and psychologically messed up. To pay child support or get in touch with them was complicated, according to him, because it was too stressful and would interfere with his business.

Although he gave many similar excuses each time I talked about his family, he said talking about it made it hard for him to do his work and would be happy with me if I stopped asking about them or about his friends. I sensed an accent when he pronounced the number five as 'fav' twice because I wasn't sure what he was saying exactly, I asked him where he was born, and he said Mississippi before moving to Ohio to work as an Engineer but quit because his boss was making fun of his accent. Despite his shortcomings, I still believed him because he was so soft-spoken and gentle like a lamb. After a while, he reduced my pay, claiming that he was not paid for some of his ad jobs and that the businesses would pay up once their sales increased.

Elisa described him as those guys that take all their money, including their last dime or nickel, to the casino, with the hope of winning big but come home without his shirt because he believes he's going to win the next merry-go round. I felt sorry for him and wanted to give him a chance, and his luck could be just around the corner, just like he says. Elisa increasingly became very upset and told me I was under his spell for sacrificing my time, life, and energy, writing to Jonathan and getting nothing in return. I stopped talking to her about him.

Once my mom called, and I told her about him and that I was doing two jobs to help him out with some of his bills, she thought I was stupid. She asked me to come back home immediately after graduation from my degree program. When I told Jonathan, he said working for someone is like a slave because those that own a business do not have two heads but prefer to act as if they have the biggest head in the world. He said I was more talented than any girl he had ever met.

I never considered myself needy or naïve but wanted to be loyal and supportive, and I never thought he was taking advantage of me, as my friend and family were saying. Although he had not paid me any money he borrowed, I believe he will pay me back when he has it or when things get better for him. He even told me that the reason he didn't send any money to his kids was that their mothers were very rich and received monthly allowance from their parents and didn't even need it unless they were bored doing nothing.

Elisa was so upset and started encouraging me to date more until I found the right guy for me. She said it was a numbers game, but the guys I've dated have been similar in personality or character. I decided to give it a try and dated another guy I met at the restaurant, who told me he was a model for the major department stores across the Midwest and travelled between Cleveland, Minneapolis, Toronto, and Chicago. During the two weeks he was with me, it seemed he didn't work because he spent more time in my apartment, and that made Elisa angry, and she wanted him gone. She referred to him as a stray cat or wounded dog and asked me to take him to the shelter. It sounds funny now, but it was not amusing to me at the time. I was in love with him until I found out he was also in love with another girl, and he told me he was going to continue loving her because he claimed she'll commit suicide if he left her. So, under pressure from Elisa, I gave him up and returned to Jonathan.

Elisa, on the other hand, had her priorities straight. Work came first, and dates or relationships were secondary. Until she met Mike, she believed only in casual dates and dumped the guy whenever she felt like it. There were times she worked a double shift or double jobs, including weekends, until she joined the investment firm. No date was too good to hang on to, more than work, and no guy could change her mind. And when she dated a guy, she got rid of him after a few dates. She referred to them as underwear, and they had to be discarded after serving their usefulness. She was passionate when she dated because she gave it her all. Maybe that was why they never gave up until they realized she wasn't going to change her mind.

Besides Mike, she only dated seriously once with this famous French chef, Benoit, that owned a restaurant in town. She dated him seriously until he relocated his business to New York City. Not sure why she felt differently about him. Maybe because he was a Parisian French, from the same city as her, or maybe because he was generous with his wealth. He paid all her bills and flew her to major cities like Miami or Los Angeles on business trips or whenever he was free.

He was a very likable rich guy, and we both thought he was attentive, and funny, and he spent as much time with Elisa as possible, almost as if he couldn't have enough of her. But she tells me it was because she was a passionate lover. He spent nights with her many times, although he had a suite at a downtown five-star hotel. How they met was when we were downtown, enjoying the breeze, and we smelled French food, and when we looked at the door sign, we noticed it was a French restaurant. We went inside, and a tall slim, dark-haired man walked up to us, smiling and saying bonjour. And noticing his accent, we replied in French, and he smiled, and in three days, he started hanging out with Elisa. The entire time he was in town, they behaved like it was their honeymoon. Always happy and playful. His place was a great hangout with young enterprising people with delicious food and a lively bar.

Benoit was a great guy and loved sports, especially soccer. Very hard-working man and fun to be around. Almost childlike in attitude and behavior. All around, a nice guy in his late thirties. More like ten years older than Elisa. I felt he truly was in love or infatuated with Elisa, but she was just having a good time and took it day by day and simply enjoying her life.

The next day, Jonathan made me work all day into the night. Retyping and changing the format for his paper and creating online posts. Also tried to create a weekly email list at the last minute, which kept me in the office for close to midnight. As I entered the apartment, I noticed Elisa was still up, and I told her that I delayed coming home because I also had to clean the office more because Jonathan said his lease at his small apartment was up and he would start sleeping in his office. So, I cleaned the place up and waited for him, but he had not arrived after midnight when I left. Elisa just looked at me, smiling but said nothing.

I just told her that I was tired and would just take a shower and go to sleep. I asked about her day, and she said, "I'm exhausted too. Her job assigned her the responsibility of training a couple of college interns. That the interns were a little disinterested as if they were forced or required to complete the course for college credit. She was sure about that, she concluded. Anyway, she was happy to be home finally. I teased her that if they were working for Jonathan and doing cleaning instead, maybe they'd enjoy it more and consider their internship a worthy lifetime experience. She laughed so hard that tears were streaming off her face. I guess it sounded like a very funny joke to her.

In any case, Elisa got up, and I noticed she was still wearing her high heel shoes, navy suit jacket, white lacy shirt inside, and a matching skirt. It just occurred to me that she had long legs, which made her look like a model. Her hair was freshly styled as if she had just come out of a salon. An exact opposite of my scruffy clothes from tidying a relatively untidy office space, which I hardly complain about nor mind.

She walked over to the kitchen counter and picked up some takeout carryout dinner boxes from Benoit French restaurant, and placed them on the table in front of the sofa. She said he thought we would need some dinner and sent them over through one of his delivery guys. He often surprises us with food boxes or drops by with containers of fresh food items and personally cooks for us. A generous guy like him would only come around once in half a dozen years.

"Have you eaten yet?" she asked, smiling and making herself comfortable next to me by the sofa. She looked at me as if I was a stranger and said, "you know, I think you can get a high paying job, painting a billboard, or better still, a mountain, or join the union and get paid handsomely at a construction site," she teased, kicking her heels off her long legs. "Anyway, Benoit's restaurant was jam-packed tonight."

"It always is busy," I replied. "Thanks for the food, Elisa." I got up and brought some plates and cutlery for both of us from the kitchen because the smell of the delicious food was making me very hungry, and I couldn't wait any longer. While I was dishing for both of us, Elisa opened a bottle of wine for us and poured it into two empty glasses that were by a set of napkins. We sat side by side and enjoyed our meals and wine, chatting some more. I knew that, despite our differences, we cared deeply about each other, just like normal, respectable family or friends.

As I was enjoying our delicious meal, I couldn't help speaking out loud what was going through my mind. Turning to Elisa, I said, "It would be nice to be relaxing at home, pregnant and nursing a little baby, instead of wasting time in a bad neighborhood office, cleaning floors, if I can help it," looking at her wistfully, as if seeking her opinion.

Elisa shook her head, "hopefully not with Jonathan," looking with honest, serious eyes, "not if you want him to support it. However, if you want to have kids, you need to be involved with someone responsible and with enough money to help in raising the child."

She knew I try to think like a grown-up but think with my heart instead of my head. She believes I gravitate toward the wrong kinds of guys, and she vowed to help me by introducing the right kind of guy that would not mind taking care of me, while I love the person as much as or even more than I give of myself to the wrong guy each time. I feel embarrassed about it and try not to think about it because the thought of embracing the fact and stepping out as an independent girl is scary, honestly.

Elisa grew up in a big city and worked closely with her supporting parents who nurtured and taught her how to be independent and strong. For me, I was either insulted or teased harshly and sardonically by my father, while my mom was almost like a silent participant. I m glad she knows about my upbringing as much as she has opened up about herself. She told me that even though she's not thinking about kids, she also told me that I shouldn't put a clock on my fertility because people healthy are giving births every day, even passed their forties. I also know that money is not everything that brings happiness to couples, but it is essential to making life comfortable when used to an end.

"I don't want kids yet until I'm comfortable in my own skin," she said as she reflected on the idea.

To share my thought on the subject, I said to her: "Actually, you can have a baby before your thirties, not in your forties." She just looked at me without uttering a word while I smiled at her and ate the food in front of us. Regardless of how she feels, I just know that I'd rather have kids now and watch them grow up, go to school or work, and spend the latter years enjoying life with my husband.

 Thinking briefly, she responded, "I'm a couple of years older than you are, Marie. Time goes by too fast, and there's so much I still want to do, to get where I want to be." To her credit, she did work a couple of years before coming to the US for her university studies. So, by every standard, she has been successful. Her high expectation does not allow her to see it as others see it. She wants more and expects more of herself.

I got up, walked to the bathroom to take a shower, and prepared for bed. A little while afterward, Elisa stepped into her room to finish a project on her laptop before she slept. I smiled as I thought about her because she is a good girl. She cares a lot. She is very pragmatic and disciplined in her ways. I'm glad we became roommates, and now, almost like sisters, supporting and sharing life experiences, counseling each other, and looking out for each other. She made me realize that we can open up and bond with total strangers that are not blood relatives as a family sometimes. Come to think of it, that is the most realistic modern definition of family.

13

On her drive to work the next day, Elisa called me to say she saw a billboard ad about Benoit's restaurant, and I told her it was placed by Jonathan. Told her that he places both paper and digital ads these days., and she was pleased to hear that. She said I must have suggested or planted the idea; else, he would be clueless. I knew she was right, but I said nothing. She said the ad brought a smile to her face because it mentioned Benoit's restaurant as a venue for good wholesome food and a great atmosphere to mingle, relax, and enjoy a couple of drinks and a cigar. It also stated that many important personalities patronize it, listing a couple of filthy rich Ohioans, basketball and football athletes, among others.

She thanked me because, according to her, the choice of words in it were things I knew and would say. I suppose it's because I absolutely enjoy Benoit's cooking and tell her how lucky she is to date a fabulous guy like him. I know she's proud of him and his accomplishment. Come to think of it, she's always proud of and admires successful and enterprising people because she sees herself in them. She even called Benoit before calling me and told him how proud she was of him. Something I've never heard her say, but besides her passions, I'm sure there are other sides to her that men find very appealing.

Like her physical beauty, she always dressed in designer clothes, often wearing short skirts, crisp white blouses, high heels, expensive earrings and necklaces, and of course, her model walk. I suppose she's what is called a total package.

A few hours later, she dropped back home and mentioned that she wanted to facetime with Benoit because she couldn't get him off her mind. I told her that's what love does, and she wrinkled her nose and shook her head sideways in disagreement. Seating across from me, she picked up her iPad and gave someone a call, and I could hear her conversation because it was on speaker. "Bonjour," I heard a male's voice with an accent from the background. I knew it must be Benoit. "Nice mention of the restaurant by Marie," he said to her. "I shall tell her," she replied and muted the line. They continued chatting for a good half an hour before hanging up. Her face was all smiles, and she was giddy like a kid in a candy store. I could tell she was very happy.

She told me Benoit had graduated from one of the top French culinary schools a decade-plus earlier and went to work at one of the top Parisian restaurants. And as luck would have its way, a very rich multimillionaire enjoyed his cooking and asked him to partner with him and open a couple of boutique French eateries. He expanded the business across Paris and wanted to travel or relocate overseas. The man negotiated a deal, and he was bought out for tens of millions, and the rest is history.

In the US, he first opened similar eateries in several cities, namely Chicago, Minneapolis, Cleveland, and Denver. I asked her why in the middle of America, and she said he wanted to start small, then expand into major cities. He plans to partner with one high-tech billionaire and go big time across the coastal parts of the States, such as Miami, L.A., NYC, and so on, but everything is still in the works. She also said he moved to the States with his model girlfriend, but since she was young and doing well in her career, she returned to continue in it, after spending about a year with him and had been gone exactly two months, the day he met Elisa.

After an animated conversation about her boyfriend, she asked me, "do you want to have dinner at Benoit's restaurant Saturday?"

"I'll check with Jonathan first. He said something about wanting to spend time with me all day Saturday. If I can wiggle out of it, I'd love to. I'll let you know."

"Sounds good." She replied, and her thoughts turned instantly to work. She was ready to return to work because she had to be present at an important afternoon meeting for all staff in preparation for a visit from a team of investors a week afterward.

According to her, the guests were planning on holding a couple of high-powered meetings on the possibility of investing a huge chunk of their money in a combination of packaged medium to long-term portfolios. Her role would be critical in explaining and sharing both the short- and long-term benefits of each option.

She checked all her facts on her laptop, organized her power points for presentations on her hard drive, and made some calls. Then got up from the sofa, waved goodbye, and headed to the door.

I decided to hurry to school for my afternoon class. With everything in my backpack, I was out of the door. I went straight to the class, which was scheduled to start in half an hour.

A couple of students were already there, talking or doing some homework. One of the girls was quarreling with a guy sitting next to her. They seem to be boyfriends' girlfriends because the issue of cheating kept coming up in their conversation. The other two girls right in front of them were in their own world, deep in their own issues. One conferred with the other that she might soon be fired from her part-time job because she was accused of causing a loss in inventory numbers at the kid's Foot Locker shoe store she worked for. That the number of shoes sold did not match the inventory sheet, she had given to her supervisor. She was stressed because she couldn't think of a way out.

However, she anticipated being fired and possibly prosecuted. She has often played it safe since she started working there but also mentioned that her supervisor is difficult to work for. It seems everybody has a problem, and finding a solution is as problematic as the issues that cause the problems. Just before the instructor arrived, the girl behind me tapped my shoulder to ask if I had an extra pen because she couldn't find hers in her book bag, and when I said no, she quickly followed up with a story about her part-time job. Stating that a new hire had made her upset because the young guy was not following instructions properly and was very forgetful.

When I asked what she thought was his problem, she changed the story. Stating that she thought he liked her because he was smirking each time, she tried responding to his questions. That he looked at her and acted like everything was a joke. When I asked her why she couldn't ignore him or try to find another job if she did not like it. Her response was that she couldn't quit because she needed the money. Anyway, I was glad the instructor finally came in to start the class because I was getting stressed listening to crazy talk.

After class, I headed home but ran into a nice-looking guy walking toward me. He smiled and stopped right in front of me. The next thing out of his mouth was a weird question: "Are you a model?"

I said, "no, why?" thinking he sounded corny.

 "You look like a girl we modeled together last week, but I left before asking for your number," he stated, sounding self-assured and confident.

"So, you are a model?" I asked him, "and who do you model for?"

"Signed up with French, Italian, and American designer brands like The North Face, Gucci, Prada, Giorgio Armani, and Louis Vuitton."

"So, how did you end up in Cleveland and not New York or L.A.?" I asked with suspicious curiosity.

"My parents live here, but I'm based in New York City," he stated bluntly.

"Ok, give me your number, and I'll call you in half an hour. Add it here," I handed him my phone.

"Thanks, talk to you soon," he replied, smiling like a lottery winner. "We'll arrange and meet for a dinner and some fun event, alright?" he sounded triumphant, and we parted ways.

Entering the apartment, I noticed Elisa was home, and she asked how my day was.

"I have a date," I responded, a little nervous. "A guy met me and wants us to get together."

"With who?" Elisa looked surprised, knowing that I was already dating Jonathan, whom she dislikes and thinks I should run away from and find someone else.

"Some guy I met on my way home. He thought we knew each other from some modelling event or shoot. I acted like he was mistaken. Or, maybe he was pulling a line just to see my reaction."

"And he still thinks so? I mean, as if he knows you?" Elisa was amused and looked at me funny.

"Of course not. I told him, but he asked me out anyway. He's a model for a couple of designer companies. He sounded like he made up a rehearsed pick-up speech."

"He must be handsome," Elisa said, "and probably has a lot going for him, instead of the sorry ass guy you are currently hanging out with, in the name of love."

"Yeah, kind of. I wasn't going to go out with him, but he made a big fuss that I sounded like I'd forgotten who he was, and I didn't want to admit I had. He's taking me to some art opening, and dinner afterward." It sounded like the kind of date Elisa would prefer for me to explore, if nothing else, at least to see where it leads, rather than dead ended. "I said I'd call him in an hour and let him know."

"I think you should say yes. Wear something hot," Elisa advised. I disappeared into my room, searched through the closet, and came up with a white cotton dress and threw it on the bed. Elisa came in a minute later and shook her head. "You'll look like you're going to the beach or park. There's a black pencil skirt at the back of your closet and a silver tube top. Wear that." I hesitated for a minute and then nodded. Elisa knew a lot more about fashion than I did. I called the guy and accepted the date, jumped into the shower, and was dressed ten minutes later, and my hair was still wet.

"Blow-dry your hair, put on makeup, and wear high heels," Elisa suggested as I headed back to the bathroom and emerged ten minutes later; and actually, looked like I was going on a date, except that I couldn't find heels in her closet. I walked into the living room shoeless, and Elisa handed me a pair of high-heeled sandals since we wore the same size.

"Now you look hot!" Elisa said, smiling at me.

Minutes later, I hailed a cab and gave the driver the address of SPACES, a venue located west of downtown Cleveland, where works of art are displayed just as you'd find in an art gallery, but it includes events throughout the year.

As soon as I came out of the cab at the place of our meeting, I saw him as soon as I walked in, and he made a beeline for me.

"Wow! You look amazing." He had his cell phone in his hand and snapped a picture of me before I could stop him.

"Why did you do that?" I felt uncomfortable and ill at ease. "I put everything I do on my online website," says Zack to me. The thought of it made me agitated, and I followed him into the crowded gallery, where he seemed to know many people.

Zack was a tall, slim, handsome man about my age, and as women crowded around him, I felt I didn't dress appropriately for the place. Sort of awkward being there. A couple of men had small conversations with me, and Zack listened in, smiling and nodding his head. The show he suggested we watch was an interpretative dance art form that was very different from my typical gallery experience. There were six local choreographers that converged to create moment poetry in a vivid portrayal of modern art. It is a kind of art form that can be viewed from a diverse perspective depending on who is viewing it.

After this event, we left the gallery and took a cab to The Bourbon Street Barrel Room in Tremont here in Cleveland, which offers a relaxed, casual, fun atmosphere while serving authentic New Orleans-style cuisine. The menu included such food choices as gumbo, jambalaya, crawfish etouffee, and beignets. The restaurant also featured thirty plus rotating craft beers plus New Orleans cocktails. It was crowded and a little noisy, and it seemed everybody knew Zack there too.

The conversation was nearly impossible once we were seated at the table, and he took another picture of me on his cell phone, which made me nervous even more. I wondered if he was trying to let people think he was on a date with some famous supermodel. It made me realize that regular dating and hanging out more gave one plenty of confidence and self-assurance. Maybe that's why I kept feeling awkward and out of place in crowded places, as well as meeting and talking to strangers the first time around. Like Elisa has told me, I need to make myself available and active to know and find the kind of guy that is right for me. I feel that it not only takes time and effort but is also suitable for one's personality too. But now that I was here, it felt all too strange. Zack was a good-looking guy, but we had nothing in common, and I doubted he would ask me out again.

 "So, what do you do?" he asked me, shouting over the clatter of the noisy restaurant after we had ordered. I noticed that his muscles rippled under the black T-shirt he was wearing with black jeans. He was in fantastic shape, and it was easy to guess he worked out every day.

"I'm a business student at Case Western," I shouted back." He looked speechless by my response.

"I thought you were a model, he said, looking at me with suspicion." I shook my head, smiling.

"No, I'm a student," I repeated. His eyes opened wider as he was momentarily confused, and then he nodded mechanically.

"I guess that's cool." I began to realize he thought I was someone else when he first met me while walking home. His wrong thought must have motivated him to quickly ask me out on a date without any formal introduction or chat. I know Elisa won't date a guy like Zack because he was too young, less experienced, and not as rich as the older men she's accustomed to dating. After a minute of silence, he asked, "do you like studying business?" He didn't know what else to say to me.

"Very much so. Do you like being a model?" I asked him in return.

"Yeah, I'm having the time of my life with modelling and getting to travel and see the world. I'm hoping to branch into movies next, and my agent is working on it. I should be hearing from him soon, based on an audition I had over a week ago." I nodded just as our dinner arrived and the noise level increased around us. We were spared further conversation until we were back on the street.

He put an arm around me when we left the restaurant and looked at me with anticipation.

"Do you want to come to my place? It's a few blocks from here," he expressed confidently.

The location wasn't an issue, but I didn't know much about him, and it was obvious that he expected to sleep with me in exchange for dinner. And handsome as he was, having sex with a stranger that I had just met in the streets, and spending time together in crowds, didn't appeal to me.

"I have to be at work at six tomorrow morning. I should get home," I said to him, not knowing what else to say. I felt that was a better and safe thing to tell him, rather than appearing rude by questioning his intentions or creating an awkward scene that would result in hurt feelings and regrets.

"Yeah, right. We'll have to do this again sometime," he said, sounding unimpressed. I could tell that he thought that if I wasn't going to sleep with him, there wasn't much point in seeing me again. He put me in a cab five minutes later and waved as it drove me home. I was feeling confused, the evening had been noisy, boring, and unfulfilling, and I knew nothing more about him than I had when we met, except that he was being considered for a part in a movie in Cleveland or California.

As I thought about the date more, I felt like the reason for this kind of date, with young men like him, was not to get to know each other but just to dress up, get out, share a meal, network at the gallery party, and if possible, get together and have sex. Although I've done it in the past, as I get older and think about serious relationships and settling down and having a family, it is not as appealing to me as in the past. Maybe that is why I'm seeing Jonathan because he looks and acts older but with an immature and quirky personality. Staying home and doing routine things with someone mature, maybe enjoying a conversation or watching T.V., would be more in line with what I'd prefer compared to Zack's world.

When I returned home and discussed the date with Elisa, she seemed to be very understanding and supportive. Elisa suggested we should take a ride to Benoit's restaurant briefly. Upon arrival, we noticed it had closed half an hour earlier, but he was inside, and we could see him through the lighted glass entrance. The kitchen staff was cleaning up. Benoit gave us some mini bottles of water and proceeded to instruct his staff on what to do before closing the door for the night.

"Welcome, girls," he commented, smiling, and opened a bottle of wine for the three of us to share. He told his staff good night, and we rode back together to our apartment. We were still up at three, talking and feeling tired.

Elisa asked again, "by the way, how was your date?"

Not being in the mood to rehash, I responded reluctantly, "ridiculous, a total waste of time. I should have stayed home with you instead. He was pretty for the eye but nothing to discuss or say."

"There are some good guys out there, so don't give up," She reminded me, even though I was skeptical.

"I think you got the last good one left," I responded with a dry laugh and looked at Benoit as he got up to go to bed, allowing us to discuss dates

"What do you expect from a model, for Christ's sake?" she snapped.

"He kept taking pictures of me as if I was a model and he was the photographer, so as to upload to his online website for his followers, according to him," I said, feeling annoyed repeating the date. I felt that he was creepy; taking random pictures of girls he barely knew and posting them online just to compare and get public affirmation was indicative of someone that's not sure about himself.

"At least you tried," she concluded.

"Talking about bad dates reminded me of another date I'd gone on many months previously," but telling Elisa for the first time. "I met this nice looking foreign-born American guy that told me after a couple drinks that he was shopping for a wife. And when I asked him what he meant, he responded that he was already engaged to a woman through an arrangement by his family, but since he was not sure if he wanted to go through with it, he decided to date as many girls as possible. To shop around, compare other females before proceeding with the arranged marriage to his fiancée.

"Nice," Elisa remarked with a smile.

"I guess I didn't do it for him because the Cleveland Star newspaper had his picture and his new wife, both wearing some colorful traditional garments from their home country," I said.

"A few bad dates are not an excuse to live like a nun or get trapped with the wrong guy. And you have no excuse," Elisa added very quickly, almost with exasperation. "A girl cannot stay home alone forever. It takes some effort to find the right guy."

"And then what? You get married and feel sorry for yourself for the rest of your life?" I responded, feeling frustrated, as I thought about my parent's boring relationship. At least they don't hate each other, but in my opinion, my father married my mother out of pity, not love. And my mother's apathetic complacency contributed to it, resulting in her current feelings of helplessness."

"It doesn't always turn out that way," Elisa insisted, knowing that her parent's situation is different, but could be better. Come to think of it, some people were not meant to be married in the first place but ended up together because of circumstances. But the current generation is more careful and a lot more cautious about who they marry and why. Or they just live together, which makes more sense to them, but still does not guarantee anything. However, their parents' reasons for getting married no longer apply. Giving up lives, careers, cities, or country for a man seems like a bad idea to most of them, which could lead to a miserable life like those of people they know or read about every day.

"Well, I guess I'll sign off on the dating department for a while," I replied, feeling relief.

"You try something once or twice, you chicken out. You never heard of a boxer or sports team quitting just because they lost a contest or game, have you?" Elisa scolded me. "You can't give up after one boring date. That's silly. If you do that, you'd be trapped with some crazy guy, like the one you're seeing right now, forever."

"Ok! Ok! I've heard enough. I'm going to bed now." I got up and headed to my bedroom and closed my eyes. Maybe she's right; nothing good comes easy. Maybe one day, I'll be lucky to find the right guy or be introduced to one through a good Samaritan. Before I knew it, I was fast asleep, like a baby.

14

Jonathan made me repaint the toilet and office walls again because he thought the previous color was 'too colorful,' to borrow his words. I didn't argue with him because he appeared to have been in a bad mood, and when I asked him what was wrong, he simply said he was stressed and needed some quiet. He also wanted me to do a search list of prospective businesses and should contact them and negotiate content requirements and create ads per specifications and industry pricing industry standards.

As I was painting the doors leading to the rental entrance, Jonathan was out to see a medium-sized company manager he said was owing to him on a previous assignment. While away, an attractive girl walked in, looking a little lost as she looked around an office space that was almost empty with dim lighting with very few windows.

Come to think of it, the place looks more like a studio rather than a newspaper mill. She had huge breasts that were nearly falling out of a man's tank top and was wearing skin-tight jeans. She had tangled, long red hair that looked as if she had just climbed out of bed or used a gym. I wondered if she wanted to place an ad since she was holding a large folder to her chest. Or missed her way and asked for direction, considering Jonathan prefers to meet his clients at some designated location rather than his shabby and not very new threadbare furnished office space.

I stopped painting and looked at her. "Can I help you?"

"I have something to drop off for Jonathan. He wanted me to drop off some artwork I've done in art class for him. Is he here?" she said, with hesitation in her voice.

I shook my head and glanced at the thick folder she was holding against her chest.

"It's a couple of artworks I put together in my graphics art certificate program. He said if he could look at the portfolio, he might provide me with a better job opportunity at his advertising company rather than continuing at McDonald's, where I'm working part-time. He seems like a friendly guy that comes around to grab a bite or buy some coffee from time to time and teases me," she said and smiling shyly. "A few days ago, when he dropped by, he asked what I did besides working at McDonald's, and I told him I was a student, and he wrote his number on a dollar bill and asked me to give him a call," she concluded.

"And what's your name," I asked her.

"My name is Angela," she stated. Something about what she said struck a chord of my memory. Jonathan had met me at my part-time job and dropped a tip with his number written on it and asked for me to come work for him when I contacted him. The type and nature of the job were never clearly defined, but he sounded very mature and believable; I thought the opportunity would be useful for me to apply my education. My head was spinning in anger and confusion as I reflected on how convincing he was, with his promises of using my marketing and business training every day. But here I am, doing menial chores and not getting paid for work done, but being used as a lover and girlfriend instead.

An alarm bell went off in my head, and I sensed trouble. "Are you a graphics designer or writer?" Angela asked with interest.

"No, I'm a business major at the university. I do odd chores for him, from cleaning, painting, writing, copy editing, online web publishing, promotions, and whatever office task I'm assigned to do.

"Do you want to leave the folder with me? I'll give it to him when he gets back," I said quietly, trying not to seem anxious or suspicious. There was no reason for her to worry either because Jonathan had every right to see anybody he wanted and do whatever he wanted. Anytime or place. Although he says and acts busy every day, he tends to blame businesses for not signing up with him or doing business with him, forgetting that marketing, networking, and promotion are critical or essential to the success of his firm. And lately, he's been borrowing funds from me to catch up on his bills.

"Do you mind if I wait?" Asked Angela, continuing to grab the large folder to her chest as though someone would try to steal it from her. I often feel the same way about my schoolwork too. More so, if it's an assignment, that would result in a course grade.

"Not at all, but he might be a while, maybe a long while, before he returns," I told her. "He usually goes out on meetings or business events and might via off to take care of some errands too."

I feel a little bit annoyed to have her stand here, waiting for the champion to come or for him to call, which is extremely rare; even when I call, it often goes into the answering service. I consider him an extremely smart man, but it could be frustrating dealing with him if or when things don't go his way or not to his liking.

So, I'm not surprised that this girl, Angela, feels and sees him the same way too. She sat down on one of two plastic folding chairs at the entrance to the office and was ready to wait while I continued painting with my hand shaking from confused fury. I could tell I wasn't doing a good job anymore due to nervousness and not knowing what might ensue when Jonathan got in.

Angela sat for two hours without making a sound, reading a book she'd brought with her, and I almost forgot she was there, but not out of my mind. And out of nowhere, Jonathan walked in, smiling in my direction as he approached.

"How's it coming?" he asked, referring to what I was doing. "Good, I hope." He beamed at me as our eyes met, and I felt my knees weaken as they always did when he looked at me. He fascinated me because I'd never met a man like him in my twenty-something years on earth. And since meeting him, I've never said no or questioned anything he says, whether right or wrong.

We both jumped when Angela spoke in a soft voice from where she was seated. I momentarily forgot about her because she was so quiet and engrossed in her reading. Jonathan turned at the sound of the voice and was startled when he noticed her smiling adoringly at him, which I saw and didn't like. The hint of something worrying was in the air.

"What are you doing here?" He asked her, obviously surprised.

"You said I could drop my portfolio off, and you'd take a look at it," she reminded him.

"Yes, I did," he said as though he'd forgotten and smiled at her. Elisa always compared him to a snake in green grass waiting to pounce on his prey, especially when his prey were women. She sometimes refers to him as a creep. But I see something in him that she didn't, and Angela talking to him did too.

"I'll read it during the weekend and let you know what I think." And then he was struck by an idea. "Would you like to go for a cup of coffee and tell me about it for a few minutes?" he offered.

"As long as you have been waiting for me, you can explain what you have accomplished in your portfolio, so I don't miss any of your intended meaning." I knew as well as he did that whatever she had in her portfolio didn't need further explanation or an interpretation from her. It should speak for itself. But I didn't say anything as I continued doing my chores and pretended not to listen.

Angela immediately accepted his offer, and they left the office a few minutes later, deep in conversation about her portfolio as she explained its content to him. And for a minute, I felt sick. I had heard it all before. He had said it all to me in the past months we've been together. And I've seen him flirt with other young girls, students, office staff; female clients in charge of contract projects or managing businesses he was seeking to perform projects from bids. I never took it seriously or felt threatened by it, but this time, for some unknown reason, I do. The girl looked so innocent but determined, and he was so intense when he talked to her.

He came back an hour later, without the girl, and explained the meeting to me, so I wouldn't worry. He didn't want me to be upset.

"Her father owns almost half of Ohio farms. He probably could be the richest man in the state, he said to me. He has a shitload of money and would be willing to back any advertising, promotion, and all sorts of marketing program we propose to him by using his daughter's contact. Her father wants her to gain outside experience before allowing her to work in his business, so we can make her father happy by making her happy. If her rich dad is willing to help us out, we sure can use his money as much as possible to help ourselves. Doing anything with her won't hurt us, at least if her daddy's money keeps flowing our way." I liked his southern accent so much that the smooth drawl that came out of his mouth made sense, and I could see why he had to spend time with her, to do whatever it takes to get her interested and happy in whatever he said or does with her.

"Sometimes, you must prostitute yourself a little to get something good. She's like an angel because through her rich father, we can get all sorts of money to get our business going." He finally concluded, with a big smile on his entire face.

I sighed as I listened to him, wanting to believe that what he said about the reason for visiting with Angela was true. I am not sure if whatever he has said is true, but willing to give him the benefit of the doubt. He also gave me the impression he liked what I've done for him, although I didn't think it was special.

"Are you going to be able to come over to my place tonight?" he said, searching my eyes as if for something hidden or to try and read my mind through my eyes.

"About what time, precisely?" I replied, just to make sure since I live with Elisa and won't want to sound blank, should she ask me anything.

"After I return from having dinner with one of my friends that is having trouble with his baby mama? So would midnight be too late?" he slowly stated, with a slow, almost whispery pleading drawl. As he said it, he pulled me closer to his body, caressing and rubbing my neck and letting his hand drift to my breast as I melted into his strong arms. He kissed my forehead, moving his lips softly across different parts of my face, and I wished he could just undress me and make love to me, there and then. When he abruptly stopped, holding my head in his hands, looking into my eyes, I remember he had asked me a question, and I quickly responded.

""No, it's fine." I've had a long day today, and I know I'd be half asleep by then, but the prospect of curling up in his arms, satisfied by our lovemaking, would be too tempting to resist. He has always been a clever lover who understood women's bodies well, and the sex we've shared has been like a drug and would make me forget everything else in the world. I am almost getting used to the long delays for him to pick me up and make love to me all night long, as he used to. The thought of tonight alone would compensate for all missed times, so whatever he decides is fine with me. "I'll come over at midnight," I said in a soft voice as he kissed me softly on the lips.

As soon as I accepted seeing him at midnight, I remembered that Elisa and I, and maybe some of her other friends, we're thinking of dropping by Benoit's restaurant on Saturday night and wondering if he wanted to join us after he returned from meeting his friend. He never said that he didn't like my roommate Elisa, but I sensed it easily, knowing how he thinks and acts. And it is mutual since she doesn't think much of him anyway. He avoided her whenever possible, and when I extended the invitation to him for Saturday, he looked vague, which is another way of saying no.

"The dinner and visit with my friend would take too much out of me. I won't be up to a lot of people and a noisy restaurant. But thanks anyway. Another time?"

I nodded and didn't insist. I knew he gave a lot to whatever he was doing out there without me.

"You go with them, though, if you want to. I'll just go home and go to bed." The invitation by Elisa had been casual for anyone with no plans. But the Sunday-night dinners at Benoit's have become a weekly tradition, and everyone came.

"Do you want to have dinner at the apartment on Sunday night?" I asked him nervously. He was awkward with my friends and almost never participated in our regular Sunday-night family-style meals. He always had an excuse to miss them.

"I have to meet with the legal contract lawyer and accountant," he said quickly. "And now I'll have to read Angela's portfolio, so we can snag her father's money as his marketing and advertising consultants. We'll have a quiet dinner together next week," he promised.

But he was always soft about plans and never remembered the nights he had suggested to me. The only way to spend time with him was impromptu, when he was in the mood and not too drained by his writing or meetings. I wasn't surprised that he'd declined. I was used to it. He was a creative person to his core and not easy to pin down, so I no longer tried.

I left him at the office and went home to shower and wear clean clothes considering he always made me work as a janitor or jack of all trades, before meeting him at midnight at his apartment. He didn't like the lack of privacy at my place and preferred spending nights with me, if or when we did, at his place. It was small and disorderly, but we could be alone for the tempting things we did in bed.

He kissed me again before I left, and Angela seemed insignificant to me now. She was a means to an end, money for his business, which I knew he needed desperately. Even his regular clients had limited funds. And a small ad business in a place like Cleveland is not a big moneymaker unless well connected or able to devise very creative ingenuity to generate revenues for clients. His niche needed diversification beyond geography or line of business, so unfamiliar clients would know of him or tap into his expertise and the nature of his promotions.

Jonathan had asked me to lend him money a few times to help pay the rent at the office, when he was particularly broke, and I had, which had left me short of money for several weeks. And I never wanted to ask my parents for extra money to help him, since he has always been negative towards them, even though he didn't know them. Whatever I gave him was money I had saved. And he was always annoyed that my parents weren't willing to help him through me, given how rich he thought they were. I never told him my father was convinced he was a scam when I described him, his personality and how he goes about his business to my mother when she insisted on knowing whom I was dating. She told me that both she and my dad wished that I focus on my studies and forget about men until I graduated. Jonathan only seems to say good things about the person he is directly connected to and negative in everybody connected to that person, whether he knows that person or not.

I arrived at Jonathan's small apartment at midnight, and he was sound asleep. His grey, dirty hair was disheveled when he opened the door, and he seemed surprised to see me and then pulled me into his arms. He had been naked when he opened the door and didn't seem to mind since it was a warm night, and he had no air conditioning in the tiny apartment. I was breathless after climbing eleven flights of stairs, and even more so when he took my clothes off and began making love to me even before we got to his bed. He made love to me, standing and bending over backwards like a dog in heat. He came over my thighs at first but got hard almost immediately, and we continued once more on the hard flow.

He quickly lifted me up and tossed me on the bed but immediately made me kneel over his face as he lay on his back so that he may first lubricate my vagina with his tongue. The operation titillates and excites me so that I amorously press myself on his mouth as I face his penis, which I never let go. He spends in ecstasy while I also felt the pleasure. We made love all night long and fell asleep in each other's arms at dawn. He was so good at sweeping me off my feet, again and again, turning my head, and playing my body like a harp. He called himself a hillbilly, but I never asked him what it meant, but he told me that his lovemaking with me was like playing a musical instrument, and my small body allowed him to flip me like a harp. He must have been a very good player because he's been pretty good at giving me unlimited satisfaction. I won't be lying if I describe him as beyond good.

.

—

Several of Elisa's friends and colleagues from work dropped by Benoit's restaurant on Saturday night for dinner. Elisa was already there; two of her other friends dropped by, Adam and Eva - boyfriend and girlfriend, and I dropped by too, which was conditioned upon my being free and not going to be with Jonathan. Since Saturday night out was always flexible and unplanned, Benoit kept an open table available for the team, just in case.

"Is Jonathan coming?" Elisa asked, looking my way and across at everybody else, hoping he wasn't.

"No," I said, "he'd be 'too tired' after his business schedule."

While those at dinner chatted comfortably, two other people showed up – Andy and Andrea, looking tan and dressed for a relaxing warm evening outing. Pretty happy they could make it after flying in from Chicago and visiting with friends from their college years.

They all ordered some French wine, courtesy of Benoit's recommendation. He also sent over some starters. The restaurant was very busy with crowds from out of town, probably due to an NBA basketball game between the Cleveland Cavalier and the Chicago Bulls. The conversation ranged from the fun things Andy and Andrea did while in Chicago to which of the two teams they rooted for; Elisa talked about her company and excited about her new clients and increased business opportunities. She also talked about her bonus and hinted that she was going to use some of the money to replace our living room set and a French impressionist picture for the wall. Adam and Eva were planning to visit Miami to enjoy their first-year dating anniversary. Andy announced that anyone that would be free and available was invited to attend a birthday party he was organizing for Andrea in another week and a half. Benoit and Elisa suggested they might rent a Utah ski resort for the weekend, and anybody free would be welcomed. And that, if anybody in this night group is willing to come along, to let them know within a few days in advance, to arrange a rental flight to and back, for the occasion. Most of the evening crowd thought it was a great idea since most are avid skiers. Only one suggested that, although not good at it, they'd go anyway, for the fun and adventure. Everybody was in good spirit and excited about the prospect of enjoying each other's company again.

They ordered their favorite dishes for dinner and tried a few new things that Benoit had introduced on the menu, as well as what he recommended. The waiter cleared the table, and orders of dessert and cappuccino were placed. Each drank their order, and after a few more conversations, they called for cabs or drove their respective cars back home for the night.

Elisa and I took a cab back to our apartment after hugging or shaking everybody's hand and saying good night. Moments later, we arrived home, and Elisa wished me good night and went to her bedroom. I did too, and after changing into my nightdrooo, I climbed into bed for the night.

———

As he had promised he would, Benoit cooked dinner at the apartment I was sharing with Elisa on Sunday night. He brought all the ingredients from the restaurant and prepared two kinds of pasta, a big salad, and steaks for everyone. He brought several loaves of French bread, freshly baked focaccia, half a dozen different cheeses, and a chocolate cake that had been baked that afternoon. Everyone was in a good mood and gathered around the kitchen while he cooked. Adam and Eva set the table. Andy opened the wine to let it breathe. Andrea made dressing for the salad. I was there, but Jonathan had his meeting with the 'accountant,' as usual, and was planning to read Angela's Portfolio after that, so he didn't come. Another couple, colleagues of Elisa, Paul, and Petra, also came, sat down, and mingled. Paul had put some music on, and the atmosphere was festive as Benoit poured the wine and Elisa set the plates down at each placemat, piled with food. It was a feast and the kind of Sunday evening we all loved. We laughed and talked a lot. It was like a family gathering of good people, good feelings in the home we loved. I seemed a little tense at first without Jonathan, but I relaxed after my second glass of wine, and since Petra wasn't going to be driving, so she drank too.

Elisa looked over at Benoit and smiled. He smiled back, and he put his arm around her as she thanked him for dinner. It was delicious, and we ate everything.

Elisa made coffee for those who wanted it, and I served it. Everyone pitched in, it was a perfect evening, and at midnight, Adam and Andrea left. Paul had an early morning project, Andy had a long day ahead, and Adam also had work to do. Others lingered for a while, and Petra and Eva did the dishes while everyone else sat and talked. No one wanted it to end. And after they all thanked Benoit for bringing the food and doing the cooking, he and Elisa went to bed. She had to be up early the next day too.

They disappeared into her room, sat on the bed, and talked quietly. He loved spending nights with her whenever he visited. He teased her about it and said it was like sleeping in a girls' dorm. He loved the warm, welcoming atmosphere. It felt like a home, not just an apartment shared by female friends. It made him feel and wish he and Elisa lived together instead. He knew he could stay with her anytime he wanted to, and he usually did two or three times a week. They both liked and enjoyed time together despite their busy lives, with jobs that demanded a lot of their time.

He lay down on the bed and beckoned to her. "Come lie next to me." They hadn't been alone all night, and in the comfort of her room, he wanted to make love to her. She had the same feeling in mind. After almost a year together, they hardly had the opportunity during the week. Sometimes, they are not in the mood if they get together late at night after leaving the restaurant. Sunday nights were special for them when they forgot the stresses of their workweek. They could just be two people who loved each other and had the time to do something about it.

They lay in each other's arms afterwards, and a few minutes later, he was sound asleep. She smiled at him. He was such a good man. She didn't know how she'd been lucky enough to find him, but she knew it was a blessing that she had. Her life with Benoit was perfect and fun for both. The apartment in Shaker Heights was her home. The women she was close to as her female friends were like her sisters. Benoit understood how much that meant to her, and he no longer tried to change it. He accepted her as she was. Independent, hardworking, successful, kind to him, and fearful about marriage.

In the living room when Elisa came to talk with me, where I was sitting on the couch, I had admitted to her that I was worried about Jonathan and told her about Angela and her portfolio project:

"I know he wouldn't cheat on me, but she's all over him, and she's so young, and she has a rich father who might help him become better off financially. What if she traps him somehow? You know how men are. They're so naïve."

Elisa thought Jonathan was anything but naïve, but she didn't say it to me and tried to reassure me as best she could without saying what she actually thought of him.

"You're not exactly old, for God's sake," Elisa said, sounding frustrated at how ignorant I was of my many virtues and Jonathan's equally numerous flaws, dishonesty being at the top of the list. She was sure that Jonathan was lying to me about the girl, but she didn't want to upset me:

"She's five years younger than you are, and who cares if she has a rich father? Jonathan is in love with you."

"I hope you're right," I said, sounding calmer and more confident than I felt. We both went to bed a little while later.

I strongly suspected that Jonathan was cheating on Angela and had been a cheater, possibly many times. There were so many nights he didn't spend with me, with thinly obscure excuses, or just didn't show up, or wouldn't answer his cell phone when I called. But I always gave him the benefit of the doubt.

Petra had already gone to bed, exhausted from work, and relaxed after the happy evening Benoit had provided for them.

Benoit left before the others got up the next morning and whispered to Elisa that he had to go to the fish market in The West Side Market to get some fresh catch of the day. He liked to pick the fish and meat and produce them himself. Usually, the cook went with him, and sometimes Benoit let him go on his own. He ran a tight schedule at the restaurant, and everyone liked and respected and loved his management style.

Elisa was at her corporate office before anyone else the next day. She wanted to get ready for her first meeting but still had to research. She wanted to read and review some prospective clients' account information before submitting a management report to her boss prior to the scheduled meeting.

With time, I quit dating Jonathan after I caught him cheating with Angela. He always made me show up in the office an hour early to clean up and prepare possible customer calls or prepare files for him to follow up with or me if he wanted me to pitch the sale. He thinks I'm a better salesperson than himself. Come to think of it, he is right because his business only breaks even whenever I play a dominant role in sales management.

In any case, I arrived early as usual and inserted the door key, but the key couldn't enter the hole due to a jam. I tried pushing it gently, and it opened because it was not properly bolted from the inside. I heard a voice that sounded like Jonathan's and an unknown female voice. I thought of going back home and calling his cell, and remembered he didn't pick it up when I called earlier. I entered quietly and noticed the open office space lights were off, but the small office further to the right side was lighted. Looking straight into the small office, I was shocked and surprised to see Jonathan's pants dropped to below his knees, and a large long fleshy throbbing thing was sticking out. The girl in front of him, whom I could now recognize as Angela, was completely naked with her heap of clothes on the floor. She got ahold of the long thing between his mid-section with one hand, and with the other hand, she looked at it, then looking at him as if in hesitation, she rubbed the tip up and down. He uttered the sound, "Ah! Ooh! I can't help it; put it in."

She rushed into his arms and covered his face with kisses; in a low voice, she exclaimed: "How I had longed for you since our last time two days ago. What a shame I must wait so long for you to give me enjoyment."

Finding his voice between her kisses, he responded, almost irritably: "What's the hurry, Angela! Do not spoil a good thing with your impatience, okay?"

With a gentle effort, he lifted her up, reclining her backwards on a couch, bought with the money he borrowed from me a week earlier. As she raised her plump legs up wide apart, my gaze was immediately directed at the gapping lips between her legs, covered with a profusion of curly hair. He quickly went to his knees and glued his lips to her crack, and I could hear the furious sucking and kiss to her delights. Not being able to restrain himself, he got up between her legs; he pushed his hard-throbbing object into her. He moved in and out of her open lips between her legs until a profusion of creamy moisture oozed out, flowing onto her thighs. As their bodies collapsed in tired enjoyment, I immediately tip-toed out without them noticing me and vowed never to set my eyes on him again.

I never told my friend Elisa the story due to shame and the fact that she'd say, "I told you so."

A few months later, Benoit moved on too, relocating to expand his restaurant empire, but kept in touch with Elisa from time to time. Their liaison continued until she met Mike at work and started a serious relationship that was more in line with her love interests and lifestyle. They later moved in together and got engaged.

I moved into another place too, and later met another guy in one of my classes named Aaron. Our relationship started on a high note but glided into a slippery slope when he got tired of my attention and desire for a long-term relationship. I kept in touch with my best friend, Elisa, on a regular basis. She was instrumental in motivating me to stop seeing Aaron and thereafter introduced me to Greg, whom I love and adore. I'm glad for it and happy to be deeply loved twenty-four-seven by him, an extremely sweet, caring, smart, handsome, successful man that is not a player. I'm honored by his desire to make me his forever partner through a flourishing, serious dating, and loving relationship that has metamorphosized into an engagement that is about to lead to a beautiful marriage. That's a reflection on the history of my love life.

15

Just as Greg had promised, he returned from his long day at work, went to the gym for half an hour, showered, and wore a comfortable lounging shirt and pants. We had our occasional dinner in bed, talking and laughing together. I shared some updates on our wedding plans, tentative dates, and discussion with the designers, as he requested. Also told him how I was reminiscing about my life experiences, especially since my college days, and how it has all combined to make me who I am today. He joked with a simple expression, "experience is the best teacher." On his part, he shared with me how pleased he is with building his client base and the growth of his firm as he navigates the current state of the economy.

As we kissed each other goodnight, our bodies resisted sleep. Our excited energy and passion turned into an intense hunger and desire for each other. To feed the fire in us with relaxation, we immediately set ourselves in motion on the path to consummate our love and craving for each other. Our lips and bodies were instantly melted together. I must have slept like a baby because I don't remember when I fell to sleep, nor when he woke up and left for work. His intense passion for love-making and work is amazing. Come to think of it, he once told me that a combination of these passions is what God created us to accomplish on earth. Regarding lovemaking, he said, 'it's the secret agreement our creator gave Adam and Eve.' 'To combine it with everything we do, to maximize the benefits of all our senses, and make memories to last a lifetime.'

Eating breakfast at the terrace downstairs an hour later and watching the colorful fish playing in the pond, thoughts of nostalgia kept creeping into my mind. I couldn't help wishing Greg was off to enjoy the meal with me. I could turn him into a dessert or snack easily because I can't seem to have enough of him. I don't think it's an obsession, but if it is, I consider it mutual. Kissing many frogs before meeting him was a life lesson for me. That's why I credit him for opening his heart and head to making it possible. If he didn't 'leave the door open,' just like Bruno Mars, the iconic musician sang, our reality of dating, loving, and engaging to be married would be just a dream. Many of my favorite musicians, like Bruno Mars, have eloquently helped people like me to actually experience 'our first time,' 'count on me,' 'just the way you are,' 'it will rain,' 'marry you,' as we navigate our daily lives while building healthy and happy relationships.

As my deep thoughts were coming to an end, the phone rang, and it was my man's voice. Just at the same time, Cooper, the caretaker of the mansion, walks in through the double doors with a bouquet of flowers. I told Greg to give me a few minutes, and I'll call him back, or he could call again in five minutes. He said he'll call shortly soon after he assigns a project to one of his portfolio analysts.

"Hi Marie, it's me again," he finally called back, juggling multiple tasks, as usual.

"Oh, hey sweetheart. Thanks for calling me back, and thanks for the beautiful bouget of flowers I just received," I responded, full of excitement.

"You are welcome," his enthusiastic voiced acknowledged, with a throaty giggle.

"What a surprise." I replied. "Plus, the card was so sweet," as I was overwhelmed with emotions.

"Oh yeah. Sure!" he expressed, sounding effusive and pleased.

"Frankly, it made me cry with tears of pleasure." I brought myself to say, overcome with feelings.

"You are welcome, honey. Just like putting fuel in a car regularly, we must feed our love and express our feelings every day." He added. His words made me realize that, for him to have a feminist side was not a bad thing at all, just like people shouldn't label women that exhibit male tendencies.

"You are one hundred percent, correct, sweetheart. Twenty-four-seven," I said.

"Thanks for advocating a sustainable, loving relationship." He stated. "This weekend, I'll fly us out of town to enjoy and reaffirm our feelings of love for each other. Where we are going will be a surprise. The only clue I'm giving you is that it will be at a beach resort in the continental United States."

"Okay, honey, see you later," I replied, blowing him a kiss, and hung up.

At exactly six-thirty, he called for me to be ready for him. He'll take me out for dinner. Of course, I couldn't stop thinking about him since the sound of his voice, so I decided to surprise him when he arrived. I'll look exactly like him, by way of what I wear. I'll wear a suit, just like him, to give an impression of going to dinner as if I were his female colleague. To eat and talk business. Does it sound hilarious and hedonistic? Yes, that's exactly my objective. To look fabulously beautiful and sexy, I wore designer dark suit pants and a half matching jacket over a finely crafted lacey open neckline shirt, delicate gold earrings and wristwatch, and rich natural lip gloss to multiply his appetite. And for shoes, the high heels would match the suit but provide a little tease of my beautiful manicured toes.

Times up, he's here, and I'm heading out to meet him now. Outside of the huge door, I could see him seated at the driver's side of his sports car. Smiling and looking at me in admiration.

"Who is this stunning glamour girl in front of me?" his deep voice serenaded, boldly and triumphantly.

"How do you like my new suit?" I asked him, smiling across my entire face.

"Very good," he responded. "You look different. Like a page out of an executive suite."

"I know it," I admitted. "I saw it when I looked at myself in the mirror before coming out to meet you," muting my smile and pretending to be serious.

"Yes! Real nice." He stated, sounding like he wanted to say something else.

"Yeah, sure. I felt it when you couldn't take your eyes off me as I was walking toward you. Besides," I continued, "I also have what you prefer. It's covered up by what I'm wearing outside and waiting for your pleasure and enjoyment." This last teasing tone embarrassed him to the extent that my confident man busted out laughing and covered his face with both hands, bubbling, "yes indeed, you got me this time!"

I climbed into the passenger's side and sat next to him as he continued to laugh hysterically. I reached over and took his hand, and kissed his palm. Turning to him with a smile, I told him I had something special to tell him.

"What is it?" he said, suddenly looking serious.

"I'm engaged," I whispered, returning his gaze.

"To who, and when?" his eyes appear confused and astonished.

"To you, of course," I responded with a laugh.

"Oh!" he said, slowly and thoughtfully. "I proposed but haven't bought you a ring yet."

"Yes, my dear. It means the same thing. Whether in America or France, the meaning is the same. Naturally, when two people's hearts are in the same place, a proposal or engagement would have taken place. So, all things considered, this first step is followed by the next step, which is a wedding or marriage, right?" He glued his eyes on me without saying a word.

So, I continued, without being interrogative but rather affirmatively: "If I must add, the scenario I'm describing would only happen between two people in love that know each other so well, rather than two perfect strangers, correct?"

"Yes, indeed. You're correct." He said and nodded his head, dropping back into his bucket car seat and laughing heartily.

He abruptly stopped laughing. With his right hand, he pulled me over and kissed me passionately. The kiss got juicier with every second, and after what seemed like a minute and a half, he slowly quit. And I begged for us to continue the sweet kisses, and he proposed for us to go eat first, then reward ourselves with more kisses later. His request was heeded, with both of us nodding our heads in agreement.

We then searched the GPS for an authentic Italian restaurant which took us to Valentis-ristorante, located at Broadview-heights, not quite far from home. Being our first time there, we were introduced to an efficient team that made sure our visit was scrumptiously memorable, from the very customer-friendly Jeannine, the owner, to Billy, the chef, the server, and the bartender. They all made us feel like we were being entertained at home.

We started with an Italian sushi appetizer of prosciutto and cheese, sun-dried tomatoes wrapped with risotto, and basil leaf. Since we were hungry, we tried a little bit of lobster delicious claw martini appetizer too. We had a seafood choice special, of either halibut or swordfish, served on the bed of risotto lime sauce. To help in washing down the meal, we ordered a Manhattan for him and a glass of Chianti for me.

Martini's choice had blue cheese olives. With orders of calamari, lobster ravioli, and shrimp scampi, fixed crispy and light, all presented beautifully and deliciously tasty. It would not be an understatement if I said the restaurant was full of happy guests, mostly couples.

While enjoying our meal, Greg was all smiles and visibly happy. We fed each other, licked each other's fingers, and reminisced about when and how we met, not knowing we would cultivate a liking for each other, fall in love and become like conjoined twins. I shared with him my very first impression when we first met. Reminded him that I've had my heart broken a couple of times, and I feared losing him, especially since he had qualities and status like no other man I'd dated previously. Also told him that there were times I would break out in a sweat, thinking that he would find me inadequate or the kind of female he'd consider as an ideal girlfriend nor to think of as a future wife.

"Don't worry about such things, Marie. I was more terrified that you would break my heart," he teased, smiling. For a moment, I thought he was saying that to make me comfortable, but as a compassionate and practical man, he meant that a good relationship is mutual.

"Good. And I promise I won't break your heart either. You're a good guy." I replied, being playful and laughing with him. His effect on me is dynamic and wholesome.

"We'll be fine," he reassured me, with confidence from a man that has never experienced anything but success in every aspect of his life. Either way, I'm glad to hear him confess his deep and abiding love and the desire to build a strong, healthy relationship with me. I believe him one hundred percent. I knew it after our first kiss and how it made me feel. He was and remained a very intense man. He is just a few years older than me but extremely passionate about everything about him, from work to hobbies, to life, and on top of the list is his lovemaking. He is so skilful, romantic, sexy, cool, and sweet. He has plenty of unlimited magic power and charm to pursue and conquer any feminine human being he sets his eyes on, but he settled for me.

—

On our drive back home, he told me how much he had enjoyed the evening. That he's looking forward to flying me out tomorrow to get some fresh air and show me some love. It sounded like a short shuttle around the Midwest or East Coast since we won't be gone for long. To where exactly is unknown, because he said he wanted to surprise me. Whatever the mystery, I'm all for it. All he requested of me was to have casual warm clothes and any other regular comfortable female items for a few day's trips. The sound of his voice, consideration, and desire to make me happy exceeded my expectation because I was already happy and overjoyed being with him every day, cuddled up, and enjoying the comfort of his arms.

Upon arriving home, he asked me to wait a moment while he went around to open the passenger's side door for me. He opened it and complimented me with a kiss as our faces met before walking me to the door. I felt like I was walking on the moon. Climbing the staircase to the second floor, we couldn't take our hands off each other. We stopped and kissed. Then hugged. He smelled so good, as I could feel his warm fresh breath. We simultaneously took little bites and nibbles of each other's ear lobes and neck, then hands and fingers, while slowly walking towards the master bedroom of the second floor. Our eyes were half-closed and glued to each other, but we found our way to the super king bed in the middle of the room.

We slowly undressed each other until there was nothing else left on our soft glistening skin. With a gentle effort, he picked me up like a baby and placed my body at the edge of the bed, facing him. With my butt on the bed, he raised my legs until my knees were at the same level as my breasts. Looking at the wall mirror right behind him, I could see my luscious, pouting lips of the pinky vagina, slightly gaping open, in a most inviting manner, as my legs were wide apart. The only cover on it was an abundance of beautiful curly brownie-black hair, which I occasionally shave like a bald eagle.

He slowly moved his hands to my sides and pulled both of my breasts together, and sucked on the nipples, one after the other. The sensation tingled through my entire body, but mostly at the tip of my nipples, vagina, thighs, and toes. Just as I was experiencing a convulsion between my thighs, he went down on his knees immediately and glued his lips to the open love button between my legs, sucking and kissing furiously, to my delight. Resulting in intense sighs and wriggles with pleasure. When he realized he could no longer restrain himself, he quickly got up, placing his knees between my legs. He placed his throbbing penis at the center of the open vagina and ran it all the way in, until the entire throbbing hard penis was completely buried inside my belly. We laid still for a moment, enjoying the passion of our two inseparable melted bodies.

As soon as I raised my bottom to swallow his huge penis inside my vagina, he responded to the movement by shoving it in and out slowly, then followed with rapid quick succession. The movement was so exciting that I could feel it all over my body, and when I looked at his penis, I could see the shaft working in and out, like a ticking clock, shining with flowing juices, while the lips of my vagina cling to the penis, each time of withdrawal, as if afraid of losing some once in a lifetime delightful box of hot chocolate.

Due to the very intense excitement and furious movement of our bodies, we both collapsed into a spasmodic embrace and fainted in each other's arms. Upon opening my eyes slightly, I could see and feel the abundance of creamy moisture oozing from my vagina as we both lay on the bed of enjoyment after our marathon of lovemaking. We kissed each other deeply as if sucking on a pacifier. We wrapped our hands around each other, smiling and whispering our undying love for each other. Without either of us know what time it was, we fell asleep like baby piglets.

—

We woke up early, showered, and were dressed up by seven-thirty. We were ready to start our trip by eight o'clock. I was wearing a sheepskin coat in a natural color, and good-looking boots, with dark blue jeans and a matching jacket, over a pink t-shirt. Greg was well dressed, too, in his plaid jacket over a blue t-shirt and dark blue jeans, and Texas leather boots. We got in his Mercedes – Maybach GLS and drove straight to Cleveland's Hopkins International Airport and exited toward a designated road that led to a private plane hangar. He drove closer to one of the larger airplanes that were not only huge but very beautiful. He still did not tell me where we were going, but I was all in for the surprise.

"I intended for us to fly to Toronto, Canada, for a day or two but decided on Rochester, New York instead," he said finally, as he leaned over and kissed me. "There are some beautiful beach walks along the lake and beautiful Lake Ontario resorts and inns where we can have lunch and dinner, as well as spend the night. We'll return to Cleveland, Ohio, tomorrow or the day after, but I'll let you decide." I was speechless as I walked up the stairway to the plane, where a flight attendant waited to greet us.
The captain and co-pilot had clearance for takeoff and said we'll be leaving in a few minutes as we sat down in the big comfortable seats. A few minutes later, we were off in the skies, and the flight attendant served us breakfast.

"Are you okay?" Greg asked me gently, noticing that I was eating our breakfast quietly as if lost in thoughts. When I looked up at him with a smile, he reached over and kissed me. His warm kiss was sweet. The breakfast was delicious as well. I had scrambled eggs, blueberry muffins, and a cappuccino, and he had waffles, bacon, and black coffee. We chatted a lot during our brief two-hundred and forty nautical miles flight between Cleveland and Rochester, and I only realized we were about to arrive as the plane was preparing to land. The view around us was scenic and beautiful. The pilot had rented a car for us that was waiting when we landed, so we could drive around alone. Before Greg could drive us away from the airport, he turned to me, and I knew he wanted to kiss me before saying anything, so we kissed passionately. His hand on my inner thigh created a sensational and tingling feeling all over my body, and when I looked down between his pants, I could see his passion rising, and all I could think of is wishing we were together in our own private space or room. Being in a public space, we immediately pulled our hands away from each other before we reached a point of no return.

"You do crazy things to my head, mind and body," he said in a low deep voice, and I smiled.

"You do the same to me," I whispered, and he began driving again before we could get carried away in the car. He teased me about it, and more, and we both laughed.

"You make me feel like a kid again, Marie. Like a naughty kid who's about to get into trouble."

I teased him back, saying it wasn't only his fault because I was experiencing the same sensations and feelings and wouldn't change a thing.

Fifteen minutes northwards later, we were passing several cafes, restaurants, and gas stations. Other interesting sites and signs in our view were mileage signs and driving directions to art centers, historical sights, and museums such as the Planetarium and the renowned Strong National Museum of Play. A few minutes further north, we passed more signs leading to water sports, hiking, and skiing areas of the city. We then drove sixty feet towards the direction of a private beach frontage, facing a fabulous private vacation spot. Pulling up to a huge home, we were greeted by a very manicured garden that led to the cobblestone yard. Driving further inside towards the assigned parking area, we were welcomed by the cottage charm that engulfed the entire huge property.

Parking, facing the massive columns, we stepped out and made our way to the back of the mansion, noticing the beautiful views and a deck beckoning us to come in and relax after our flight. To our right was a set of stairs leading down to a private strip of beach. I noticed the gradual slope, which allows for the perfect stroll down the beach, suitable to cool off our feet or to simply take a dip afterward.

Just as we were taking in our view and enjoying the fresh breeze from a man-made lake with swans in them, a man emerged from an attached bungalow that was next to the mansion and introduced himself indirectly to me as Joseph, the property caretaker. Indirectly because he and Greg did know each other. He was tall, clean-shaven, and distinguished. Greg gave him a handshake, and I nodded his way as our eyes met.

"What do you have for us, Joseph?" Greg asked.

"Welcome back to the Rochester property, sir. Glad to see you again, and affording me an opportunity to meet your family," Joseph said, looking in my direction as he uttered the word 'family' with a genuine friendly smile. For almost a year now, I have moved in one hundred percent with Greg, so technically, we were family in every sense of the word.

"When I received the message about your arrival, sir," Joseph turned to Greg with smiling eyes, "I immediately prepared a variety of seafood meals for two, as you directed. The catch is local, from your smaller pond across from the pier." He pointed in the direction of a pier that could be seen from where we were standing.

"Please show her around," Greg urged the caretaker while following behind us.

"Yes, sir," Joseph replied and turned to me as we walked towards the double door entrance: "The private dining is on the same floor as your master bedroom, leading to your private deck, jacuzzi, and pool overlooking the beach. Please make yourself at home. My job is to be of service and make your stay completely comfortable and memorable. I'm a call away on house phone number zero." He concluded, bowing to both of us, and walked out through the ceiling-high mansion's entrance doors to offload our luggage to the bedroom suite.

As soon as the doors closed behind the caretaker, we turned to each other; Greg looked at me mischievously like a naughty boy, and I reached out to hold his hand. He pulled me closer, and we hugged for a good minute, kissed passionately, and he whispered in my ear for us to go eat our lunch.

I hesitated for a moment as our eyes gazed at each other. Although I was hungry, I was enjoying our warm intimacy and didn't want it to end.

"Honey," I told him, "I loved you very much and would forever appreciate the fact that you made time for us, despite your busy schedule. To specially create a beautiful and romantic moment for us together, away from home, is so sweet of you.

"Sweetheart," he said, closing his eyes for a moment as though my words were too sweet to hear, and then opened them and looked at me. "I want to thank you for the kind words. I love you, Marie. I know it sounds crazy to say, but I think we were meant to be together. So, I want to thank you, too, for finding your way into my life. I don't believe in accidents. The fact is that we were ready for each other, and the time was right."

We kissed deeply. When we opened our eyes, without a word, we walked towards the dining area, which was richly decorated with Antique and natural color leather tables and chairs, surrounded by china cabinets, a mini wine cellar, serving carts, and buffet sideboards. Knowing we were hungry and a little tired, we quietly sat across from each other while I dished moderate quantities of the course of meals for both of us, starting with the salad. Greg then poured some California white wine into the glasses for both of us. It tasted like one of the best associated with the south of France. We ate and conversated about the things and places we passed along the way. I extended my hand to feed Greg a piece of salmon I was eating, and he opened his mouth to receive it. As he was chewing, he held my fingers up and licked two of them, saying they were complementary to the food, which made me laugh. As I also wanted him to drink from my glass, he responded by having me take a sip from his too.

After emptying each other's glasses, he got up, reached out for my hand, and asked if I was ready for the dessert. Looking into his mischievous eyes, I told him I was more than ready, and we both busted out laughing. We headed through an adjoining door that led to an oversized four-piece Windsor Court California king-size bedroom set in metallic antique gold with a down comforter. The room was lavishly adorned with high-end Armoires, vanities, dressers, and chests. Our suitcases were visibly placed on a twin dresser set in the middle of the walk-in closet. Through the transparent walls was a view of the terrace, which housed a breakfast nook and a couple of Rustic Espresso chairs, with a view of the swan lake and beach a few feet further. At one side of the bedroom was a fireplace and flowered chintz. Facing it was a Valentina loveseat in a dark champagne antique mix of white and black copper.

Holding hands and walking towards the fireplace, we immediately sat side by side on the loveseat and started kissing. We couldn't get our clothes off fast enough as our bodies intertwined, our hands searched desperately for each other, and we kissed as we tried to take each other's clothes off. I whispered in his ears that his dessert was ready for him, and he couldn't restrain his laughter as he replied that he was extremely hungry for it too. Before he could finish his words, I realized my hand was holding his hard-throbbing penis, which I had suddenly let out of his restraining pants. The warmth of his hard penis sent a titillating sensation all over my body. Simultaneously, his hand slipped under my clothes and frantically played with my wet clitoris, as I could feel the wetness flowing towards my thighs.

"Ah! Oh! Oh!! Play with it more. It feels so good. Better still, put your penis in honey," I begged, as my entire body was trembling and yearning for more.

He whispered the words 'love you, Marie' and smothered me with luscious kisses, thrusting the tip of his tongue between my lips. As my thighs relaxed and opened to receive his strong fingers, I experienced a spasmodic contraction. Our bodies and arms clasped each other closely around the waist while our lips were making audible sounds resembling a mixture of kisses and sighs. As our smiling eyes met, we both realized what had happened. My cunt was deluged with warm creamy spend from his frigging, while his juices were spurted all over my clothes and hands.

Without a word, we got up and helped each other's clothes off. We left them on the floor and loveseat. We walked to the comfortable king-size bed, and he gently and quietly lifted me off the ground with his strong warm arms and placed me on the edge of the bed. Kissing my lips, then my neck, he stopped and looked into my longing eyes. Without saying a word, he lifted and moved me to the middle of the bed.

With my hands wrapped around his neck, I kissed him hungrily, and he responded with intense passion and excitement. Between his hands and lips, he set out to explore every sensitive erogenous zone of my body. This heightened stimulation generated a combination of multiple sexual fantasies and arousal in me that I couldn't help but have a convulsive orgasm. I urged him on with my submissive and yielding body, as well as some mumbling words. To hurry up and make love to me, and he responded instantly and vigorously without hesitation. I dare say it was one of the most passionate sex I've ever experienced in my life. A kind of lovemaking that is born of desire and need, coupled with our desperate hunger and thirst for each other. We slept like babies after several hours of bedroom lovemaking in an out-of-town indoor romantic escapade.

16

We were up before sunset and requested our brunch in bed. After taking our shower and dressing up for the day, we decided to have our sumptuous meal, which was awaiting us at the terrace. The setting was perfect for an intimate romantic meal. A combination of sautéed mix veggies, flavorful filet mignon and scallops, clams for an appetizer, and a bottle of Cabernet Sauvignon to water down the meal. We enjoyed the tender chewable bites from the appetizer to the main course. We fed each other, chatting and laughing with no care in the world. We were spoilt by the intimate dreamy setting, which was combined with natural fresh, breezy air from the beach, and the outdoors green surroundings.

As my mind was filled and my body soaked in the wonderful atmosphere and pleasing delicious lunch, Greg turned to me and held my hand, and pulled me closer. He said, "I've been looking for you all my life, and I want to take the opportunity to let you know that I'm glad we found each other." As he said it, our lips were glued together. As we kissed passionately, I was so aroused, and since I was lost for words and holding my tears of joy in, I reached over and pulled him up. He followed me back into the bedroom. We made love again and again. And again, for a couple of hours, until nightfall. Another milestone of a sporadic romantic escapade.

I held him in my arms against my breast as he fell asleep with a smile on his handsome face. It was a deep, peaceful sleep of a satisfied, contented, happy man. My heart was so full of joy that I couldn't help but text messages to everybody I loved. These include family and friends that I've not communicated with for some time. Among them were my grandparents, my parents, a couple of nieces and cousins, Greg's parents, and brother and sister-in-law. And last but not the least, my best friend Elisa and Mike, her husband. I not only told them I loved and missed them but assured them that I was not only doing great but that they were also in my heart every day.

A few hours after writing up my schedule of the plan of events and activities for next week, I decided to order room service of mixed fresh fruits, macarons, a bottle of champagne, and water. I proceeded to kiss Greg gingerly and softly on his lower and upper lips, progressing to the side of his lips and ear lobes. As I loved to his neck and chiseled chest, he made a grunting noise, and I stopped momentarily and looked at his face.

First, he opened one of his eyes, then the other, followed by a smile. I took the opportunity to apologize for waking him up and asked if I could feed him some snacks before he went back to sleep. He obliged by nodding; then pulled me to his chest for a soft, delicious kiss. He sat up while I moved the bedside food tray closer. I requested for him to allow me to feed both of us. He smiled and kissed me as a way of saying yes.

In between a bite and chew of his strawberry, macaron, and sip of champagne, I said to him, "honey, I want to thank you for welcoming me into your life."

"I love you from the bottom of my heart and to let you know that the feelings are mutual," he responded. He has proved it numerous times, especially since our trip arrival, as well as a moment ago. Truthfully, he hasn't stopped loving me since the first day we met, and the pendulum has been on the upswing ever since.

"This is just the beginning," he continued. "My wish and desire are to love you every day and build a happy family and memories to last a lifetime."

"Thanks for your sweet words," I hastened to respond. "I also want you to know that you have loved me beyond expectation, and I would forever be indebted to you," I added, looking at his knowing, soft eyes full of compassion and kindness.

"We are in it together, sweetheart," he stated with reassurance. "It takes two to tango, as my parents often say to each other. I pledge to be by your side, through thick and thin, as we journey together. I picture us raising mini you and mini-me to carry the torch of life, generations beyond us," he concluded.

Listening and replaying his last statement, I responded with tears of joy streaming my face. I rushed and held him tightly across my breast and mumbled words of love and promise of everlasting love between us. I shared some dreams I've had about us, including a dream of delivering our first set of twin babies, a boy, and a girl. He was speechless and quiet. After a second's reflection, he said he would be grateful and thankful for whatever gift we receive as a couple. He took a sip of champagne while I continued to feed him and myself some snacks quietly. Like a businessman that he is, he asked me how far I've gone with our wedding plans, and I told him very far. He looked pleased and urged me to 'hurry up,' but not necessarily placing any deadline on me. In many words, I see that we both want it very badly and possibly soonest.

"Tomorrow is our last day here, and we'll be heading back to Ohio the day after," he reminded me, as I could hear in his voice and see in his eyes that he was not quite ready to go back yet.

"True," I replied. "It feels like we just got here for sure. And come to think of it, it feels like back in Ohio. Whenever we're together, and wherever we go, I feel very excited just knowing I'm with you. Being with you is like being a kid at a candy store. I can't have enough of you. Thanks for helping me find my inner joy and happiness and knowing what true love means."

"You are welcome. Thank you too for seeing the qualities and attributes you've illuminated in me," he contemplates for a moment.

He continued, "we would spend tomorrow engaging in some outdoor activity or adventure and depart the day after. Let's make the best of every minute and treasure whatever we choose to do, as long as we are both happy. And before I forget, would you mind if we attend a Tequila Gala in honor of our last night tomorrow?" he concluded.

"Good idea, I'm a hundred percent in, honey," I responded as we nodded in unison. Smiling and looking at each other, we proceeded to kiss and cuddle, punctuated by expressions of love and the joy of making time to enjoy our relationship and make happy memories together. We cuddled and kissed some more. Shortly afterward, we fell asleep in each other's arms until the next morning.

I woke up to use the bathroom and noticed it was already eight a.m., according to the wall clock. There was a card under our bedroom door, and when I opened it up, I saw that it was left by Joseph, the caretaker. It was addressed to Greg and family, thanking us for visiting and letting us know that breakfast was ready at the terrace nook, as designated. I left the notice where Greg would see it, walked over and kissed his lips lightly, and headed to the bathroom. Bubbled up the heated bathtub with some sweet-smelling natural aromatherapy fragrances to soothing my skin. Got into it to relax a while before cleaning up and getting ready for breakfast.

Half an hour into the dreamy relaxation, I looked up to see my Greg standing in a white lacy robe, slightly showing his chiseled body frame and chest, all the way to his toes. He looked so delicious, and I wished he could join me. I couldn't help inviting him to join me. When he did not resist and accepted the invite, I quickly got out pull him in before he changed his mind. I wasted no time in disrobing him, tossing it on the floor, and helping him into the bathtub.

As he sat directly across from me, he kissed me good morning, and his lips tasted like a mixture of hibiscus and tropical roses. A friend of mine once told me that less than half a percent of the world's population has his type of fresh and healthy breath when one wakes up in the morning. Regardless of the art or science of the statement, I'm just blessed to be enjoying an unlimited supply of amorous warm kisses daily from the love of my life.

Anyway, we soaped and scrubbed each other up until we were as clean as a whistle. We were then ready to go dress up and have our breakfast. But before we got out of the bathtub, we decided to indulge ourselves in short and sweet lovemaking. Since it was a 'quickie,' it could only count as an appetizer in my book.

Wearing our casual sunshiny outdoorsy clothes, we were finally ready for breakfast by the terrace. Oh yes, we were dressed for the outdoors. Greg complimented my white filigree gown, natural lip gloss, and satin sandals, and I told him he looked very handsome and fabulous in his designer khaki shorts, Hawaiian shirt, and aloha charcoal beach sandals. I was jealous of his beautiful physique – a combination of his height, chiseled body definition, lovely face, dreamy eyes, succulent lips, and the whole work. Although I'm an attractive woman, he has always drawn the most attention whenever we are together, which has been consistent since our first encounter. If you throw in his charm and smarts, I won't even be a fly on the wall. I'm glad he thinks the world of me and is ever appreciative of my being in his life.

Talking about the breakfast meal, it was finger-licking good. Very mouthwateringly delicious. We both finished our omelets, and the fruit bawls and freshly squeezed orange juice. I also thought the fragrant smell from the bouquet of flowers was refreshing, as it mixed with the breezy outdoor air.

"Sweetheart," he squeezed my arm as I turned to look at him. "I know we discussed going out to a party later tonight, but I want you to know that in addition to it, we had other options, like the opera, symphony, and ballet. Since the party was planned in advance, we could enjoy those other events on some other occasion, okay?"

"Thanks for letting me know as well as the reassurance honey," I smiled and touched his hand to let him know that we were on the same page. "I'm not ashamed to tell you that I've never gone to either an opera or symphony show in my life, except watching on television. In any case, I can't wait to enjoy them with you in the future, whenever your time permits.

"Regarding ballet, I took some lessons as a kid in the small town I grew up in a while staying with my grandparents. That was how I also learned how to sing and paint," I concluded, smiling while squeezing his fingers.

"That's nice. You definitely accomplished a combination of artistic skills that most kids couldn't afford in the States. By the way, I appreciate your letting me know. And thanks again for the beautiful painting you gave to me during my birthday party a while back," he smiled and padded my thigh while I leaned over and kissed him for his kind gesture and acknowledgment.

"So, my Greg, can we engage in some water sport after we step out of the building?" I inquired with a grin.

"Of course. Any suggestion?" He asked and smiled.

As I listen to his voice, I'm also beginning to feel a warm sensation all over my body as his hand on my thigh moves slowly and makes little rings all over it. Even my nipples are getting hard against my top. The only thing in my head right now is wanting to make love to him. I'll just have to suggest a couple of things and include lovemaking without him knowing that is the number one thing in my head.

"Yes, my dear. We could go fishing, kayaking, swimming, beach walking, hiking, hunting, museum exploration, or make love. Any combination is acceptable, honey." I responded, bashful that his smart brain would be able to figure out what was in my mind.

He laughed hysterically, which I'm sure, was due to my many choices or squirmy feelings from his touch. In any case, I was enjoying every minute of our time together, regardless of what we did.

"Okay, let's take a walk to the pier. Before we do that, I'm going to call the caretaker to arrange for us some fishing accessories like a line winder, spinning rod and reel, and any related items we might need in a medium-sized yacht. Plus, have him include some supply of snacks and drinks in lunch packages inside its mini freezer. You are welcome to bring along your bikini, shades, sunscreen lotions, windbreakers, and so on." He concluded after rattling out so many options.

After I agreed to his suggestions without pinpointing anything in particular, we got up and went back inside the room to get ready for the outdoor trekking.

We got up and quietly walked into the bedroom, and without a word or second thought, we went directly to the loveseat and sat down. My mind immediately played back the picture of us wrapped around each other in frantic romantic rapture. Although I was not against our going out to the pier or attending a party later tonight before our departure tomorrow, I was beginning to think we should skip the day trip and enjoy the evening's outing, which would include Greg's friends, instead of just us. Plus, this trip was about us going away from our home base or comfort zone.

So, I just wanted to enjoy our time together as a couple as if we were on our honeymoon. Not necessarily because I am a jealous female, but just eager to express my feelings for him and have deep conversations about us and our future together. I'm also looking forward to letting him know that, regardless of where we were or whatever we are doing, we certainly have always maximized our pleasure together as a couple. He has often encouraged me to be comfortable and direct in sharing and communicating my feelings and wishes with him, while he does the same to avoid misunderstanding and conflict.

To that end, I turned over to him and started my monologue:

"Sweetheart, I have a request to make of you. We both enjoy the outdoors as much as the indoors, and since this beach mansion is just as equipped as your beautiful home back in Cleveland, I suggest you cancel the arrangement you have with the caretaker, except to prepare our meals and be on the stand-by for errands or to get us any basic essentials we might need. Rather, let's spend our time and just take a walk to the pier and around the garden or poolside. Then relax and enjoy each other in the comfortably pleasing indoors, until our night party. What do you think?" I concluded, probing his eyes and awaiting his thoughts.

He cleared his throat and started:

"Thanks for your thoughtful suggestions. I absolutely agree with everything you've stated because my primary objective is happiness. And by that, I mean my head and heart have long told me that you're always looking out for my best interest, one hundred percent. To add to that, I believe that our feelings and love interests are unambiguously mutual." As he responded, my eyes were fixated on his handsome face, which was covered with smiles from his curved lips and soft brown eyes.

I continued: "Talking about love or, more specifically, our love, this mansion pleasing to our eyes and senses, well suitable and functional for the expression of our feelings and love for each other. Let's take advantage of the trip as a time, place, and space to discuss and bond with each other. To express and melt our hearts and body together. To cement and solidify our love into eternity," I concluded my monologue as my voice trailed off. We both smiled while he reached out, placing his warm, strong hand on mine and playing with my fingers.

"Marie, you know why we balance each other so well?" he paused momentarily. Since it was more a rhetorical statement than a question, he continued: "You were born a dreamer, while I was born a person of action. Since we each had half of what the other needed, we were bound to meet and complete each other."

I smiled and quietly rose from the loveseat and pulled him up with me. We kissed for about a minute, and when I opened my eyes, I saw an old grand piano in the corner of the room. It reminded me of my childhood years while staying with my grandparents. I held his hand as we went up to it. I seated myself and began to play. I played a simple hymn, which I'd heard my grandma sing at Sunday services or monthly family dinner gatherings. As the hymn slowly died out and I arose, Greg kissed and hugged me very tightly and whispered in my ear, "you certainly have a lovely voice."

Without uttering any further words, we walked quietly towards the terrace and looked across to the lake and flower garden. We looked into each other's eyes, smiled, and walked toward the staircase. I could see and smell the beautifully kept and fragrant garden with violets. Since we both had a strong love and passion for flowers, we stepped onto the garden walkway. We found lilac blossoms growing in the lane side.

Following our impulse, we continued up the side of the garden that led to the beach, which had deeper masses of flowers, leading further towards the pier. Close to where the pier meets the beach were carved granite stones benches on both sides. We sat on the left side, which provided us with a more beautiful view of the beach scenery.

I kissed him when he turned to look at me. He pulled me closer and kissed me some more. Holding his hand and squeezing his fingers, I decided it was the right time to continue to have a conversation about how we felt for each other, as well as discuss our wedding plans and expectation.

Looking into my eyes, he sensed there was something in my mind, and he immediately asked: "Honey, it seems you have something in your mind, and probably about us. So, you're welcome to go ahead and say it," he stated, with curiosity written all over his face. I cleared my throat, looked into his eyes, and started:

"Greg, I want you to know how grateful and thankful I've been since our first meeting at your company's client party.

"More importantly, I want to also let you know that it was not an accidental meeting, thanks to my friend Elisa and her current husband, Mike. I must take the opportunity to let you know that you didn't know anything about me or my life experiences at this time. However, I knew more about you in advance. Not because I was snooping around or deliberately trying to get involved with someone like you, but because of the circumstances of what I was going through in terms of relationships at the time.

"To give you a context on what I mean, it would be clearer if you remember the word you used in describing me, as a 'dreamer.' Due to a combination of my personality and how I grew up, my idea of a good or healthy relationship, was all wrong. In pursuit of it, I was met with letdowns and broken promises until I was invited to meet you.

"I know people like you existed, but my head and heart could only imagine it as in terms of movies or something meant for only a certain class of people outside of my worldview. Thanks to you, I've been given an opportunity to know what a real man is and how relationships are supposed to be, not just in dreams but in action. You've shown me that fairytales do exist. My present life, lifestyle, and experiences are literally and figuratively; it's the true definition.

"As a dreamer, I always believed there is such a thing as love at first sight but lacked the ability to understand the type that is combined with healthy encouragement that ultimately creates success and happiness for the couple and their loved ones.

"So, I just want to let you know that I loved you the very first time we met. From a physical point of view, you were extremely handsome and looked unmistakably an ideal guy every woman would want. You were very charming, pleasant, and in total control of every person and situation at the party.

"Outside of the crowd and getting to know you personally, I greatly admire your adventurous nature, confidence, intelligence, and intuition. In bed, your passionate and very romantic nature is the best in my dictionary.

"Thanks again for accepting me completely and for wanting to marry me. As my husband-to-be, I promise I'll do whatever it takes to create a happy and healthy relationship for us."

When I was done speaking, Greg rose up from the bench, pulled me up by both of my hands, placed one of his arms around my neck, and laid his face against mine, his eyes looking mine with rapt devotion. With our bodies melted together, we kissed passionately. When our lips separated for a second, he turned to my left ear and whispered, 'you are very beautiful and inspirational.' My body shivered from hearing his deep, reassuring voice and words. He reflexively hugged me more firmly and murmured, 'I love you, Marie. With all my heart.' I turned my face to him with an expectant smile, and he responded with a kiss and reclined me on the bench and sat next to me.

Thrusting his hand into his short's pockets, he touched something, and when he pulled his hand out, he had some lilac, and I remembered I had placed it there as we were walking towards the pier. It smelled nice as it blended with the cool breeze.

"The sweet smell is a treat, Marie," he said, smiling mischievously.

"Is it?" I said with happy excitement. "You really think so? I like to hear you say that."

"Yes, my heart and head say so." I smiled as he continued:

"Our journey together was meant to be. Started the day by watching the sunset from the terrace of my mansion. A few hours afterward, one of my senior executives, Mike, arrived for brunch in the company of his girlfriend, Elisa. Over the meal, they asked if they should invite one of their close female friends to my firm's clients' party. No details about you were provided, but I said sure, I'd love to meet her.

"Anyway, after they left, I closed my eyes and figuratively pictured you for a moment. I immediately did a double blink upon setting my eyes on a vision of you."

"A vision?" I repeated, looking at him excitedly to make sure I heard him correctly.

He nodded without uttering a word and continued.

"Sure, a vision. Not sounding brash, she was tall, slim, and very attractive."

I didn't try to argue about what he was saying but smiled.

Then, I asked: "What was she like?"

"If I were to describe her with the kind of phrases you females would describe another person, you'd laugh at me. So, picture yourself standing in front of your best friend, holding something special that you want to share with her. And because you are very excited and happy to share something special, your eyes are wide open, full of love and emotion, and your lips are curved in a half-serious smile as you look down at what you're holding."

"Oh my gosh! You have an extraordinary imagination, Greg," I said before he could continue.

"This is a true story," he continued. "The girl in the vision was you. And what she was holding was me.

"And she spoke as well as smiled. Her French-accented voice was soft and musical but clear and full as a subtle kind of witchery. The exact same voice and accent that you have."

"My dear Greg, your poetic perception and expression of us affirm the limitless love you have for me, and my heart would forever be grateful," I responded. Smiling with tears of joyous gratitude, I turned to him and melted in his arms, exchanging profuse kisses and hugs.

17

As our dreamy smiling eyes glued to each other, he excused himself for a second to make a quick call to Joseph, the caretaker, to get our meal ready since we were about to go back in. We first retraced our steps back to the mansion. Then headed straight to the bedroom.

Inside, we sat side by side at the edge of the comfortable king-size bed. Looking at each other with smiles on our faces, I wrapped and pressed my arms tightly around his midriff. He responded by kissing my neck and ears. I felt proud to call him my lord, which often produces a smile on his face. The keeper of my charms and pride. Every one of his touches results in a convulsive spasm of ecstatic excitement in me. So, calling him 'god's gift' is not sarcasm.

We've been together a long time, calendar-wise, but it seems like yesterday. Our hours and days in months together are filled with experiences of sweet delight; while meeting endless heavenly transports every night.

When we lovingly chill out in any number of our soft silky beds, whether within our home base, or out-of-town locations, we can't help generating intense temperature in each other with our passionate slow-jam love-making exploration. These timeless amorous aerobics overtakes our body and senses until nature yields to our delicious indulgence.

As fierce desire and endless lust inflame us, we become melted and connected in love's most warm embrace, with pressed soft kisses on our every loveliness, from toe to head, followed by limitless reruns.

And yes, around my alluring soft and wet opening, his pliant limbs are entwined. Finally, I resign to his love seat of bliss. We pant! We throb! We tremble! We experience heaven on earth.

We continue to experience whatever passion feeds our bodily fibre without question. We heaved! We wiggle! We squirm! We bite! We laugh! We tremble! We sigh! We groan!

We taste heavenly bliss. Then fondle. And then pass out.

An unforgettable cherished beautiful routine.

--

After taking our shower and pampering our bodies, we enjoyed a scrumptious seven-course meal, followed by dressing up for the night party. I wore my elegant body-hugging Burberry black dress and diamond earrings, which had the effect of making me look like a beautiful black rose. To complete the angelic look, I decided to wear matching high heel closed Toe Pump shoes. Greg wore an open-neck long sleeve shirt, plus dark blue jean pants and classy black oxford hand-crafted leather shoes.

With a big smile on his face, he held my hand, walked out of the house, and headed towards the pier; he stepped down to the bank and unfastened a beautiful ocean blue and the milk-white yacht that had his first and last name initials on it. He leapt into it and called to me. With his extended hand, he helped me into its platform.

Filled with excitement and exuberance, I bounced to my feet with the impulsive delight of a girl at the sight of a yacht. Expected nothing better than rushes, reaching out to him.

"Is it yours?" I exclaimed, with eyes wide open.

"Come in and see for yourself," he said, smiling mischievously.

I hurried in towards the water's edge and looked at its luxurious insides and at his initials.

"How did it come here?" I asked, searching his smiling eyes and curved lips.

"I paid a cargo ship to drop it from the skies, about the same time of our arrival," teasing.

"I see," I said, looking serious.

He laughed.

"You know I'm not a magician. I plan things, and this trip was a surprise trip for you."

I laughed hysterically.

"I forgot that; how silly of me."

He got me settled in securely. I noticed he was looking at my exposed shapely thighs and legs, smiling as his eyes were raised to meet mine. We both giggled as the words, 'my beautiful fiancé' were uttered out of his lips. His words and deep voice sounded pleasurable to my ears and tickled my heart.

Turning slightly towards me, he grasped my hand and the other, my arm. Holding it for a moment, he made sure my cushion and seating were firm and comfortable. Then he gave me a quick kiss, and we immediately initiated our take-off.

When he noticed that I leaned back and dropped one hand in the water and did not resist the impulse of closer communion with the water, he decreased the speed slowly across the stream to enable me to enjoy my vanity.

It was almost twilight as we made our way to ripping gold and turning my hair a rich brown. As his eyes rested on my face, it made me remember a very memorable longest running time we made love. Oh, how it feels like yesterday. After many hours of passionate luscious sex, waking up to breakfast in bed, he described my face as exquisite beauty and freshness and purity. Concluding that, it sank into the depth of his soul and made him vow that beauty was the one thing worth living for. I branded him as the most consummate, passionate, romantic man ever.

Unconscious of his absorbed observation, I leaned back, my eyes fixed on the water, my whole attention captivated by its pleasant-sounding current as it ran through my fingers.

In silence, he turned the yacht engine off, slowly and noiselessly. Ahead of us, I could see a beautiful large mansion. How beautiful everything looks around here. Feels like a dream. He helped me out and held my hand as we took the manicured walkway towards the lighted building. Feeling the warmth of his hand in mine, I raised up his hand and kissed his fingers.

When our eyes met, I asked him: "Were you upset that I wanted to change your plans with my own suggestions or my attempt to cancel the rest of your itinerary before our return to Ohio?"

"Not at all; why?" he replied, nudging me to say more.

"Every place is so beautiful. Like this mansion, and the mansion we just came from, and this yacht. Who exactly lives here?" I asked. Curious for a more robust and clear explanation.

"My university friend, who is also my architect. He is from New York, another county not far from here. He got married, moved, and settled here. He designed and built my mansions in Ohio and Rochester, the place we are staying on this trip."

"You mean the mansion we are staying in right now and the yacht that took us here tonight belong to you?" I asked, with my eyes wide open in surprise.

He nodded lightly, "Yes."

"You own a great deal. I've heard you're very rich. It must be nice," I said, looking at him with a smile of disbelief.

 "Not really," he replied. "You know, one cannot tell until one has been poor. I don't think it is a big deal because it doesn't make one happier. As a human, we always have a hunger for something until we die. Like an endless quest."

"So, what would you possibly have a hunger for?" I asked, smiling at him.

As it seemed he was in deep thought and taking too long to respond, I then asked:

"So, you are very happy?"

"Was it some poets that say, 'count no man happy till he dies?' "he echoed.

"Maybe we can both conclude that it's a state of mind?" I resolved and urged him to take me to the party before we turned out to be the last guests.

We rang the doorbell and were ushered in to be introduced and greet other dozen-plus guests and handed each a glass of mixed drink. The butler described it as 'sex on the beach.' It tasted sweet and weird, and Greg told me it was a tropical cocktail containing a mixture of vodka, peach, schnapps, orange juice, and cranberry juice. We definitely had fun at the party until our outbound yacht ride.

—

We hated to fly back as we woke up from another all-night love-making upon our return from the party. I enjoyed meeting Greg's New York investment and former university colleagues and friends. Thanks to him, too, for exposing me to viewing money as just a means to an end, not the end in and of itself. I'll forever be a student of work-life balance.

We flew back to Cleveland early evening, and just before our touchdown, Greg smiled at me, and we automatically reached out for each other's lips and kissed passionately.

"Marie, I want to thank you for coming into my life," he said to me.

"I love you with my whole heart, Greg," I eagerly responded. "Our trip and time together would forever be embedded in my head and heart forever," I added.

Flying over the city of Cleveland, the lights and every scenic surrounding looked so beautiful. I felt as though I was seeing it through a set of new eyes. The plane landed a few minutes gently, shortly as we held hands. My heart tells me that my whole life with my husband-to-be has just begun. My excitement is so great that I can't wait to make him proud and happy for accepting me and making me his wife until death does us part.

Before I fall asleep, I will write myself a couple of notes, among which would be putting the finishing touches to present to him the final arrangements and summary for our wedding event. This upcoming week would be very busy for him. However, I'm confident everything would run on as speedily and fruitfully since he has an assemblage of an effective and efficient team to work with him. I look forward to liaising with him, as I've always done, and providing him whatever support he expects and seeks from me, twenty-four-seven. He's correct when he stated that the world would not function properly without team spirit, just like the littlest body part needs the biggest organ to function efficiently and effectively.

—

The weeks flew by as we spent our early and late hours together, within our home and Cleveland's cityscapes, indulging in our perpetual sweet cravings and passions. He calls me several times, first thing in the morning, after he settles into his day's schedule, or just before he returns home.

I always look forward, especially to his funny text messages that make me laugh for hours. More than anything else, my heart is always in joy whenever we share our feelings of love and yearning for each other daily and express it in person as kids in a toy store. I also adore his regularly delivered, surprising, beautiful bouquet of flowers in various assortments, from peonies to roses, lilies, orchids, sunflowers, ranunculus, as well as some sweet-smelling ones I've never heard or known in my life, from the best florists in town. More importantly, I'm enamored and very excited that we are both ready to start a family.

In less than an hour, he's expected home early for dinner to celebrate my birthday. In memory of my roots, I commissioned the chef to prepare our occasional French cuisine as a treat. As my thoughts of him were still in the air, the main door opened, and he entered, bringing along the fresh flowery air indoors. He looked so distinguished and elegant in his three-piece suit. From head to toe, he could pass for any of the models in GQ magazine any day or time.

With a warm and intimate smile, he pulled me closer for a warm embrace. We hugged and kissed for a good minute plus, and pulling me away from his body, I noticed he was mesmerized by me, checking out my tight jeans and pink sweater, with plenty of cleavage showing. As he smiles and examines me further, he notices my perfectly manicured nails and nail polish to match my sweater. With our smiling eyes glued to each other, we simultaneously tilted our heads forward while feeling both his soft, warm hands on both sides of my neck, gliding smoothly across my hair that hung loosely down my back and kissing me passionately. Of which he interrupted briefly to whisper in my ear how beautiful and adorable I looked.

Hugging him, I asked for us to go upstairs for some mystery surprise I had for him. He looked at me searchingly and curiously but wasn't quite sure what it was. In any case, he followed me quietly, and we ended up in the master bedroom. I texted the caretaker to prepare and set the dinner in the first-floor dining area, placing our favorite aromatic flowers from our garden at strategic locations within the dining room and the adjoining area.

I helped Greg off his shoes, suit jacket, pants, and shirt and replaced them with his lounging clothes. I then poured two glasses of fruit juice and handed one to him. I took my clothes off too and wore my house lacey frock.

When I finally sat next to him by the bed, he turned to me and said:

"Marie, you know, unlike you, I never dated as such until after I graduated from the university. Maybe due to shyness and the desire to excel in my academic pursuits, as well as in a few competitive sports. Anyway, that was the case until I graduated, then headed on to graduate school. Led to the pursuit of a comfortable and safe professional career that I was also passionate about. I enjoyed what I was doing because it provided an avenue to contribute to society as well as to make an effective living.

"Thanks to you, I discovered something deeper and fulfilling, relationship-wise, like what I saw in my parents. Besides professional success and independence, I'm glad I gave myself an opportunity to truly get to meet and know the opposite sex upon setting my eyes on you. Meeting and looking into your eyes for the very first time was magical. I was immediately transfixed and desired to get to know you more. The look in your eyes deeply moved and excited me. Although I couldn't put it in words, I felt a change in my heart; just like I've expressed to you in many other ways in the past, I knew it was time to give love a chance.

"Without knowing what the outcome would look like, I was guided by my heart rather than my head. Your eyes and demeanor told me we were ready for each other, and I decided to jump into a relationship with you with both my feet. And to tell you the truth, dozens of months since, my feelings for you have been on overflow until this moment."

As he uttered the last word, he stretched out and held my hand. He then requested that I close my eyes for a moment, of which I obliged. The warmth of his touch transmitted kinetic energy through my whole body, and my heart skipped for a moment. As his voice stated that I could now open my eyes shortly after undetermined minutes, I noticed he had taken a shiny gold-lined black box out of his suit jacket pocket and dropped down on one of his knees. Also noticed, we were surrounded by heart-shaped red and white roses and strategically placed lighted candles.

With glowing excitement and love in both our eyes, he stated:

"Sweetheart, it's your birthday today, and soon would be our first-year anniversary. If you would permit me, I want to take this moment to let you know that when you find your soulmate, you not only know it with your head but also feel it in your heart. We have been glued together as conjoint twins since our first date. Our relationship has been an exciting gift that gave us an opportunity to get to know each other at a close range. We celebrated my birthday together. And now, we are now celebrating yours. Mine was marked by formal words of the proposal, and now, we are marking yours with a formal engagement. I'm excited to continue our next chapter with you as a couple, forever. Marie, would you accept this engagement ring to be my future wife?"

"Yes! Yes, my dear. There is nobody on earth I'd rather spend the rest of my life with," I responded as he placed the ring on my finger. "Thanks for giving me the opportunity from day one to build and nurture our loving relationship together. I'm excited to be called your wife and can't wait to be the mother of your kids soon," I concluded.

 As I quietly reflected upon what he had said to me, I couldn't be so thankful to him for helping me to erase the past fears and inadequacies I experienced in previous relationships. Thinking and replaying his powerful words in my head, I knew one hundred percent that he was a loving, caring, gentle and kind man. His sincerity has always calmed me down to the extent I 've almost forgotten every bad experience in my past. Fighting tears from my eyes, I just wanted to melt into his arms. As he felt the shivering in my body, he picked me up in his strong arms, with our faces and bodies glued together, smiling and hugging each other.

"Marie, I love you with my whole heart and will love you till my last days on earth. You complete me," he said as his reassuring eyes met mine.

"I love you too, Greg," I responded, laying my head on his shoulder. He smiled into my eyes, kissing my forehead while running his right hand's fingers through my hair, then lifting me up slowly for a tighter hug. Placing me back down gently, he whispered that we should go downstairs for dinner since it was obvious we were both ready to feed our hungry appetites.

At the dinner table was a variety of exceptional French cuisine to whet our appetite. The caretaker, Mr Cooper, was on hand to see to our dining enjoyment and pleasure. From the rich flavorful appetizers to the sweet-smelling entree's choices of servings and filling portions; to exquisite desserts and unlimited pours of curated wine selections were visibly available to satiate and nourish our palatable craving.

After dinner, we adjourned to the living room large foyer area where I wanted to surprise Greg with pleasant and cherishing piano music and singing by one of my favorite female artists. His soft eyes were covered with joy and happiness, and just before I ended the song, he walked over, took my hand, and kissed it. Then whispered in my ear for us to take a stroll in the lighted garden by the pool.

When we went through the back door, a few steps brought us onto the soft gravel pathway that was lined with miniature palm trees and benches facing the pool. We walked slowly, holding hands, with almost noiseless footsteps. With one of his arms around my waist, we stopped and kissed passionately, and to steady our steps and get more comfortable, we sat on one of the benches overlooking the pool that reflected a combination of the clear moonlight and lighted pathway.

"How lovely the blooming flowers smelled," I said between our kisses. Greg intensified our delicious kisses while we groped in the dim obscurity.

"Not as sweet as between your legs," he teased, smiling. He asked if I preferred for him to kiss my pussy, and I nodded multiple times before he could finish his request. His soft, firm fingers playfully twisted their way into the soft folds around my wet hungry love button.

 "Oh! Yeah! More! More!" I sighed softly as my hands clung around his neck.

"My sweet lady, I am ever pleased to render any quality and quantity of delicious pleasure your heart desires," he added, as our eyes smiled at each other.

"You will experience your usual most heavenly sensations," he continued confidently.

From his urging, I raised my house dress and reclined backward on the bench, as I was now excited with passionate expectation. He immediately asked me to kneel over his face as I reclined on my back at full length on the seat. He proceeded to suck and finger me at the same time.

Sensing intense excitement from my reaction to his magic tongue and fingers, he clasped me very firmly round the butt with one arm and used his right hand; he rubbed my clit further, which resulted in increased excitement as his tongue moved around every inside part of my vagina. With the increased excitement and pleasure, my whole body trembled and wriggled over his mouth as he licked the creamy juices that were flowing from my vagina.

I grabbed his neck as I couldn't stop shaking from excitement, and I whispered in his ear: "Oh dear. You are so nice to me. It feels so delightful. So pleasurable and beautiful, I can't help thanking you for making me happy."

My desire for more enjoyment with his penis was so intense that I wanted him to also enjoy my warm juicy cunt, so I sat up on the bench very quickly and took his seat next to me. As soon as I made him recline on the seat, my hand at once pulled his penis out of his house pants. I bent over and kissed and licked it furiously. I immediately straddled over him and guided his throbbing hard penis into my pouting wet cunt. I started to jump up and down in a frenzy of voluptuous enjoyment. I rested a little bit, intensified bouncing more but only rested for a short moment to enjoy and indulge in the devil's bite. That is the delicious pleasure of enabling my pussy's cunt to contract and squeeze his huge throbbing penis to create and increase the sensation for both of us.

"Oh! Oh! Oh!" I sighed. "Oh Greg, I'm dying from your love. So much delicious pleasure. I don't want it to stop." I begged, moaned, hugging, kissing, biting, licking every part of his body in fondest abandon.

As the throbbing and contracting and squeezing and swelling increase, our bodies experience increased tingling sensation and shivering. The physical sensation of trembling and wriggling was so pleasurable that I couldn't control my endless involuntary movements.

At last, we both produced orgasmic creamy juices, which left us in an ecstatic lethargy of love, and I almost fainted on his warm, strong body that was glued to mine.

When we had recovered a little, we sat back up on the bench. I placed my hand around his neck and kissed him passionately, thanking him for being so loving and caring and passionate. He pulled me up, whispered, 'I love you,' and we walked quietly back to the house, climbed upstairs, and went straight to the bedroom.

We used the shower together, soaping and scrubbing each other's bodies. After drying and putting lotions on, we went straight to bed naked and covered our bodies under the soft sheets, spooning and kissing some more. As I enjoyed his warm body next to mine, he told me several funny stories and made me laugh with a mixture of fairy tales and his childhood experiences.

Our evening together has been wonderful, from a very delicious dinner to romantic moments, passionate lovemaking, and more. Every minute or daily moment with him is filled with beautiful romantic adventures. He has always gone out of his way to assure my pleasure and create very happy memories for me. Mostly beyond my dreams. I feel totally at ease with him and very special around him. Everything about him draws me closer to him, to the extent I want to melt into him.

As the clock ticked, I noticed its midnight, and he'd be starting his day early as usual. Just about that moment, he turned over and hugged me intimately as we felt each other's warmth. I enjoyed his strawberry kisses for endless minutes until our bodies were heated up. He raised his head and kissed my forehead and whispered goodnight, and I responded in kind. I noticed he was fast asleep, and I lay awake, half asleep. My body, mind, and heart are filled with him. Thoughts of Greg are always tender, loving, and joyous. At last, I close my eyes and sleep the night away.

18

How fast does time run when one is enjoying multiple fun things. A little over a month has passed since our last out-of-state trip. Plus, our anniversary is right behind us, as if we just met yesterday. As I think about my other half, I can't help smiling as I look at my left hand and feel the expensive and luxurious engagement ring on my finger. Yes, it is meant to bond and seal our love forever as a couple. It has a rare kind of emerald design that I've never seen before. Especially as I examine its baguette diamond with a platinum foundation that was specially commissioned for me. I reckon very few girls like me have ever seen such a 35-carats precious stone, with a magnificent and beautiful appearance, ever!!

Dreaming about my Greg and every moment we've spent together, our over one year together, it seems like a minute when one examines any gazillion things we've done together. Maybe because our whirlwind romance started and remained in a honeymoon state, from day one, through this moment. My experience has been nothing but uncountable rewards.

Talking about rewards, I'll have to tell him pretty soon about how my body is changing and feeling lately. When we bring a child into our world as a couple, life will no longer be about us or me or him only. Where we go or what we do would require maximal responsibilities beyond us. I am so excited and ready to embrace my role fully as a mother, lover, wife, and partner for life.

As I present to him the assigned wedding arrangements, which he awaits this week, I know he is also planning and ready to share with me when we discuss every detail to ensure that everything works out for us.

He has told me a million times that I'm always in his head, heart, and mind, no matter whatever in life occupies his day. The fact that he has sacrificed so much for me and loved me wholeheartedly speaks volumes about his character, unselfishness, kindness, and endless overflowing love from the depth of his heart.

For the three hundred and sixty-five plus days we've been together, he has showered me with countless daily texts and phone calls, beautiful poetic notes, and messages that often accompany a bouquet of flowers and beautiful gifts.

Not to talk about weekly dates and exciting, surprising out-of-town trips to beautiful and secluded resorts across unknown horizons. Moments that are filled with twenty-four-hour conversations, expressions of endearing love, and romance. Being with him is but a dream come true.

While awaiting his arrival from work, Mr Cooper, the caretaker, brought in a beautiful bouquet of flowers and a card from him to me. Among other sweet and kind things in it, the card states that we would be traveling to meet my parents in the next few days so that he can formally ask for their permission to marry me. I'm over the moon and excited about the trip to France, and especially to see my parents again. On our way there, I'll share several good news with him, starting with our wedding itinerary, which would detail where, when, number of guests, and seek any suggestions, among other things. And conclude with my secret good news, which I'm a hundred percent sure will gladden his heart.

In less than half an hour, Greg's sports utility rolled through the gates, and I could see him smiling and waving to the caretaker. Meeting him at the double doors, we kissed, and I thanked him for the flowers and beautiful words on the card. He hugged and kissed me some more, and he held my hand as we took the stairs to the second floor. I helped him out of his suit, which was replaced with comfortable house shorts and an open chested floral shirt. I rang for two cups of hot cocoa for us while awaiting our dinner.

 "How nice to be home and be sitting here with you," he whispered, smiling at me, with one hand around my shoulder and the other on his thigh, as we sat on the sofa.

"Oh, how sweet of you; I'm just as excited to see you too, sweetheart," I replied and reclined my head on his lap, stretching my body across the comfortable cushion. I raised my head to give him a quick kiss and relaxed my head back on his lap, and looked into his soft big brown eyes. As I increasingly got drowned in his dreamy eyes, I rested one hand on the lump that he seemed to have in his pocket shorts, pretending as if I was trying to make myself comfortable.

To get him aroused further, I teased him: "Do you prefer for me to wear pants or dresses, mostly?" and slowly pulled my dress up a little, showing my long legs and part of my thighs.

"You do have beautiful legs, babe. As a matter of fact, I think your creator spent months sculpting your gorgeous body, from head to toe," he responded with a measured tone that sounded like music to my ears. Little by little, I could feel his shorts pocket swelling under my hand, and I could tell it was due to the warmth of my hand that was placed on his shorts, combined with the subject of our conversation. The thought of it makes me so bashful because I'm always raising a feverish desire in his blood, which his calm demeanor is unable to control the majority of the time.

Moments like this create a vivid reminder in me about our luscious sex this morning before breakfast and his departure for work. With an effort, he slightly shifted himself in order to remove my hand further down to his thigh.

Excited with an unusual flush on my face, I smiled at him as our eyes met and seized the opportunity to let him know that I might be expecting. He nodded his head quietly and pulled me closer to his chest, kissed me passionately, and uttered the words "God's will." I excused myself for a moment to get our two cups of chocolate drinks.

Less than half an hour later, we were seated at the terrace for dinner and taking the view of the pool downstairs after discussing our trip and wedding plans. He suggested that, based on the surprising news from me earlier, we'll have to move up the wedding arrangement and be flexible on all essential celebrations, as we consider necessary. My health and welfare, we both agreed, should be our priority going forward. Meanwhile, we were all set and ready for our chartered flight's departure the following midnight hour.

"You are looking stunning for the flight, honey," Greg said as he turned his attention to me next to him. He pressed his hand against mine, massaging my fingers, which often sets me in the mood to melt into him.

I was wearing a bright yellow coat over my tan outfit, with matching darker hue thigh-high boots. For him, he decided on a classic style, featuring a pants and jacket grey suit, over a dark blue shirt and tie, with dark handcrafted leather shoes.

"Thank you, sweetheart, you look very handsome and distinguished as usual yourself," I responded while leaning my head on his chest. Turning over and looking directly at his smiling eyes, our lips met and glued together, as often as we always do when our bodies are close together. The kiss lingered about a minute before we climbed into the plane. Moments after we settled into our respective cozy leather seats, we again indulged in more soft lingering kisses, only to be interrupted by the pilot's announced preparation for take-off for our nine-plus hour flight to Paris.

Looking out of the window, I see the dispatcher in his tower signal our pilot to go ahead. The engine roared lustily, and the plane shot down the runway, lifting smoothly into the air. With accelerated speed westward, the aircraft slashed into the semi-darkness in a slow climb. Cleveland faded behind us as we sped over the fertile farmlands.

As I turned my head slightly to look at Greg, I noticed he was turning at the same time, glancing at his iPad. Squeezing his arm gently, I proceeded to relax my head on the comfortable leather chair. With a mixture of excitement and anticipation, I welcomed the opportunity to close my eyes and have some rest.

Going between sleep and wakeful moments for a better half of an hour, I was woken by the voice of a flight attendant walking the aisle, asking if we were ready for a complimentary meal and juices, and I nodded my head in response. Taking a closer look at the menu she handed to me, a quick glance at the meal menu showed choices of omelet or scrambled eggs, baked lamb, chops and potatoes, mixed steamed veggies, blueberry muffins, waffles, bacon, freshly squeezed orange juice or apple juice, a cappuccino, americano, tea, and bottled water. After selecting a combination of choices for both of us, I glanced through the plane window and noticed the field blazed into a blue-white glow as the soft hum of the plane motored steadily.

We chatted with Greg briefly, and I realized Greg's eyes were staring straight in the direction of the pilot's cockpit. Without turning my way, he said that we were traveling a little more than a hundred miles an hour based on the airspeed indicator reading. He concluded that the wind outside must be blowing a storm. Looking at the route map on the screen in front of me, I noticed we were passing through a field that was parallel with a river. At this time, we'd flown slightly over an hour and a half already.

Meanwhile, with two-plus hours behind us, one of the two flight attendants was already dozing off at her cabin location in my view. Or perhaps, just resting her eyes in anticipation of a refreshed morning, which was several hours ahead prior to the scheduled flight arrival time. Meanwhile, Greg's head was turned, facing the window, comfortably relaxed. It was so quiet around me, except for the humming beat of the plane's engine. Between reading and watching the tv screen, I closed my eyes again and resolved to take a nap that was more like a long sleep.

Over nine hours of flight time had come and gone. I was awoken by Greg's warm kiss on the side of my forehead. He welcomed me with his beaming, smiling eyes and soft lips when I opened my eyes wide to look at him. Picking up his water glass from the table in front of him, he took a gulp of water, placed it in front of him, then picked it up and handed the second glass of freshly squeezed fruit juice to me. I drank half of it and placed the cup back on the table in front of me. As I did, I immediately noticed that our flight had ended, and the plane had fully descended Paris major airport and settled on the tarmac, with the engine still humming.

Picking the cup up again, I emptied it in one gulp, then turning to him, I whispered in his ear, "I'm engaged," and he busted out with laughter and reminded me that the last time I said that to him, it was called a proposal and now, it was fitting to be referred to as an engagement. He held my hand, running his fingers from my elbow down the length of my arm, massaging my palm, lingering and circling my ring finger. I smiled and nodded as I felt his warm hand around my fingers.

I turned to see the flight attendant that just stopped by the aisle next to me. She's letting us know that an arranged private luxury transfer sedan was awaiting us outside the plane, on the tarmac. We were scheduled to be driven to the Hotel de Crillon, overlooking the illustrious landmark, Place de la Concorde, a good ride away from this airport. It took but a few minutes for our luggage and us to be seated for the hotel ride.

As the luxurious sedan cascaded the cobblestones, gliding onto the smooth major street, I turned to Greg, asking, "honey, have you thought about what you'll say to my parents, especially my father, when you meet them yet?"

"Actually not. However, whatever words come to my lips, after an initial pleasantry, I'd take it from there," he responded practically, with his seductive, disarming smile.

Remembering that he is a very charming, personable, competent businessman, I know he'll feel totally comfortable at home with them, regardless of the situation. Although I've not seen either of my parents for quite some time, I know they'll like him from the get-go. Smiling with a feeling of happiness and contentment, as the thought lingered in my head, I reached out to squeeze his hand.

He responded by gently wrapping his right hand against mine, lifting it towards his face, kissing my fingers, and slowly letting go. Tingled by his warm lips, I turned to him and placed my left hand around his neck, massaging it, while my other hand rested on the crotch of his pants. Feeling a rising bulge due to a combination of his size and the warmth of my touch. I also was beginning to feel a hardness, which I knew, was arousal from my magic fingers.

He turned slowly and glued his eyes to mine. He had a blush written all over his soft eyes and handsome face. Instead of speaking in response to this voiceless appeal, I kissed him blissfully, eagerly, and with a reflective intensity, hungrily sucking in the fragrance of his sweet breath and warm, soft lips as I trembled at the same time.

Opening my eyes fleetingly, I realized that the chauffer-driven sedan was moving at a slow pace. I also observed that the uniformed chauffeur had deemed the lights in our compartment with the exception of the base of the car that was illuminating glowing orange lights that originated from around the four-legged gold-rimmed mini tray that was arranged with an ice bucket of champagne, two crystal glasses, matching bowls of mix fresh fruits, plus miniature spoons and delicate soft white cloth napkins.

I closed my eyes again as my hands continued to slowly caress and kiss every part of his body, from the firm flesh of his neck, ear lobes, and warm lips, to the hardness in front of his pants. He whispered into my ear, between breaths: "I'm tempted to make love to you right now. Right here. However, as a gentleman and out of civility, we'll have to wait and make it up upon our hotel arrival, my dear Marie."

"Yes indeed," was my whispery, inaudible, instant response, as the echo of his deep voice pleaded for my patience.

Meanwhile, our yielding bodies that were devoid of common sense and reason accelerated into top gear. Our kisses and caresses increased, as the thrill of emotion shot through our blended sensuous human anatomy that had become synchronized at this moment. Time stood still, as I lay almost motionless in his strong, warm arms. As one of my hand rested on his thigh, and our bodies melted together, I could feel his throbbing hardness as the sedan slowly turned towards the hotel entrance.

19

At the curb in front of the auspicious hotel establishment, the luxury sedan came to a stop. The look and feel of the Hotel de Crillon, is that of a luxurious, understated French palace. Two uniformed valet parking attendants approached the vehicle, smiling and greeting in English with a French accent. They simultaneously opened the doors as Greg, and I stepped out. Aided by the driver, the immaculately dressed hotel attendants proceeded to retrieve our luggage to take to the concierge or reception area. We walked towards the large entrance doors and were again greeted by another well-dressed uniformed, smiling doorman as we entered. I noticed that each uniformed staff wore wool suits with blue overcoats and gold pins. As Greg is handling the check-in process, I've decided to look around and call my family to know that we've arrived and arrange dinner with them later.

I'm amazed that the setting is very unlike any other hotel lobby I've ever been to. Instead of the typical imposing reception desk, I see a sit-down reception section that provides intimate in-room check-in, considering our reservation was made in advance.

What impresses me about the insides of this hotel is the fact that it creates a calm feeling in me as I walk through the soft violet glow of the lobby and across the immaculately polished marble floors that stretch to the hollowing stone walls. Besides, the crowning jewel is the magnificent floral arrangement of the gold-and-crystal chandeliers that hang from the ceiling, displayed on marble tables and in alcoves. Greg and I can't ask for any more intimate and magnificent romantic grand holiday resort than Hotel de Crillon.

Looking across the lobby at some well-heeled couples and business guests from the US, Europe, Asia, the Middle East, and Africa, as Greg was walking towards me and chatting with a well-dressed gentleman, I heard a voice of a female standing by a chess table with a young man that looked like in his twenties. I immediately recognized her as Madonna and her young boyfriend. Standing next to them is another young female who looks like her young daughter, that has modeled across several runways across London, New York, and Paris. A few yards from them were Justine Bieber and his model wife and a couple of Hollywood actors that I've seen in movies but couldn't place their names at the moment. To the left of them was a great French actress who had every charm but a youth. She has looked delicate and exquisite for several decades.

She was very animated as she was chatty with a tall, pale-faced man, whose French seemed to be as perfect as his attitude in the company of the actress. In French, I could also hear the voices of others paired individuals discussing the latest upcoming movies. I recognize one of the French Cabinet Ministers who once ran for president. Right behind them was a very beautiful young female, tall and fair, with grey-blue eyes and a wealth of golden, yellow hair, chatting up a very wealthy famous wrapper cum movie writer-producer. A little further in the background, a younger-looking well-dressed man was exchanging an excitable banter with a beautiful famous, African petite model turned actress.

Just as my brain and eyes were absorbing in and feasting on the spectacular scenic views of the hotel interior and the many beautiful and captivating celebrities, Greg arrived, gave me a quick kiss, held my hand, and we headed to our reserved suite.

"We're finally here, honey," I said to him, smiling, "and ready to rumble," giggling.

"Oh yes. I'm excited too and looking forward to us enjoying each other."

He added, "did you notice and/or recognize some of those stars?"

"Sure, several of them are some famous faces I've seen in the movies, as well as in pop music. Did you notice some, too?" I mused, curiously looking at his smiling eyes.

"Of course. Two of them are my clients. I've had the opportunity to manage their assets for a few years and have received good referrals from them in the past month," he concluded with the glowing air of a price fighter.

"And by the way, they're in France for the Cannes film festival in the French Riviera that's scheduled in a few days' time. Perhaps, they're in Paris now for an ongoing fashion show, which should be rounding up shortly," he concluded.

"Good to hear, my man. Oh, by the way, I did call my parents and invited them over for dinner, as we agreed on." I reminded him.

"Great. Thanks. I can't wait to meet them, finally." He nodded, looking thoughtfully.

"Are you hungry yet?" he asked expectantly.

"Definitely, sweetheart. I'm starving and could eat a horse." Laughing out loud as I uttered the words. And added: "We'll also enjoy a delicious snack, okay?"

Chuckling, he responded: "Of course, my dear Marie. Room service sounds good?"

"Absolutely. I'm all in. I'll call in as soon as we get in our suite." I responded, feeling very pleased.

"Actually, our top-of-the-line Signature Suite comes with private butler service. And since you have a surprise for me tonight, I have one for you too. In fact, two. After handing me our wedding plan, I was able to quickly arrange our wedding date by moving it forward and changing the location. Before I share the surprise, here's the reason: you're expecting and minimizing the stress on you by initiating a speed wedding and honeymoon.

"We'll have our wedding here in two days' time, and I've chartered a large plane to bring my parents, family, and our friends from the States. I've also arranged a large luxury bus to bring in your family and friends on your list that are here in France. Second, we'll be heading from here directly to our honeymoon destination, and to keep it a mystery to surprise me, Greg has added a twist in the arrangement and hinted it would still be our arranged Hawaii location or some exotic island destination that he said, would be equally exciting. He then whispered in my ear: "Are you in agreement, sweetheart?" He concluded, sounding a little serious and eager for me to be flexible.

I nodded my head, knowing his surprises were always thrilling and very intimate for both of us. I kissed and hugged him to assure him that I was on board with his plan.

Our Signature Suite is larger than the largest Parisian apartment, richly furnished with dozens of luxurious accessories such as many-hued marbles, bronze, moldings, crowns, curated art, a variety of antiques, and classic books, and handcrafted woodwork.

Modern items include modern electronic toys in the form of TVs, Bluetooth sound systems, light fixtures, floor heating, tubs, and dozens of other forms of amenities. To crown it all, the Suite provides a terrace and panoramic views of Paris' Grand Palais and the Eiffel Tower. It also available for connection to the 2,500-square-foot Suite Bernstein, which has a six-person dining room and a 1,200-square-foot terrace overlooking Place de la Concorde, with views of the Beaux-Art palace and the iconic tower.

I've gone ahead and ordered a traditional French cuisine and a bottle of wine on ice through our in-house butler to be placed by the terrace within the hour. First, we've both changed into our housecoats, followed by our grey marbled underfloor heating baths. I decide to use the extra deep soaking tub, while Greg decides to use the walk-in shower.

Just as Greg was toweling his body, I got out of the tub, and he helped dry me, and we both lotion each other. We wore our house clothes and went to the terrace for our meal, where the butler was a skip away for orders or requests, should we need anything.

The view was spectacular, and the custom leather seats and dining area were very comfortable. We thoroughly enjoyed the scrumptious, mouthwatering smoked salmon plus caviar and oyster. After drinking the special vintage house wine, we retired into the comfort of the luxurious master bedroom to relax and continue our conversations and enjoy our special time together.

The Porthault linens and Drouault pillows and duvets on the huge super king bed were so inviting that we immediately made ourselves comfortable, seated side by side. I turned my face to Greg, searching for some sweet word to say to him, but ended up kissing him blissfully, sucking in the fragrance of his sweet breath until my whole body trembled with emotion.

He responded with his hands caressing the firm flesh of my neck, slowly working their way towards the heaving breasts; with his deep voice, he whispered, "I notice your beautiful boobs have developed and firmed more than the last time. I could remember, my dear Marie."

As he uttered those words, fire and thrill of emotion seemed to shoot through both of our bodies. For a moment, we laid almost motionless in each other's arms, with one of my hands resting on his naked thigh. I immediately felt the hardness between his legs, and the arousal in me forced me to say, "honey, please, we must not stop here. Make love to me now."

He responded by hugging and caressing me more. Then after kissing me for a moment, he said, "how thoughtful and delightful for you to make a formal request. Your request is granted and extended indefinitely throughout the duration of our expedition."

He continued, "my dear Marie, what can be more pleasing in life than to balance work and life with the one you love. To build up and cherish each other, in faith, hope, joy, and romantic pleasure."

Before he finished saying the word 'pleasure,' I pulled his face closer to mine and kissed his lips passionately. When his soft, warm lips met mine in a fiery embrace, my hand searched through his pajama shorts hungrily and let out his throbbing hardness. In response, his hands responded by slipping off my house robe. Lowering his right hand, he took possession of my wet crimson vagina. My thighs immediately began to experience involuntary contractions due to the tickling effect of his magic fingers on my clit.

In a great state of excitement, I gasped and whispered in impatience, pleading, "please, Greg, hurry up and make love to me. I can't wait any longer."

With a gentle effort, he reclined my body gingerly on a pair of soft linen pillows. And to enable his hard, throbbing penis to have a grandiose entrance to my luscious-looking pouting lips of cunny, he opened my legs wider apart. His glowing, smiling face is suddenly transforming into a famished male specimen that's ready to indulge in his favorite delicacy, and indeed, it's my pleasure and an honor to serve him.

Realizing that we'd not pleasured each other since our flight here; and knowing that our time in Paris would revolve around entertaining family and friends, we're both conscious of how precious every minute of time together is crucial. To make it up, we definitely must allow special moments of together-pampering prior to engaging others.

Just as these deviating thoughts were spinning in my head, Greg was momentarily down on his knees, with his lips glued to my crack. To my endless delight, he sucked and kissed me for over a minute as I continued to sigh and wriggle with pleasure.

He could no longer restrain himself. Getting up with his knees between my legs, he brought his shaft to the charge, and to my astonishment, he drove it right into the wet soft crack till it was all lost in my belly. We laid still for a few moments, enjoying the conjunction of our private parts until I heaved up my butt, and he responded to it with a thrust, then we commenced a most exciting twirling. I could see the manly shaft as it worked in and out of my love button, shining with lubrication, while the lips of my cunny tried to cling to it each time it moved in and out as if afraid of losing such a delightful sugar stick. This did not last long. Our movements got more and more furious until we both met in a spasmodic embrace. We almost fainted in each other's arms. Our shiny, glowing, satisfied faces were transfixed on each other for a moment. From the corner of my eyes, I could see a profusion of creamy moisture oozing from the private part as we both lay in the exhaustion of pleasurable enjoyment after our battle of lovemaking.

—

Thirty minutes later, our private butler buzzed the suite with a sealed envelope. Greg responded and asked him to drop the message in the mail slot. Essentially, we've been notified that my parents arrived and have checked in. I immediately called their room to request for them to freshen up or relax for a while. Also informed them that we would be meeting for dinner in two hours. I'm excited to hear their voices again and to know that they're only a skip away from us now. I can't wait to welcome Greg's family tomorrow too.

Meanwhile, I've asked the butler to get us a tray of two bowls of mixed fresh fruits, two cups of warm chocolate juices, and a bottle of champagne with glasses. To momentarily be placed on the terrace for us while we prepare to meet and welcome my parents at dinner time.

An hour and a half later, we were well-rested and ready for our welcome party. I'm also anticipating the type of reception my parents, especially my father, would have with Greg when he formally announces his marital wishes with their daughter. I wonder what my father would say or how he'll react, knowing his temperament. I could be wrong about his reaction since my judgment of him is based on how he treated me growing up. It's simply my way of not allowing him to relate with me as if I was still a little girl. Sometimes, our childhood fears linger with us into adulthood. That's why, for me, I fear he would treat me like a child, forgetting that I'm a grown-up adult now. It's strange that most of our conversations over the years have been on the surface or through our mother. Come to think of it, I shouldn't be worried because he's an experienced businessman, and since Greg is a successful entrepreneur himself, they'd probably connect like kids' gloves. And for me, he probably would be a different man compared to what I think of him due to our history together.

And for the family dinner get-together, I decided to wear my light blue, short sleeve dress, midi skirt, and tie, which pairs perfectly with my grey heels and matching blue hat. Greg also decided to complement my outfit with his grey suit, white shirt, and pale blue tie. A nice combination that goes well with his signature leather black shoes. We both look like a perfect couple that is ready for a family magazine photoshoot.

We leave the suite, heading to meet my parents at the arranged hotel restaurant. At last, we are at the Murano glass chandeliers, and smoky mirrors and a server directs us to a reserved area at the fine dining L'Ecrin. An immaculately dressed couple was seated in our direction, speaking in French and clearly lively and joyful. As we approached, the man's voice dropped to a whisper, and I immediately recognized it as my father's voice. He quickly looked our way, and as our eyes met, a glow of sunshine showed through his entire face. As I turned to look at the woman next to him, I was overwhelmed by the broad smile and curve on my mother's lips. Her face was still that of an exceedingly beautiful woman that could easily pass for an older sister. Her lovely eyes held the clear candor of a young woman, and as I smiled back at her, her lips quivered with deep emotion of love. Beaming with excitement and open arms, they both stood up to welcome us.

Taking a step ahead of Greg, I received a hug from my dad's open arms. He smiled broadly, whispering my name and saying in French, 'my little girl has grown up to become a beautiful adult woman. He added that he was so happy to see me and very proud of what I've become. I then turned to hug and kiss my mom while Greg stepped forward. He reached out and gave my dad a firm handshake and handed him a limited-edition French bottle of wine that was specially ordered to coincide with my dad's year of birth. He accepted it with two hands, repeated thanks twice, and kissed Greg on the chic. As my mom ended our chitchat, she released my hands as she turned to greet Greg. I introduced them in French, and she teased me if I found the handsome man through a beauty catalog. I replied, 'of course,' and giggled as she turned to hug Greg. He handed her a beautiful, freshly picked bouquet of flowers, and she thanked him in French, referring to him as her son-in-law.

We were now seated at L'Eorin intimate restaurant for our fine dining together and adorned with Murano glass chandeliers and smoky mirrors. A glance at everyone's smiling eyes assured me that I wasn't the only one with an appetite, ready for a serving of Haute French cuisine of duck foie gras with black truffle and veal chop for four. The two waiters in attendance ensured we were provided we all had abundant restaurant feast of food, and wine combinations from the private subterranean wine cellar, La Cave.

The dinner passed most pleasantly, for our first meeting since my departure for university, and especially, coming back to visit as an engaged young lady, bringing my fiancé along. My dad was very pleased to see me and excited to meet my handsome husband-to-be.

After several taking glasses of wine, and in the middle of the desert, he looked contemplatively at Greg, and then, to me, he suddenly asked, "how did you meet?"

"Well," I started, "We met at a professional dinner get-together," and turned to Greg to see if she needed to add something.

"Yeah, sure," Greg added, clearing his throat. "During one of my company's annual get together for our consultants and clients, Marie was invited by one of my executives' girlfriends, Elisa, a friend of Marie from her university."

"It sounds like a web of love stories. If you're not uncomfortable, I'd love to hear some details, such as, what drew you guys together beside a chance meeting," my inquisitive mom asked, laughing while refilling her wine glass.

I squeezed Greg's thigh under the chair, and he winked at me; I requested that we move to Jardin d'Hiver, a more relaxed lounge of the hotel famous for tea and Coutume Café coffee. And if we desire, we could also have light soup. My parents agreed. After emptying our glasses, we were shown the way by a waiting attendant.

My mom touched one of my hands, and when I turned to look at her, she whispered in my ear, 'you have a perfect gentleman for a husband-to-be. And once we were settled down, she asked me, more loudly for the benefit of all four of us, "what attracted you to him, or was it the other way around?"

"Mutual, I believe. The moment we set eyes on each other and were introduced, we had instant chemistry. Before I say more, I have to give credit to Elisa, a Parisian girl I met at the university. We were initially roommates and became very close friends, and after watching my dating experiences with what she referred to as 'losers,' she decided to introduce me to Greg through her boyfriend, Mike. They are happily married, by the way.

"Anyway, compared to any guy I've ever dated, Greg has qualities I could only dream of in a life partner. He's very handsome, tall, and soft-spoken. And as we started dating, I came to realize that he is extremely caring, nurturing, kind, humble, and very generous, despite his extremely busy professional schedule. For example, early in our relationship, he sensed that I acted as if I didn't deserve him, but he quickly helped me to think differently by letting me know that every relationship is mutual, and we deserve and complemented each other."

My parents were very quiet, and I noticed my dad was nodding his head the entire time I was speaking. With glowing eyes, he turned to Greg and asked: "Don't be offended, please. What interested you in our daughter when you could date or marry any girl you wanted?"

Greg took a sip of his tea, smiled, and stated: "Actually, I've not dated or been involved with girls much until I met Marie. The way I was raised, most of my time and energy was focused on academics, sports, and spending time working in the family business. So, although I was not looking for someone to create a future together, as I got to know her more and more, I saw a girl that was not only physically attractive but also intelligent, pragmatic, loving, nurturing, compassionate and fun to be with, twenty-four seven.

"And why I decided to propose and marry her is because she has exhibited these qualities every day we've spent together, as well as while interacting with my family and friends. I'm proud to have had her by my side daily for a good year plus and ready to settle down with her as my wife, for better or worse." His big deep voice boomed and reverberated around our enclosure, excepting the throaty sobs and tears of joy from my mom.

As if her cries were a prelude for him to tell my parents the reason for visiting, Greg seized the opportunity to continue: "You are wonderful parents, and I know Marie's loving, kind, caring, and rational mind today is due to both of you. She means the world to me, and I hope to spend the rest of my life proving that to her. I came all the way across the ocean to ask for your permission to marry me, and I would be honored to have your blessings." He concluded as he squeezed my thigh, smiling as he looked at both of my parents.

My dad decided to respond to his request: "On behalf of my wife and myself, I want to let you know that we are honored to have you in our midst. In our current modern days, young people like you are not bound by tradition to seek marital approval like in the past. Traveling a great distance with the specific intention of acquiring our approval for your marriage t our daughter signals to us that you are fully and completely committed to marrying Marie and willing to go to great lengths to do so. We thank you from the bottom of our hearts."

As soon as he concluded his acceptance, two uniformed butlers handed each of us a glass of champagne, ladies first, then the guys. After gulping the drinks in one or two successions, we all got up from the comfort of our leather chairs, taking time to give and receive multiple kisses and hugs between us, then wished my parents goodnight. I took a few minutes to remind them of tomorrow evening's planned wedding here at Hotel de Crillon. Although they're aware of the details of invited guests, such as my grandparents, nieces, and cousins, I also reminded them that a large plane would be flying in our other guests from the States, such as Greg's family and our friends. And since our day would start early, I urged them to return to their suite for some rest or relaxation and be ready to meet again in the morning for breakfast.

Upon entering our Signature Suite, we quietly took off what we wore for the dinner outing and replaced them with our usual comfortable house clothes. I walked towards the panoramic view of Paris from the terrace, followed by Greg. Partially closing the glass compartment, I sat on one of the comfortable chairs facing the glowing fire in front of me and ushered Greg to sit on the one next to me. He proceeded to pour a chilled glass of champagne into two glasses that were arranged by our butler and handed one to me. We exchanged smiles, took a sip, and he reached out to kiss my lips when he noticed I was looking at him mischievously.

Throwing off my shawl, I displayed a beautiful form and voluptuous body, which was becoming more obvious due to my pregnancy, especially when wearing a loose house gown, which concealed neither shoulders nor the two fair and ample breasts, whiter than alabaster, giving me form a luxurious fullness.

While sipping a glass of champagne slowly, my eyes meandered ahead of where we sat and then turned to look at Greg. Noticing I was looking his way, his smiling eyes turned to me, lingering admiringly upon the exposed beauties of my growing breasts, examining my delicate features, which were beginning to look girlish and attractive, as he's teased me several times when we shower together.

Realizing that we are relatively young and deeply in love and knowing how strong his passion for me has been since we first met, I'm not surprised about his feelings for me because we both have strong desire and excitement for each other, regardless of time, place, or what we are doing. Following my dreaming thoughts, I instantly reclined and relaxed my head on his lap. Then looking up with my eyes half open, I decided to enjoy the effect I was having on him.

Laying on him, I deliberately rested one hand on the lump that he seemed to have in the pajama shorts he was wearing. Playing with his thoughts, I decided to ask him a series of questions at the same time: "My dear, do you think my body or legs and breasts will change in shape permanently? Do you think I should stop wearing short pants or short skirts, and only wear long dresses? Do you think I'm being bashful about the changes I'm experiencing because of pregnancy?"

Not waiting for his answers which usually are likely, going to be thoughtful and long, my feelings immediately went to the effect my questions were having on his body's reaction, specifically, inside his pajama shorts.

Slowly, his private part continued to increase in size, and I felt it throb under my hand. Thinking I was unaware of his sensual reaction, which is inherent in human nature but controlled by mental restrains, he tried to slightly shift sideways so as to remove my hand lower down onto the thigh.

In fact, the opposite was the case because he found himself being gradually overcome by the most tumultuous sensations. Knowing his body like the back of my head, I noticed his heart was palpating uncontrollably, his breathing grew hurried and irregular, and he could hardly restrain himself from clasping me to his chest with energizer strength.

Knowing that I had excited his passions, I raised my smiling eyes to his face and glanced at him with a soft smile on my lips, full of tenderness and invitation. Greg pulled my face to his with his two hands and whispered: "Thanks, sweetheart, for enticing me with your dreamy eyes and unspoken irresistible passion. I accept to love you, always and forever, until the end of the world."

He encircled my slender waist with his arm and then drew me to his throbbing penis, which instantly entered my eager ripe and welcoming wet vagina lips. Thus, resulting in both our hearts and bodies being transported into paradise lost. And for over an hour in this voluptuous magma, our exquisite bodies bathed in a sea of rapturous delight, mixed with our dizzying brains, hearts, and amorous souls. At last, we found ourselves in the comfort of our king-size bed, sleeping and dreaming about our next day's wedding.

20

At about eight AM the next morning, we received a message from our butler, notifying us about the arrival of the rest of our guests, both those that flew in from the US and those within France that were bused in numbering a little over one hundred. Those from the US, numbering about less than half the total number, will be staying in Hotel de Crillon, while the rest, mostly my French relatives and friends, will be housed in Paris Ritz, inclusive of meals and entertainment. All the wedding guests are notified to be available at the historical Salon des Aigles where the wedding will be taking place in the early evening, per distributed schedule to all invited guests. Our wedding planning management team would be responsible for the entire arrangement and liaise with our special adviser as the need arises. Summaries or necessary short notices would be forwarded to us as planned.

I've also followed up by making scheduled calls to meet both our parents and Greg's brother, Bill, and wife, Sara, for a nine-thirty breakfast. Mike and Elisa are also invited since Elisa will be my Bride mate, while Bill will be Greg's best man. We plan to meet at Brasserie d'Aumont restaurant, here at Hotel de Crillon. I've also informed them to dress in athleisure if they intend to join us at the Sense spa shortly after we eat.

Meanwhile, Greg took a quick shower and had to make some zoom calls in the Suite conference room. I used the bathtub and now relaxing and listening to some of my favorite French songs that I've not listened to for years.

In approximately forty-plus minutes later, he was back in the suite and getting dressed for our breakfast with the family. Full of smiles and exuberance in his eyes, I could tell he must have had a sweet deal or two. In his usual deep business voice, he stated that he was able to seal three deals out of five, which, according to him, is an excellent batting average in the investment or sports phraseology. I don't remember which is, but I'm happy he's able to close a couple of deals that he's been working on for months while on his wedding excursion. According to him, these European billionaires are heads or founders of a global aluminum group, founder of an oil, gas, and pipeline company, and head of a conglomerate that include beverages, apparel, and perfumes holding corporation. He plans to have the three deals under management in thirty days, providing him and his team sufficient time to finalize everything.

On our way to Brasserie d'Aumont restaurant, we met and walked together with Bill and Sara, and they said Greg's parents were already at the restaurant. We exchanged hugs and pleasantries while acknowledging that they had a smooth flight here. We're excited to see them again and to hear that they're doing well. Sara whispered to me that she was expecting and asked if I was too. With a shock and surprise on my face, which she noticed, she quickly added that I looked like I was too, and I quickly said yes indeed, and we hugged in confirmation.

On entering the restaurant, I could see Greg's parents and my parents very chatty and animated as if they'd known each other previously. Everybody stood up as we exchanged hugs and kisses. My mom and dad said Greg's parents were a wonderful couple. Greg's mom also added that she was very pleased to meet my parents too. While I was introducing Bill and Sara to my parents and giving them a little bio on who they were, Mike and Elisa also entered the restaurant. I quickly added them into the introduction, resulting in a further exchange of hugs and kisses between us. Elisa informed me that she and Mike had met Greg's family previously before Greg was introduced to me. We laughed together while she turned and spoke French with my parents and reintroduced her husband, Mike, to them. As we were busy chatting among ourselves, the two chefs from the restaurant that were assigned to serve us called our attention to be seated in an adjoining reserved area for breakfast.

They informed us that several breakfast options were available, namely: A French version of scrambled eggs which simply were eggs, cheese, and butter, but the butter was meant to enable the other ingredients to shine and shimmer. It also came with truffle salt to provide extra flavor or the addition of veggies for healthy eating.

Other menu options were a delicious French toast roll-up that was filled with the flavor of French toast, apples, and cinnamon sugar. What's special about it is that it can be eaten by people that enjoy sweet foods with varied fruits.

The croissant was another food item, which is buttery and flaky. A pastry that could go with any finger-licking good breakfast meal. It came with jam, and one of the chefs suggested it could be made into a sandwich if we so desired.

Another suggested breakfast meal was the Pain au chocolate, which is a French breakfast treat that melts in your mouth while eating. To crown it up, it has a ton of rich chocolate flavor.

Chaussans aux Pommes is another breakfast pastry option that we were told goes well with a family gathering like what we're doing. My parents laughed when the chefs said it while looking at them as if for approval.

Next was a toasted ham sandwich, which we are told, would go well with coffee. This Croque madame, as it is called, is filled with delicious flavors that would put the typical western equivalent to shame. My mom whispered to me that it's because they combine the usual ham sandwich ingredients with melted cheese, fried egg, and creamy bechamel added on top.

For drinks, we are offered a café au lait, which is a perfect morning coffee drink that can be combined with just about any type of drink we desire because the milk will balance any flavor we choose to add. So, experimentation is the key.

A second drink suggested to us is hot cocoa. This French hot cocoa has an addition of chocolate syrup, plus key ingredients like vanilla extract to help the chocolate stand out. And, of course, there's ice water, freshly squeezed fruit juice, and champagne.

Minutes after we had finished breakfast, the chief wedding planner dropped by to see if we had an additional suggestion that needed to be included in the wedding schedule. Such as: if we desired any changes to the assigned prelude music before the start of the ceremony or music preference for the procession or bridal entrance, had any questions concerning wedding ceremony scripts, the speeches to be made and by whom, order of ceremony we desired, any specific rules or expectation or request we wanted to be implemented, during officiating, words of welcome, introductions, readings, officiant address to the couple, exchange of vows, exchange of rings, the kiss, unity ceremony or ritual, during the ceremony, nuptial blessings or closing remarks, and the recessional. After a brief animated conversation, we affirmed the schedule and excused the planner to go ahead and implement their responsibilities.

—

I walked with Elisa and Sara as we headed to the Sense Rosewood Spa, while Greg walked with Mike and his brother Bill to chit-chat or catch up on their unfinished business. Elisa whispered to me that she was expecting and shared with her the surprising discovery Sara shared with me earlier. We all wondered why such a coincidence occurred with the three of us, at the same time, just a few weeks apart. Regardless of its spiritual meaning, we were very happy and wished for a successful delivery for all of us. They asked if we had any honeymoon in our plans, and I told them that Greg had hinted we'll be flying out to Hawaii or another similar beach island in the Caribbean after the wedding for a brief honeymoon before returning back home.

The Spa had a huge, incredible Art Deco-style lap pool with gold mosaic tiles, an overhead skylight that provided natural light, with walls that provided visual texture. The three of us decided to use the three solo treatment cabins, while Greg and my parents took a turn to use the couple's suite. Our three guys used the fitness center to work on their cardio. After that, we women decided to use the David Lucas hair salon, while the men used La Barbiere de Paris men's grooming studio. Before we left for our respective Suites, we took succession and received facial and body treatments by Maison Caulieres. Our happy family crowd adjoined for the morning with hugs and kisses between us one more time and promised to meet again for the wedding ceremony at the appointed venue and time, scheduled at the historical Salon des Aigles, with all our illustrious invited guests, for the occasion.

Back in our Signature Suite, Greg and I walked over to the terrace, holding hands, hugging and kissing passionately for about a minute. When we opened our eyes, we scanned the panoramic views of Paris, mostly the views of the Grand Palais and the Eiffel Tower. It was a beautiful view to behold.

Back inside the living room area, we sat on the divan. I dimmed the lights and searched through the Bluetooth sound system for some soft tunes while Greg opened the mirrored minibar to get us two small bottled water. Just at that time, the butler rang to ask if he could be of service. I told him to get us some Coutume Café coffee, bowls of fresh mixed fruits, champagne, and caviar.

When he returned momentarily, he said our chief wedding planner wanted to have a brief conversation and was waiting in the visitor lounge, next to our private living room. I acknowledged the message and instructed the planner to wait half an hour.

We started out eating our caviar and a sip of champagne. Discussed our smoothly; the day had gone so far, and we hoped for a successful wedding celebration by nightfall.

"Of course, Marie," Greg uttered after taking a second sip of his glass. Holding my hand, he smiled and said: "Sweetheart, you've done a fabulous job of working with the wedding team from the beginning to this moment, and I'm very certain the entire process would end on an excellent note." He concluded with confidence in his voice.

"Thanks, honey," I re-joined and gave him a kiss.

He responded by pulling me closer and kissing me passionately. We couldn't keep our hands off each other but had to stop, to continue later. Most likely when. We're officially certified as man and wife, which is only a few hours away. I can't wait to melt into him.

After chewing a spoonful from his bawl of mixed fruit, he turned to me and reminded me of the qualities in me that he's thankful for, such as my beautiful and effervescent personality, ideals, and values in life, compassion, and emotional maturity.

I replied that I'm also thankful for his having the same qualities, as well as his decision to take a chance on me. Plus, his wholesome and pragmatic outlook on life, his passionate nature, and his tolerance for ambiguity. I added that when I look back on our time together, I'm inclined to think that we were meant to meet and fall in love.

So, I'm very grateful we took advantage of the opportunity to build a future together. Finally, I'm thankful for the beautiful and happy memories we've built together. And cementing it with marital union promise to continue to build, cherish and sustain our relationship for the rest of our lives.

"I agree wholeheartedly and promise to honor and always nurture my love for you and the family we are bound to create," he added as he reflected on our thoughts and relationship tête-à-tête.

After a second of silence, our eyes met, and I noticed his soft brown eyes were smiling back at me. His smile broadened further to the rest of his face as his eyes meandered to other parts of my body as if he was checking me out. It reminded me of our first meeting when we couldn't take our eyes off each other as if we were transfixed. As he noticed I couldn't take my eyes off his handsome face, he instinctively shifted his weight towards me, reaching out and holding my hand in his. Squeezing my fingers and placing them against his warm lips. With his deep voice, he whispered the words, "I love you, Marie."

I'm so happy that our love for each other has been in the honeymoon phase for over a year, and grateful for recognizing that we are not perfect but perfect for each other.

In response to his quiet words, I nodded my head repeatedly and added, "yes, and forever love and passion." We both laughed, and I gave him a quick kiss. Then getting up, I hurried to the lounge to meet Stacy, our wedding planner.

At the lounge, the planner stood up to say hi, and I reached out to shake her hand.

"Hello Stacy, what's new?" I said to her, smiling.

"Good day and nice to see you too, Ms Marie," she replied, her voice sounding hasty but with genuine pleasure and an opportunity to be of service.

"I apologize for coming to update you in person at a moment's notice. It's about a few things before the commencement of the wedding ceremony, which is due to take place very shortly." She concluded, momentarily awaiting my response or approval to proceed with her schedule update.

"Not at all, Stacy. You are doing your job. And I'd do the same if I was in your shoes," I responded, assuring her with a smile.

"Thank you very much," she replied, nodding her head. "Please let's sit down so that I can share with you some pre and post-wedding ceremony programs on specific items in the schedule for your information."

We walked to the conference table next to the couch, and she opened her iPad to show and describe to me exactly what she'd come to discuss with me.

"As you already know," she began, "first, you and your fiancé would arrive early to work with the glamour and luxurious beauty team. They will create your facial dream look, hairstyle, and freshness for both of you. Thus, setting the stage for your happily ever after.

"Then, followed by the dressing team. Males and females. Coordinating with each of you separately on each of your roles, as well as combined roles throughout the ceremony.

"Hundreds of pictures would be taken of both of you, at the helipad, surrounded by breath-taking panoramic views of some of Paris's major attractions, overlooking the courtyard and a 398-square-foot, as well as overlooking Place de la Concorde, with views of the Beaux-Arts palace and the iconic tower. Drone filming would also be taking place during the entire pre and post-wedding celebration.

"Luxurious décor and fresh gorgeous red roses would be provided in porcelain vases and strategically placed in the entire yard space, and after the ceremony, a limited access section would be allocated for the two of you and your immediate family members and special guests.

"A team of security would be provided, as well as a catering team throughout the ceremonial and celebratory occasion.

"Multiple indoor/outdoor spaces are provided pre and post-wedding shoots, a glam lounge for entertainment, enjoyment of exclusive cocktail creation, paired with a variety of aphrodisiac dipping chocolate dipping sauce and long-stemmed strawberries.

"Specific spaces for all the invited guests would be the 60-seat Les Ambassadeurs Bar on Place de la Concorde, which features sumptuous Old-World décor, including a hand-painted ceiling. Guests would be provided surplus cocktails, champagnes, and caviar. Piano music would be provided initially and replaced by a DJ set team for the pleasure and enjoyment of the wedding attendees and celebrants.

"Early morning tomorrow, all the invited guests staying either at Paris Ritz or here at Hotel de Crillon would be invited for breakfast with the newlywed couple at Jardin d'Hiver's all-day lounge, famous for tea time, light lunch (soup, Croque Madame) and Coutume Café coffee. Sweets and pastry would be available for takeaway.

"Finally, guests' return trip transportation would be provided for guests that came by luxury bus two hours before noon. Those that flew in would be shuttled to the airport for the late afternoon-chartered return flight.

"Thanks for your patience and taking the time to listen to my update Marie. Do you have any questions?" The wedding planning director concluded as she took a gulp of water from her glass.

"I don't have any questions, Stacy. Could you please forward a copy to my phone please? I'll follow up with a note if Greg or I have any questions. For now, assume that everything is good to go." I concluded and reassured her with a big smile.

We both stood up again, shook hands, and confirmed to meet as planned.

"Thanks again for coming, Stacy. See you in a few."

"You too. And bye for now," she replied., and I watched her step out to take an elevator. I then walked back inside our Suite and shared the information with Greg.

21

Yesterday was our wedding celebration. And everybody, a little over 300 people-strong, had a fabulous time. Family, friends, friends of friends, and people we've known for decades or not too long ago, on both sides of our relationship, had a special day in their calendar to remember, based on their exhilaration and speeches yesterday.

It's apparent that we did have a real wedding after all. But we didn't want it to feel like one. We'd wanted to somewhat gather dozens, or hundreds of friends and family together and literally have a party to last a lifetime. That's what we tried to have. So, our celebration could aptly be described as a "family and friends' festival of love."

My newly minted official husband, who I absolutely adore, is the most caring, nurturing, romantic, sweet, cool, generous, and unassuming smart guy I've ever met in my entire life. At our wedding and celebratory party, his infectious and bubbly energy was shared with over two hundred invited guests. I love him beyond words. Our friends and both our family members love him very dearly. Our relatives love him equally. Our guest visitor logbook is full of accolades and statements of praise, kindness, and genuine goodness that he extends to others, including strangers.

This helps to explain why we are so much in love. As a matter of fact, we literally fell in love from day one upon setting eyes on each other. To test how deep our feelings were for each other, we moved in together, and my life and outlook on relationship turned into a fairy tale story that can only be associated with what is seen in movies or books, more like something resembling heaven on earth. We've not only enjoyed a most passionate, loving, happy relationship for over a year together, but he has always religiously taken time out of his extremely busy schedule to send me flowers and love notes. Texting me regularly, regardless of how hectic his work schedule demands. And the way he has described it, he believes we complement each other. The way I see it, he completes me. He's more like a male feminist than anyone I know.

For what we wore and how we looked for the ceremony, I was wearing a long, lacey wedding gown and hairpiece, specially designed and fitted for my body. Greg also wore a form-fitting tuxedo suit, as well as our accompanied delicately crafted wedding gear, such as jewelry and shoes for both of us, which made us look like we literally had jumped out of an international magazine cover. I certainly would give credit to our world-class Italian wedding designer, as well as the Brazilian shoe designer. Thanks again to the Brazilian for adorning my shoes with crystals and making sure Greg's signature oxford was as comfortable and very fitting with his matching suit and tuxedo. Also, thanks to the New York jewelry designer and clothier, whose family has been in the business for over three hundred years. Also, the wedding ring and band I'm wearing, including Greg's band, are one of a kind in the whole wide world, courtesy of our new friend Phillippe, the famous French designer that was recommended by one of Greg's billionaire clients.

Talking about the nuptial ceremony, I couldn't believe we kissed for a long time when the officiating pastor declared, "now you can kiss your pride." Greg's kisses were so sweet, so measured, so warm, and delicious that I didn't want to stop kissing him, which made the audience laugh and clap. Strangely, I wasn't embarrassed, but thrilled, and I have dozens of pictures as proof. Or, it can be viewed in live or online local TV news or magazine clips, or better still, through a multitude of sources like social media outlets.

Also, my excitement was on cloud nine during the signature cocktail. Starting with the authenticity and delicious taste, which can only be described as definitely highbrow. It is said to have been in the French culture for thousands of years.

The wedding planning team did an excellent job in ensuring that we made happy memories from the ceremony to cocktails, from the reception to the live band, followed by DJ music that showcased songs that spanned the entire American music genre and pop culture. From the 80s and 90s to the current variety of top 40s. And a combination of sorts, from Europe, Asia, Latin, and Africa.

The speeches made me cry buckets, especially all the glowing statements about my early childhood years from my grandparents, relatives, schoolmates, and best friend, Elisa. And more importantly, those from Greg's brother, his childhood friend, and his professional colleague, Mike. As well as his friends that flew in from across the US, providing in-depth insight and picture gram about the man I married. This wedding ceremony has not only united us but opened a bond that we will scramble to embrace, enjoy and appreciate each other daily as we navigate our earthly existence. Memories to cherish and pass on to those we'll leave behind.

And before our celebrants or wedding guests left for their respective homes or places of their choice, we made sure each and every one took a special memento of us home. A gold-plated emblazoned wedding picture of Greg and me, accompanied by a token of appreciation for taking time out to enjoy our company. It was indeed a pleasure to bond with them as family and friends of varied and varying stripes. Love is beautiful.

—

We finally took our chartered jet on its way to our honeymoon island destination. The 'secret' destination was shared with me as we were about to board the plane - finally.

The nurse onboard visited with me briefly, informed me about her role, and left me with a brochure on available services and comfort en route. These included but were not limited to a resting bed, relaxing lounge, and compartment for beverages and snacks.

The plane crew was cheerful and cracked a few jokes to put some smiles on our faces. Overall, I'm pleased about Greg's arrangements, as well as happy about his choice, deferring to him since he's been an avid world traveler since birth. Come to think of it, he's been very good at looking out for my care and welfare. I'm proud of his constant consciousness for comfort and safety. A good example is his renting a helicopter that is fitted with a bed, kitchenette, and lounge, with appropriate staff on board, including one with medical and hospitality training or experience.

We are finally in French Polynesia and slated to spend our romantic and relaxing honeymoon together. Upon arrival, the welcome team from Motu Tautau resort took us from the airport by boat to the resort. We enjoyed the spectacular view of the bright blue ocean. The VIP suite was spectacular, featuring a glass-bottom floor and a stairway that led from the room directly to the ocean.

We were a little tired and requested for room service champagne meal from our assigned butler. Although we had options of meals from across every known continent, we opted for French. Feeding each other and reminiscing over our wedding trip and our visit with friends and family, we decided to relax in our bed to rejuvenate for our all-day next-day outdoors tour. We are excited and looking forward to checking out this jagged remnant of an ancient volcano that is said to rise suddenly above 2,400 feet from the surface of a sparkling, turquoise lagoon.

In bed, finally, we took each other's clothes. Naked, we got on top of the soft bed covers. I deliberately displayed my beautiful, voluptuous form liberally for Greg's enjoyment and pleasure. He took notice by slowly and bashfully scanning my unconcealed shoulders, as well as my two fair and copious breasts that provided me with a luxurious fullness.

I provided him sufficient time to enjoy the sight and satisfactory discernment, and then, in my seductive soft, sexy voice, I said to him, "my newly minted husband, you are cordially invited to this house and chamber of yours to behold every day of our life, till death do us part."

"Say no more, my dear angel," he replied with a broad smile, "we are destined together, and I'm thankful, grateful, and happy for it."

After uttering those words, my husband was overcome by the most unrestrained sensations. With our bodies intertwined together, I could feel his palpitating heart. He could hardly restrain himself as I was clasped to his chest. Our lips found each other, and his sweet breath grew irregular with excitement. With an equally excited passion, I raised my eyes to his face and glanced at him with a soft smile that was full of tenderness and invitation. He responded precisely as someone that has known my anatomy and heart for over a year. He wrapped his arm around my slender waist and drew me to his throbbing penis, and instantly entered my awaiting vagina.

His hungry lips were all over every part of me, from my open, invited lips to my shoulders, soft neck, nipples, rapid electric movement, and sensational feelings he was offering me from his throbbing penis. As my senses were reeling, my amorous soul bathed in a sea of rapturous delight on a dizzy brain, I could only be thankful for a husband that's not only the best for me but also the possessor of a heart that beats in unison with every noble, generous, and kindly feeling that the world has ever offered to our mother earth.

-

We woke up, scrubbed and showered together, dressed causal, ate our warm continental breakfast, and were ready for our fun island expedition. We have our camera with built-in binoculars for photo ops.

Upon pickup from Vaitape Pier, we start our full-day tour with a 4WD voyage tour in an open-sided truck. As it takes off, the truck, which easily scales mountain terrene and roadway to several viewpoints along the way, circles the volcanic island and makes occasional stops at several lookout points of interest and scenic views. The professional guide took us around a 20-mile circumference of the island and stopped at East Matira, Faanui Cancon, and Amanahune Bay lookouts with beautiful postcard views that we captured with our camera to share with our friends and family.

I thought the volcanic formations from the island's ancient caldera were fascinating and note-worthy. My artistic interest was heightened during the observation of the production of coconut oil and tie-dye sarongs by local artisans at a craft workshop, and more importantly and memorable was the enjoyment of the tropical fruits sample at a small plantation.

After our morning section of the island tour, we enjoyed a delicious lunch which was included in the tour schedule, before transferring to our boat for the afternoon cruise portion of our tour.

We then settled under the sunshade as our tour captain navigated to a calm lagoon where we first observed from our boats and then mustered enough courage to snorkel in waist-deep water close to tame stingrays. After this close-up experience with the stingrays, we're taken to another spot where black-tip reef sharks glide past our vessel. The final snorkeling spot was over colorful corals teeming with tropical fish.

Before ending our day-long tour, the guides also taught us about local culture and the artifacts left behind by the US troops after the second world war. At the end of the magnificent sightseeing tour, watching Mount Otemanu changing colors as the clouds covered and progressed to bright sunshine that was followed by lashing rain streaming storms, I couldn't trade these once-in-a-lifetime amazing sea shades for anything else.

-

Our ten-day honeymoon trip was jam-packed with a full day potpourri of a to-do list that was planned out for us by the resort executive for our enjoyment and pleasure. The clock was switched to 'our time.' Our daily activities included making love, sipping cocktails, ordering room service, which included breakfasts, finger foods, and champagne brunches, or enjoying a variety of dinners from all continents of the world. Other activities that we engaged in included using the fitness center or salon spa, outdoors 'trekking,' laying out by the pool, jet-skiing, learning how to paint seascapes, and enjoying everything the ocean provided.

Regarding the delicious dishes from many countries, I'll mention some of my favorites, which include but are not limited to Le Corail. We thoroughly enjoyed sipping wine and eating finger foods or dinners, facing the lagoon or within a refined and air-conditioned atmosphere. This was perfect whenever we dressed up as we always did back in the States, for an elegant romantic date night, instead of a home-cooked meal. It's not an open secret that I enjoy exquisite French cuisine from an 'a la carte' or tasting menu very much. And, of course, the choice of selecting our own wine since we are told it is supplied from the largest wine cellar within French Polynesia. Besides the meals and drinks, the restaurant provided exceptional service whenever we frequented it.

Other great restaurants were St. James, a waterside restaurant with a spectacular view of the sunset, which provides a variety of memorable cocktails and a food menu of flavorful, mouthwatering meals. Their management team was exceptional and a joy that lingered and made the visit memorable. Others with similar but different gastronomy included La Villa Mahana, Bora Bora Yacht Club, Bora Bora Beach Club, Far Niente Ristorante, and Lagoon Restaurant by Jean Georges.

Our trip was finally over, and it was time to return home. Before departure, we had to get a couple of souvenir gifts for our family and friends. We were glad the local shops provided a variety of handcrafted jewelry with top-quality pearls, which I'm sure, everyone will enjoy.

—

It's been several weeks since our return from our wedding honeymoon trip. We've also been enjoying each other, and I'm happy my husband's business is thriving beyond his dreams, thanks to his competent and able team. He spends more time with me and personally drives me to my monthly checkups. I can't be happier and count my blessings. He sent me a bouquet of flowers and a handwritten card stating his undying love and joy in having me as his wife. It brought tears to my eyes, and I texted his phone and told him I loved him and for him to expect an in-person expression of thanks from me when he arrived home a little over an hour from now.

Minutes after, the butler had notified me that our dinner was ready, and I informed him that my husband should be arriving any moment. He proceeded to set the table while I freshened up to go to the dining area downstairs and await his arrival.

Seated and sipping a cup of water and looking at the flower garden through the glass door, my husband arrived, unbeknown to me, and hugged me from behind. He kissed me on the lips as we walked to the dining table for dinner. We ate as if it was a feast and reclined on the couch in the living room library, which was next door through a double glass door. After summarizing our day's events, I reached out and held his hand, kissed it, and proceeded with thanks to him.

 "Greg, I know you already know, but to remind myself and help you understand what I'm about to say, I'll dive a little into my past, okay?" he nodded with a smile.

"Before I met you, the men I dated only gave me either their heart or head, which were not one hundred percent sufficient to sustain a healthy long-term relationship. For those reasons, I want to thank you for being a 'feminist alpha male.' By opening both your heart and head to me, you've not only allowed me to feel complete but enabled us to grow and express our passion and identity as a couple. I thank your family for bringing you to this world, as well as mine, for enabling me to learn and develop an appreciation for the different sides of life. I pledge to love you, support you, and be an exemplary mother to our children, to the best of my ability." I held his hand in his as I concluded.

He pulled me closer. Hugged and kissed my lips and neck; his warm lips nibbled my ears.

He whispered, "we are better and stronger together."

He continued: "To similarly affirm what you just said, I want to let you know that our feelings for each other were mutual. Our first twenty-four hours together made me realize that you were the kind of woman I needed as a life partner. My father told my brother and me shortly after university graduation that he and our mother were grateful for our completing one milestone. They'd be very happy if their second milestone for us was around the corner. Specifically, deciding to settle down and raise a family, just like they did.

"He said some men get married because they have to. Others because they want to. I want you both to settle down for both reasons. Smiling, he hugged us and said he and our mother were proud of us as their children." Greg concluded, looking at me silently.

"So, what exactly did he mean 'both reasons' or did you guys know?" my inquiring mind wanted to know.

He replied: "Although we didn't understand what he meant, neither of us asked for clarification. Instead, we thanked him and went to our respective rooms for the night."

Still curious and eager to know, I said: "That's an illuminating statement. So, have you figured it out yet?"

"Yes, of course!" He responded, almost immediately with his signature deep voice. His entire face was full of happiness, combined with an exciting glow in his eyes.

As if by a prompt, we kissed, and simultaneously took a sip from our champagne glasses. Then, I quickly placed mine back on the coffee table to listen to him further.

"Can't wait to hear it," I replied, smiling and making myself comfortable on the sofa.

 Clearing his throat, he continued: "beginning from the day we started dating, we certainly showed genuine love and passion for each other, which exponentially escalated after we moved in together.

"I knew that you were the kind of girl I won't have trouble spending time with, come rain or shine. And the dozens of months we've spent in building our relationship have enriched and solidified our relationship beyond our expectation." He concluded.

"Very true," I replied, nodding my head. "We have so much in common in terms of our personality traits and have continuously increased our diverse interests and passionate love for each other, for life, and our future together."

"Yes, indeed, sweetheart," he stated and thanked me for reminiscing on where we've been in terms of our love, and now, as newly married.

We're both looking forward to the delivery of our twin babies in two weeks. We've decided not to know the gender of the babies, but I suspect they'll be male and female. Either way, we will be very happy and do what every loving, nurturing parents would do, in raising them to become well-adjusted global citizens.

THE END